I0594410

SPILL

MELANIE PICKERING

Copyright © 2021 by Melanie Pickering

All rights reserved.

No portion of this book may be reproduced in any form without written permission from the publisher or author, except as permitted by U.S. copyright law.

This book is a work of fiction. Any names, characters, companies, organizations, places, events, locales, and incidents are either used in a fictitious manner or are fictional. Any resemblance to actual persons, living or dead, actual companies or organizations, or actual events is purely coincidental.

First edition.

Print ISBN: 978-0-6452945-0-7

Ebook ISBN: 978-0-6452945-1-4

Cover art by Jacqueline Hayley www.jacquelinehayley.com

For anyone who has ever felt invisible-

I see you.

Blood will tell, but sometimes it tells too much.

-Don Marquis

CHAPTER ONE

AMY HAD NEVER DELIBERATELY kept anything from the boy she loved, and that knowledge scraped her conscience raw as the train slowed into the brightly lit station. It didn't matter that she and Flynn weren't dating. He was her longest and closest friend, and he didn't deserve to be lied to.

To make matters worse, he wasn't the only one. As far as Amy's mum knew, she was doing an assignment with her friend Leona. That part, at least, was true. A *research experiment* was how Leona had spun it; the chance to prove an urban legend true.

What they were really doing, though, was conducting a seance in a haunted train tunnel in the middle of the night in a dodgy Melbourne suburb. Something Valerie Shipley would be worried sick over if she knew that was what her daughter was up to, and as for Flynn... well, there was more than one reason Amy hadn't told him.

Hefting her backpack onto one shoulder, she pushed the guilt from her mind as she concealed her blonde hair with the hood of her sweatshirt and stepped from the train with confidence she didn't possess.

The platform was deserted, save for a couple of policemen who eyed their little group with interest. She supposed the four of them looked as though they were up to no good, dressed entirely in black with their hoods up. It wasn't even cold enough to be wearing sweats.

Amy dropped her head, determined not to make eye contact, but she could tell they were staring as she passed. Was it obvious what they were planning to do?

Ahead of her, the others had already pushed through the ticket gates and were walking towards the overpass. A pent up breath escaped her lips as she reached for her railcard.

'You okay, Ames?'

Luka's warm brown eyes reached out to her from beneath his hoodie.

'Yeah.' She nodded, grateful that at least one of them had waited for her while cursing under her breath that it wasn't Flynn. It *should* have been Flynn. If he'd been with them tonight, there was no way he'd have left her walking alone.

But she hadn't wanted to tell him about the seance. Flynn didn't believe in anything paranormal and would have only tried to talk her out of going. So what if she deliberately neglected to mention it? Besides, he hadn't even bothered to show up at school today. It wasn't like he made it easy for her to tell him.

His loss.

Taking his best friend's outstretched hand, they ran to catch up to Leona and Kenzie, who were already waiting down on street level. Pausing at the top of the stairs, Luka turned to her, his eyebrows raised. 'Race you.'

Amy grinned back as she saddled a handrail, thankful that she'd worn slick leggings. Sliding down the two flights to the bottom, her feet hit the concrete a full second before Luka's. She fist-pumped the air. 'Burn, boy!'

He shook his head and moved to sling an arm around her shoulder. 'You got lucky.'

She shoved him off her, but then linked her arm through his. Her body had been tight with tension and she felt so much better for having let off a bit of steam. Luka was always good at that. But then he went and ruined it.

'Try to ignore the meth-heads,' he warned, as the girls clutched at each other and speed-walked down the darkened street.

Amy's heart pounded the entire time, but it only took a few minutes to reach the junction at the bottom of Bunbury Street. Here, the road sloped down towards the banks of the river, and the railway tracks leading from the bridge in front of them disappeared through a tunnel beneath their feet. The tunnel, that was said to be haunted by the ghost of Elodie Mitchell.

Amy looked at the signal lights down by the tunnel entrance. Both were glowing red, and she couldn't recall if that meant the tracks were busy or clear. The tracks ahead were quiet, but fear tumbled in her belly. What if a train came while they were in the tunnel? This wasn't Leona's smartest idea. Surely, no school assignment was worth risking their lives?

A flash of light swept over them as a lone car turned the bend, its headlights illuminating a large grinning skull made from discarded CDs that adorned the safety barricade to the tracks below.

Amy shuddered as she caught sight of the words fashioned beneath it before the darkness swallowed them again. VITA BREVIS. *Life is short.*

Gripping her backpack, she peered over the ledge. Elodie Mitchell's life had been cut short the moment she fell down there twenty years ago. Perhaps that's why the skull was there. Like a reminder. A modern-day memento mori.

Whatever the reason, Leona was attempting to raise Elodie's ghost tonight, and she was already skipping down the street, trailing her nails across the red-bricked siding of the tunnel wall as she went. 'Come on, let's go.'

About halfway down the street, the wall dipped low enough to gain access onto the tracks before rising again to meet the bridge.

Leona stopped and stabbed Luka in the chest. 'You. Watch out for weirdos and security guards.'

'Shouldn't I be watching for trains?' he asked, giving her and Kenzie a leg up, before climbing up himself. He smirked at Amy. 'Need a hand?'

She glared at him, hands on hips. 'I think you need to stand back.'

He raised his hands in acquiescence and obeyed. Amy tossed him her backpack before backing up a few steps. Then, blowing out a breath, she bounced on the balls of her feet and ran straight towards the wall. Planting her hands atop the brick, she sprang up to meet Luka in one fluid movement. He slapped her palm with a high-five.

'Your parkour training is paying off.'

It was hands-down one of her best moves, and although Flynn had been stopping by her gym class of late, she still wished he'd been there to see it too. But of course, that would mean that she would've had to tell him all about the seance that she was deliberately *not* telling him about.

'Will you two hurry up?' Leona's voice rang out of the darkened tunnel ahead.

She and Kenzie had completely disappeared into the gaping maw and Amy wondered, not for the first time, why they couldn't hold the seance in the daylight. But Leona had been adamant. It had to be done as close to the time of Elodie's death as possible. *For authenticity.*

Dramatic much? Maybe they should've invited Flynn. He could've filmed the whole thing for his media class.

Amy turned and peered at the bridge behind them. It was still quiet, but she didn't know which was freaking her out the most: seeing a ghost or getting hit by a train. Anxiety made her tummy clench.

Eager to get this over with, she marched into the blackness. 'Where are we doing this?' Her voice echoed off the brick. Stopping under the expansive void that Elodie fell through, she looked up. 'Hey, isn't this where—'

'Not there,' Leona retorted. 'I don't want junkies throwing needles and beer cans down on us.'

Luka appeared beside Amy and whispered in her ear. 'You know this area's not that bad, still, she makes a fair point.'

Amy jerked her head back. 'You know you just contradicted yourself, right?'

Luka spread his arms wide with a smile to match. 'Then call me an *oxymoron.*'

Despite her best efforts, Amy snorted, then burst out laughing.

'What's so funny?' Kenzie called from about twenty feet away. She was lighting a circle of tea candles on one of the tracks. Amy frowned. Leona was taking this séance thing too far. Did they actually need all this crap?

'Nothing,' she murmured, watching the flames flicker and settle into a steady glow. 'Luka's just being... Luka.'

Kenzie nodded, but Amy sensed her stiffness. It was no secret that Kenz adored Luka, yet the guy seemed totally oblivious. Amy stepped over to her and laid a hand on her shoulder, knowing just how she felt.

'Remember what to do, girls?'

A clatter of stones halted Leona's pep talk and all three snapped their attention towards the tunnel mouth to find Luka throwing handfuls of gravel at the wall.

'What the fuck, Luka! You're supposed to be keeping watch. How old are you, three?'

His face paled as Leona spat something in Mandarin. Amy's lips twitched. The poor guy. Leona was bound to curse his penis to shrivel up, or something equally as bad. She was all bark and no bite, yet she scared the boys shitless.

'Can we get this ghost party started?' Kenzie puffed out an irritable sigh.

With a scathing glance at Luka, Leona set her phone to record a video and placed it face-up on the track between the candles. Her plan involved them linking hands and calling for Elodie's ghost three times, like summoning Bloody Mary at a tween sleepover.

Except none of Amy's sleepovers had ever been like that, and she didn't know what to expect. Taking a shaky breath, she closed her eyes as Leona began the chant they'd been rehearsing all week.

'Elodie, Elodie, sing for us a melody. Make yourself heard.'

Amy held her breath, listening hard, but heard nothing but her own pulse beating loud in her ears. This was a complete waste of time. She should be curled up in bed asleep right now and dreaming of Flynn, instead of standing in the middle of some godforsaken freight tunnel. Something—most likely a moth— whizzed by her ear, making her flinch. As she turned her head, she caught the faintest rumble coming from deep inside the tunnel.

Chest constricting, she strained to hear over Kenzie's chant of 'Elodie, Elodie, sing for us a melody. Make yourself seen.'

With a pounding heart, Amy couldn't help turning her head toward the approaching sound. Even with her eyes shut, light was turning the backs of her eyelids red—light, which was now accompanied by the sound of squealing iron wheels and firing pistons.

Oh, crap.

Leona's hand squeezed hers, as Amy tried to pull away, but Leona's grip was like a vice. Panicked, she blurted her own line. 'Elodie, Elodie, sing for us a melody. Make yourself whole.'

Hit with a rush of air, she opened her eyes to two white lights boring down on them—a freight train approaching from the far end of the tunnel. It was too dark to tell which track it was on, because the candle flames had snuffed out.

'Move!' Luka's voice exploded behind them. Startled, Amy launched towards him as he sprinted toward her.

Dim blue light spilled through the void in the roof where Elodie had fallen, and Amy ran towards it, her only thoughts on escaping the tunnel. Pressure was building in both ears and pain exploded in her head as they popped. She screamed, as everything turned white.

'Get back!'

Luka's hands were on her shoulders, his voice muffled as if he were talking underwater. Then next thing she knew, she was body-slammed back against the bricks, mere seconds before a second freighter rocketed past on the very track where she'd been standing. Instinct kicked in, her palms bracing behind her, but it didn't stop her head from ricocheting off the wall and cracking against Luka's jaw.

Pain splintered across her skull as she tried to make sense of what just happened. Over Luka's shoulder, the freight cars continued to flash by; the dim light from above causing an odd strobing effect. In the dark spaces between each rail car, something was manifesting. A figure. She squinted. *Elodie?*

'Ames.' Luka was breathing hard. He shifted back a step, his thick tumble of brown curls obscuring her view. 'Are you okay?' Worry swam in his eyes and pulled at his brows.

She nodded, wincing. 'I know how to fall, remember?'

'Thank fuck. Flynn would rip me a new one if anything happened to you.'

'What?'

'Nothing,' he grumbled, rubbing at his jaw.

'Holy shit!' Leona's voice reached Amy before her body did. 'Are you out of your freaking mind?' Her friend's arms wrapped around her in a tight hug. 'I thought you were a goner. That train came from out of nowhere.'

'Tell me about it,' Luka said. 'We better haul arse out of here before we get busted.'

Leona waved her phone in the air. 'Well, ghost, or no ghost, this footage is going to be awesome.'

'Do you think it was Elodie?'

Amy swung around to face Kenzie. Had she seen the ghostly girl, too? 'What do you mean?' she asked.

'The train. The second one.' Kenzie looked to be on the verge of tears, her green eyes huge and shimmering. 'Do you think she sent it?'

Amy put her arm around her friend's shoulder. 'No, Kenz. I'm sure it wasn't her.' She flicked a glance at Luka, who stared back, unmoving. 'Let's go home.'

The walk back to the train station was silent, except for Leona replaying the video over and over on her phone, trying to see if they captured any paranormal activity. Amy wasn't interested. It only proved to remind her of what she'd done tonight.

Lied to her mum. Kept a secret from Flynn. Risked her life.

And for what? Some creepypasta footage of them almost getting hit by not one, but *two trains*?

She boarded the Metro with a sigh. The carriage was empty, so they all grabbed their own seats. Close enough together, but far enough apart to get lost in their own thoughts.

Amy only had to travel one stop, yet she stretched out, exhausted, and struggled not to think of what might've happened if Flynn had been there to rescue her instead of Luka. Would he have taken her in his arms? Maybe even kissed her?

Heat crept up her neck. Ever since the day she'd met the tall skater-boy-next-door, she'd fallen for him. Hard.

It had been back at the start of the year, in the middle of summer, and one of those scorching hot days when the sun beat down on your back, making you lose your shit over the tiniest things. It didn't help that she and her mum had been moving yet again. This would've been their sixth home in the four years since her dad had left. And she'd liked their last flat—unlike this dump—but they hadn't been able to afford the rent increase, and so there they were dragging their belongings up two flights of concrete stairs. Again.

Amy hadn't even reached the second half of the stairwell when the crappy plastic wheels on her suitcase had snapped off. She'd watched helpless, as they rolled over the edge and clattered onto the weed-encrusted concrete below. She was already hot, tired, and sore. Determined not to cry, she'd sat down and pressed the heels of her palms into her eyes. Once she'd pulled herself together, she'd noticed a boy sitting on the retaining wall beside the drive.

Partly camouflaged by the shade of the trees, he was watching her, all the while rolling a skateboard back and forth under his feet. She'd stared back as he got up and retrieved the broken wheels, climbed the stairs, and handed them to her in his open palm.

She still remembered the feel of his skin when it brushed hers. Warm, with long, strong fingers.

'Unit six, right?' he'd asked. Deep ocean-blue eyes looked straight at her through a scrappy black fringe.

So captivated by his open gaze, she'd barely noticed the heat from the concrete step searing through the back of her denim shorts. He'd picked up her bag as if it weighed nothing, and carried it to her front door. When she found the sense to get to her feet and thank him, he'd shrugged it off.

'If you need anything, I'm next door. Number five.' Jerking a thumb over his shoulder, he'd turned away. Amy's heart had been pounding so hard, she hadn't even thought to ask his name.

That had been ten months ago. And even though she and her mum had moved to yet another apartment, those dark blue eyes still watched her with equal parts amusement and intensity. She still ached to run her hands through that messy black hair. And oh God, don't get her started on his lopsided grin that she longed to see every day and dreamed of kissing every night.

Amy blinked. In the darkened carriage window, her reflection was pink and glistening. She wasn't sure if it was the night's excitement or thoughts of Flynn that made her cheeks so flushed. She twisted away to grab her backpack as the train slowed into South Kensington and caught Luka watching her with a thoughtful expression.

'Do you think Flynn will be at school tomorrow?' she asked him.

He shrugged, twisting his hair into a messy bun. 'With him, who knows?'

Amy nodded. Flynn had bunked off again this week, and now that she was no longer living next door, she never knew when she'd see him next. She still worried about his mum's boyfriend. The guy was a complete arsehole and liked to push Flynn around, even though he was more than capable of looking after himself these days. Her cheeks heated. The boy had grown into his body rather well over the past few months.

Warmth spread low in her belly as she thought about his muscular arms and gentle hands. Despite his rough upbringing, Flynn Powell was the kindest and most caring person she knew. Yeah, there was a pretty good chance he would have comforted her tonight. *Damn it.*

Saying her goodbyes, Amy stepped from the carriage and quickened her pace through the darkened park to her housing complex. She needed to get home before her mum finished her baking shift at one in the morning and realised Amy wasn't where she said she'd be. Still, she slowed as she passed the playground across the road. She and Flynn often hung out there whenever he walked her home, but tonight the swings were empty.

How many more nights were they going to have together? Their senior year was almost over. She couldn't let him slip away.

Vita Brevis. Life was too short, and so she made a resolution.

Tomorrow night, after gym class. There, on the swings in the dark. That's when she'd tell Flynn how she felt.

CHAPTER TWO

T HE SKY HAD ALREADY darkened with heavy clouds by the time Amy stepped through the door of Pierre's Patisserie, after school.

Her mum's boss greeted her with open arms. 'Ah, bonjour Amy, mon amie!'

'Hi, Pierre.'

'Non, non, non!' He waggled a finger and smiled mischievously.

Amy laughed. 'Pardon. Salut, Pierre!'

'That's better,' the Frenchman said, with his usual Aussie accent.

Amy grinned, shaking her head. 'What do you have for me today?' she asked, peering at the half-empty display cabinets.

'Whatever you'd like, *mon cherie.*' He waved towards the row of sandwiches.

The ham and cheese looked good. 'I'll have the—' She stopped herself just in time. Pierre had been teaching her basic French, and she was proud to recall the name. 'The croque monsieur.'

'That's quite heavy to eat before your gym class, isn't it?'

Amy sat down on a nearby barstool. 'Nah. The class got cancelled. My coach is sick, or her kid is, or something. Anyway, I'm going to spend the evening helping at The Mission, instead.' She patted her stomach. 'So, I'm going to need all that protein to get me through.'

'I see. And will young Flynn be there tonight, too?'

Heat rose to Amy's cheeks, and she turned her face away towards the window. 'Hopefully.'

It was soup kitchen night at The Mission, and even though Flynn hadn't turned up to school, Amy knew he'd never miss the opportunity to give back to those who'd helped him in his own time of need.

'Here you go.' Pierre returned with the toastie, and Amy took it gratefully.

'Merci.' She grinned, taking a huge bite, while mindful not to let the melted cheese drip all down her fingers.

Pierre waited by her table, observing the commuters pushing their way past the store towards the tram and train stations, eager to beat the rain.

'It's going to hose down any minute,' he muttered. 'At this rate, I might as well close up early.' He flicked the sign on the door to CLOSED and turned to her. 'I'll bag up all the leftovers, and you can take them to The Mission with you when you've finished eating. I daresay they'll get a good crowd tonight.'

Amy nodded as she swallowed. She didn't want to get caught in the rain, either. Eating quickly, she shouldered her backpack and took the bags from Pierre. Leaving via the back entrance, she stepped quickly down the narrow alleyway, dodging stinking industrial bins and the occasional puddle. Up ahead, Flinders Lane was a tide of mostly black suits and coats flowing in both directions.

Fat raindrops were falling by the time she reached the curb, and it was obvious she wouldn't have a hope in hell of crossing the lane and cutting through to the wider thoroughfare of Flinders Street. Parked cars and traffic clogged the road, and she cursed not being able to duck and weave her way through the pedestrian sea using her parkour skills. Laden with bags full of rolls, croissants and pastries, she was forced to wait for a gap in the rush-hour crowd before she could venture out onto the narrow footpath.

Heading west towards Queen Street, the buildings and shops she passed were a lot more fashionable and newer than those along her usual route. Older structures were getting refurbished, and scaffolding crowded the already narrow footpath. Ducking to avoid getting her eye poked out by an umbrella, she stumbled over a sandbag and fell sprawling onto the wet pavement. So much for knowing how to fall—she was lucky she didn't break both wrists.

'Are you okay, love?' A workman in a high-vis vest and hardhat rushed from the construction site and helped her to her feet.

'Yeah, I think so,' she winced, brushing dirt from her stinging palms.

A couple of the bread rolls had fallen out, and he gathered them up quickly. 'Luckily no one stood on these, but they are a bit dirty,' he added with a smile.

'Thanks, but would you mind just holding onto them for a minute, please?' Her palms were all scratched up, filthy, and oozing blood. 'I'd better clean up first.'

The man steered her safely out of the way, into the entrance of the construction site. 'Do you need some water?'

'No. I have some, thanks.' She knelt to fetch a bottle from her backpack, and as she rinsed her hands, Amy caught sight of the building adjacent to the construction site. It was a four-storey Victorian, with a cream facade and red-bricked siding.

'No way,' she whispered. Pulling out her phone, she snapped a photo of the newly exposed western wall. Usually covered from view, an aging advertisement was painted on the side of the stately building—a ghost sign.

She must have walked this way dozens of times in the past, but if they hadn't been demolishing the old carpark next door, she would never have seen it. Hell, if she hadn't tripped over that bloody sandbag and fallen, she wouldn't have had a reason even to look backwards. Ghost signs were common in a city as old as Melbourne, but this one was different. And Leona would totally lose her shit once Amy told her what she'd found.

Her heart sped up as she turned back to the workman. 'Excuse me, but what are you building here?'

He shrugged. 'Apartments, I think. We're only the demolition company. We don't do the new builds.'

Amy gasped. 'You're not knocking that one down, too, are you?' She tipped her chin towards the Victorian.

'No. See, it's marked for restoration.' He pointed to a sign tacked onto the building's wrought-iron fence she'd failed to notice. 'Now, are you sure you're okay? Because I have to pack up for the day.'

'Oh, yeah. Thanks for your help.'

'No problem.' He tipped his hardhat. 'Be careful in the wet, now.'

She retied the bag that had split open and hurried towards The Mission. By the time she'd rounded the corner ahead, the street lamps had come on, illuminating icy needles of rain as they fell. Amy cursed under her breath. Not only were some of the rolls covered in dirt, but now they'd be soggy as well. Pulling her hood over her head, she hunkered down against the rain and practically ran the rest of the way.

Pierre was right. The Mission was already brimming with the city's needy, volunteers shepherding them towards the dining hall. Keeping an eye out for Flynn, Amy threaded her way through the crowded foyer to the kitchen.

Roger, the kitchen manager, met her at the door. 'Amy, you are an absolute angel!'

She smiled at him. 'Don't thank me. I'm only the courier.'

'In any case, I'm grateful. It looks like we'll have a full house tonight with this weather.'

'Is Flynn here yet?' she asked as she helped him put the rolls into the oven to warm up.

Roger nodded. 'He's helping the fellas unload the trucks out back.'

Of course he was. Flynn never shied away from hard work. It was one reason Amy was so drawn to him that first day they'd met. Other than those eyes, the hair, that smile. Was she grinning like an idiot?

Roger tilted his head toward the rear door, a knowing look on his face. 'You can go out and see him if you like.'

Cheeks heating, Amy fled through the kitchen storeroom to the rear loading dock. The big roller door was up, and Amy could see the rain now falling in heavy sheets outside. A couple of guys were unloading a truck full of trays of tinned goods, but she couldn't see Flynn anywhere. Staying out of the way, she skirted the edge of the dock to find him hauling a crate of vegetables from a nearby van. He was absolutely soaked to the skin. A white t-shirt clung to his chest, exposing well-defined pecs and the crucifix that he always wore tucked close to his heart.

'Hey.' His eyes lit up as he saw her. 'I missed you last night.'

He gave her one of those lopsided smiles as he swept close by, taking the crate into the storeroom. She followed him, trying not to stare at the way his biceps bulged with the weight of it. He smelled like rain and sweat and *Flynn*. Her mouth went dry when she raised her eyes to find him gazing at her. It wasn't until he lifted a dark brow in question that she realised he had been asking her something.

'Sorry. What was that?'

'Are you going to your gym class tonight, or will I be waiting around in the rain for you not to show again?'

Oh crap. He'd waited for her last night?

She'd been so caught up in keeping the seance from him that she'd completely forgotten their usual Wednesday night routine. After helping at The Mission, Flynn usually dropped by the gym to watch the last few minutes of her class and then walk her home, before legging it to wherever he was staying for the night, dependent on whether his mum's abusive boyfriend was home or not.

Double crap.

Her stomach plummeted. She still felt bad about keeping things from him, so she settled for the half-truth.

'I was helping Leona with an assignment, and you know how full-on she is. It got late, and I totally missed my class. I'm sorry. I didn't even think to let you know.' She added a wince for good measure.

His jaw twitched. 'So, are you going to the gym tonight?'

'No. My coach is sick, so it's been called off. And thank God, because I wouldn't be able to do it anyway,' she said, showing him her hands.

He frowned. 'What happened?'

'I tripped over on the way here.'

He raised a disbelieving brow, and she shoved at his wet chest.

'I know. I train enough, I should know how to fall properly. It isn't funny.'

'I didn't say it was. And for the record, I'm not laughing.' He reached for her fingers. 'Let me have a look.'

Amy's breath caught as he tenderly stroked her oozing palms. 'These will need a good clean. Wait here while I get the first aid box.'

She hefted herself up onto a nearby workbench, nibbling on her bottom lip as she watched him disappear out to the dock. Lying to Flynn didn't feel right, and she hated herself for it. But before she could berate herself, he was wedging himself between her open knees, and all other thoughts were forgotten. She kept her head down, focusing on the little tendons that moved in his forearms as he sprayed antiseptic on her wounds and cleaned them up with some gauze. Then he peeled the backing off two huge adhesive plasters and covered both her palms. By the time he finished, she looked like a prizefighter.

'It's not that bad.' She joked, looking up at him.

His eyes were fixed downwards as he packed up the first aid kit. 'Just keep it on overnight. Trust me. I know a few things about hand injuries.' His smile was tight.

She didn't doubt it. She'd seen the split knuckles on more than one occasion. 'Thank you, Flynn.'

His gaze lifted. Lingered.

'Anytime.'

He was standing so close to her that she could feel the heat radiating from his body through his wet clothes. Heat that she seemed to absorb through osmosis.

'I, uh... I better get back to helping Roger.'

'Yeah, of course,' he said, stepping back as she pushed off the bench. 'I'm going to head home, anyway.'

'You're not staying around to help?' she asked.

'In this state?' He shook his wet hair like a shaggy dog, sending her squealing and ducking for cover.

After squeezing the excess water from his shirt, Flynn followed her through to the kitchen, where Roger sent them both on their way, citing they'd helped enough already, and he had ample volunteers for the night.

'Come on. I'll walk you home.' Flynn handed her an umbrella and ushered her through the front doors. 'Can't have you getting home looking like a drowned rat.'

'Like you, you mean?' she teased, shoving him with her shoulder.

'Yeah, like me.'

Once they were outside, Flynn turned to her. 'So, is everything all right, Ames?'

'Yeah. Why?'

'I don't know,' he said, eyeing her sideways. 'You tell me.'

'Tell you what?'

'Did your assignment involve you bailing on your gym class *and* *me* so that you could play chicken with a fucking freight train last night?'

Her mouth dropped open—while Flynn locked his, a little muscle ticking near his jaw.

'Luka told you, didn't he?' She grunted in exasperation. *Bloody Luka.* What she wouldn't give for one of Leona's curses right now. 'I didn't tell you because I knew you wouldn't be interested, and I didn't want to worry you.'

He halted in the middle of the footpath, forcing people to step around them.

'Oh, so you knew just how dangerous your little stunt was, then? That didn't stop you from traipsing through Footscray like a little troupe of fucking girl scouts.'

'It wasn't like that.' Oh, who was she trying to kid?

Flynn looked away, nostrils flaring. 'You just don't get it.'

He strode off suddenly, leaving her to stand in the rain, tears pricking at her eyes.

'Why do you even care?' she called out, her voice cracking.

She watched him turn and storm back towards her, his eyes like cold chips of sapphire.

'Amy, if you think I don't care about you, you haven't got a fucking clue who I am. But, you know what hurts the most?'

'Yeah,' she interrupted, her voice rising. 'What hurts, is that I actually wanted to tell you about it. You should have been there with us, Flynn. But you're never around anymore. It should have been you saving me, not Luka!' She shoved at his hard chest, her voice cracking as she bit back angry tears. 'I wanted it to be *you*.'

He shook his head, hurt writ large across his face. 'No, Amy. You lied to me. You fucking lied.'

She reached out a hand to him, but he pulled away from her. Sure, she'd messed up, but why were they be fighting? This wasn't them. It definitely wasn't like Flynn to be so distant, especially not after the tenderness he'd just shown while tending to her wounded hands. She clenched the umbrella handle and ground her teeth against the pain.

'I never meant to hurt you,' she said, trying to meet his eye. 'I'm sorry. It won't happen again.'

'You got that right.' His voice was cold as he turned his back on her and stalked off towards Flinders Street, leaving her standing in the rain. Alone.

No, no, no! Tears threatened to spill down her cheeks, and she wiped at her eyes with her sleeve. Everything was going to shit. It wasn't supposed to be like this.

She'd had it all planned out... tonight, on the swings in the park.

I was supposed to tell you I loved you.

Chapter Three

F LYNN HAD WALKED AN entire block before he realised Amy wasn't following him. He turned to see her still standing outside The Mission; the red umbrella she held winking at him through the wave of pedestrians like a warning light. *Stay away.*

She might've pissed him off, but he wasn't an arsehole. He typed out a quick text.

r u coming?

He watched her pull her phone from the pocket of her sweatpants, look at the screen, and then at him. But she didn't move. *Come on, Amy.*

Finally, she began walking towards him, and Flynn released a long breath, though it did little to ease the tension in his shoulders.

Neither of them said a word to each other as they rode the train to South Kensington. The carriage was full to brimming with commuters, so they stood in the centre aisle near the doors and looked in opposite directions. When the train slowed into Amy's station, he moved to exit with her.

'You don't need to walk me home.'

He clenched his fists and bit back a retort. The latter was an act of self-preservation he'd learned early in life. *Just keep your fucking mouth shut, Flynn.* That way, he couldn't hurt himself or anybody else with his words.

But it was already too late for that. Amy was already on the verge of tears, and he hated that he'd been the cause of it. Hated that she reminded him of his mum—weeping over another loser who'd used and abused her. *The fuck he was like one of those bastards...*

He sighed. The fight had already leaked out of him, leaving him deflated like a saggy balloon. Trailing behind Amy, he stepped from the train and kept his distance as she left the platform and headed towards the park.

As they reached the playground, Flynn paused. Probably more out of habit than anything because he didn't feel like engaging in conversation. He wasn't going to make that mistake twice. He hung back, leaning against a nearby tree, as Amy brushed the rain from her favourite swing and sat down.

He jammed his hands in his pockets, and focused on the rough bark at his back. It was solid. Grounding. He inhaled. Exhaled. And tried to ignore the tingle in his side.

'You were right,' Amy said, making a divot in the mulch with her feet. 'About everything.' She huffed and looked skyward.

The rain had turned from drizzle to that kind of mist that resembled snow, and he watched the tiny drops crystallize on her nose and cheeks.

'I mean, trying to conjure a ghost on the train tracks? It doesn't get any crazier than that, but you know what Leona's like.'

In addition to being Amy's best friend, Leona Liu was a pocket rocket of intimidation and misplaced determination. Frankly, he tried to keep his distance from her as much as possible.

'Did you know she cursed Luka?'

Flynn felt the corner of his mouth tug. 'Doesn't sound like her.'

'Oh, yeah. He was throwing stones, and she went right off. Like, *right* off. I thought he was going to lose an appendage if you know what I'm saying.'

Flynn snorted, wondering if Luka knew about that part. He'd told him everything else. About the seance and getting trapped in the train tunnel. That had pissed him off, but wait up... Amy had also said something about Luka saving her.

Flynn bristled. His best mate had kind of left that part out. Had she been in more danger than Luka let on? What the fuck was up with that?

'—it doesn't matter anyway. Elodie's a lost cause. But I might've found something better.'

He blinked. Realised Amy was still talking. 'What?'

'I think I've found the Butcher's House. In Flinders Lane.' Her eyes were shining. 'What do you reckon?' She held her phone up for him to see.

He stepped closer and peered at the screen. A photo depicted a faded advertisment painted on a brick wall. The letters were old-fashioned, their colour still a garish red.

Dr Boucher
Flebotomie for Women
Consultation Free

'That's got to be him, the Infamous Butcher of Flinders Lane. Remember when we were talking about urban legends in English at the start of the year, and Jimmy kept banging on about that French blood-letter who murdered all those women?'

Nope. It must've been one of the classes he skipped.

'He just sliced them open and watched them bleed out. Apparently, he got off on it too, you know—all the blood. Ms Baxter said it was all just hearsay. But still... He was a real person. This proves it.' She was gushing, clearly excited.

Flynn closed his eyes and tried to repress a shudder as the tingle in his side became a persistent gnaw.

'Just what are you planning, Ames?' He swallowed. She better not say what he thought she was going to.

'Can you imagine? That place must be teeming with ghosts. And not only that, this is our chance to prove the legend. Maybe Leona was onto something with her assignment idea. What if the Butcher left something behind? Those floors are rumoured to be stained with the blood of his victims. And the building's about to be renovated, so we're running out of time. I think we should check it out this weekend. You up for it?'

Jesus Christ. Her eyes were no longer shining. They were absolutely luminous.

'You realise the building hasn't been locked up for the past century, right? Tell me you're not seriously thinking of breaking in.'

She didn't answer.

He ran a hand through his hair. 'So tell me this. Why the sudden fascination with ghosts?'

They weren't real. Didn't he know that better than anyone? How many times had he asked his dad for advice, only to be met with silence? There were only so many times you could speak to the dead before you realised they weren't talking back.

She gave him a baleful look. 'You know why.'

Flynn dropped his head. She'd confided in him the very first day they'd met, telling him that she was used to fading into the background every time she moved schools.

He didn't realise she still felt like a ghost, and didn't know how to tell her that she wasn't invisible. Not to him. Not to anyone who mattered. Her douchebag of a father didn't count. Is that what this was about?

'You don't need to prove yourself to him.'

She eyed him with an expression he didn't understand and simply said, 'Thanks for walking me home.'

Great. He'd gone and opened his mouth and completely fucking blown it. There was so much he wanted to say to her, and yet he dared not. He just wasn't good at that shit. So, all he said was, 'No problem.'

Amy got up from the swing and paused beside him. 'Guess I'll catch you later, then.'

For the briefest moment, he could almost feel her lean into him before she straightened her shoulders and stepped past.

—◦✦◦—

Flynn waited until Amy was safely inside before he sagged against the swing, clutching at his side. Impulsively, his fingers sought the ridges on his skin. He closed his eyes and tried to focus on his breathing. No. This wasn't happening now.

It'd been *ten months* since he'd last had the urge to cut. He was stronger than this.

And he had Amy to thank for that. From the day they'd first met —when she'd climbed up onto the roof and asked his name—she'd been his saviour, his happy place. His most favourite moments were of the two of them, up on the rooftop of their block of flats; him riding his skateboard, and her watching him glide by with smiling eyes, her feet twitching like she wanted to join him.

God, he missed her. More than seeing her every day, he missed their easy friendship and who they used to be before she moved away. Maybe he'd take her skateboarding tomorrow, after school. It'd been so long since they'd done anything fun like that.

Sudden goosebumps prickled his arms. The light had well and truly dropped, causing him to shiver in his wet clothes. Pulling his t-shirt off, he tucked it in the back of his jeans and broke into a jog, determined to take the long way home.

He needed time to think, and hopefully, if he stayed out long enough, Mick-the-Prick would have fallen asleep in front of the TV, allowing him to slip in unnoticed. If that boozing bastard hassled him about coming home late again, he'd tell him to get fucked and walk out. He could always break into the sprinkler shed at school and sleep in there. It wouldn't be the first time.

Fuck. Was his bad influence rubbing off on Amy? Was that why she was trying to get herself into trouble? He could have punched that tree when she'd asked him to go trespassing with her.

Didn't she get it? She was sweet and smart, and surrounded by people who loved her. She sure as hell didn't need to throw all that away and risk getting a police record for breaking and entering. The tingle returned, and he pushed his legs harder into a run. If Amy thought he would sit around and watch her throw her life away, she was in for a rude shock.

Luka might've saved her last night, but Flynn wasn't ready to put that kind of faith in someone else. He needed to get her mind away from ghosts and back to the living—all on his own.

The only question was how. As his feet hit the bitumen, he tried to come up with all manner of ideas to make her forget about the Butcher's House. But she was just so damned obsessive. Once Amy got it in her head to do something, nothing would stop her. She'd just go break in there, anyway. And now he knew she'd most likely lie about it, too.

Flynn swore out loud. Even though it went against everything he stood for, the only solution he could come up with was to join her. At least that way, he would be there to keep her out of trouble.

Arriving home, he found the flat in darkness. Pausing at the door, he laid an ear against the thin wood, listening for Mick. The only discernible sounds were coming from the TV. Either the prick had fallen asleep in front of it, or he wasn't there tonight. Flynn hoped it was the latter. Pushing his key into the lock, he opened the door as quietly as he could.

The place appeared empty, but a rhythmic squeaking emanated from his mother's bedroom as he crept past. Holding his breath, he slipped into his own room, locked the door and stripped to his underwear. Falling into bed, he threw the pillow over his face and let his body sink into sleep.

A strong pounding on his door roused him awake some hours later. *Mick.* Pulling on a pair of sweatpants, Flynn unlocked the door and cracked it open an inch. 'What do you want?' he deadpanned.

Mick glared at him. 'What time did you sneak in, you little shit?'

'Depends—' Flynn yawned. 'How long have you been fucking my mum?'

'Watch your mouth, boy. For some reason, she worries about you.'

He flicked a glance past the man to his mother's room, where he could clearly hear her loud snores. 'I seriously doubt that.'

Mick kicked the door open. 'Show some respect, kid.'

Flynn squared his chest and levelled his gaze. 'You want to have a go at me, old man? You're thirty years my senior, remember. *Thirty.* You still want to have a go?'

Mick eyeballed him for what felt like an entire minute. 'Fuck you.'

'No thanks,' Flynn replied, closing the door. 'You're not my type.'

With shaking fingers, he slid the lock in place and ran his fingers through his hair. Unable to sleep, he sprawled across his bed and composed a hundred different texts to Amy before deleting every single one. By the time he heard Mick leave, around three in the morning, he'd settled on just two words.

I'm in.

Chapter Four

THE RAIN CONTINUED THROUGHOUT the next day. Flynn watched it stream down the classroom windows, wishing he was at home in bed. He'd already put off yet another appointment with the school's guidance counsellor that morning—by feigning a headache and trying to catch up on a few hours' sleep in the sick room. But it hadn't been enough. The room was as cold as a morgue, plus it reeked of disinfectant and vomit.

Then some junior kid came in with a nosebleed, and while the nurse cleaned it up, Flynn had to sit on his hands to stop himself from nicking the scissors out of the first aid box. Not that they'd be sharp enough to ease the dull ache in his side. Eventually, he asked for a couple of painkillers and headed back to class.

Ordinarily, he would've just slipped out and gone home, but he didn't want to risk another run-in with Mick. Plus, he wanted to see Amy again. To make sure everything was cool between them and do something fun together after school, just the two of them. They couldn't go skateboarding now because of the wet weather. And going to the movies felt like schoolwork. There wasn't much to do indoors, except hang at the arcade or maybe try that new indoor trampoline place. Amy would probably love that, but he wasn't too keen.

Slinking into his media class, he found his seat in the dark and stretched out his legs. The teacher had already started a film for them to analyse: an overly-popular Disney movie about two sisters. He groaned, uninterested in studying sibling dynamics—he was an only child, after all—but once he'd suffered through the first few songs, the main character's long blonde braid and bright blue eyes sparked an idea in him.

Flynn snickered, unable to believe his luck. Amy was wearing her hair like that today, so it must have been a sign. Grateful for his position at the back of the class, he shielded his phone from view and did a quick search online. Checking the session times, he grinned and sent a quick text to Amy.

pick u up at 5

dress in layers. include something warm

Then, leaning across his desk, he dropped his head onto his arms and fell asleep for the next hour and a half.

—◦✦◦—

'You're not very thorough in your instructions. You know that?' Amy quirked a brow at him as she opened her front door.

'What do you mean?' he feigned offence, glancing at his wrist. 'It's five o'clock. Layers. Something warm. It's not that hard.'

'This is Melbourne. We always dress in layers, so that's not helpful,' she scowled. 'Something warm? Could you be any vaguer?'

She put her hands on her hips. 'Will this do?'

His teeth sunk into his bottom lip, suppressing a laugh. God, he loved seeing her flustered. Lounging against the doorframe, he let his gaze run over her. She wore a white sweater that was so loosely knit he could see her hot-pink bra underneath, her usual frayed denim cut-offs over a pair of ripped black tights and white high-top sneakers. Her hair was still in the braid, but bits had come loose and were now framing her face.

He cocked his head and let the smile loose. 'Yeah, you'll do.'

To be truthful, he hadn't known what to expect, so he'd gone with jeans, a regular tee and tied a hoodie around his waist. He figured if they were going to be cold, at least they'd be cold together.

It was still pouring outside, so he'd snagged someone's golf umbrella from the laundry under his flat, and they huddled under it all the way to the train station.

'So, are you going to tell me where we're going?' Amy asked as they boarded the train.

'Nope. It's a surprise.' He sat across from her, his back in the direction they were heading.

'It's going to be like that, is it?' She huffed and lifted her legs, resting her feet on the seat beside him.

'What, you don't like surprises?' He smirked and started fidgeting with her laces.

She flashed him a sweet smile. 'I swear to God, Flynn, if you tie my shoes together, I'll kick you in the balls.'

He laughed out loud. So loud that a woman seated at the end of the carriage turned around to glare at them. He gave her a cheeky wink, then leaned forward and rested his elbows on his knees.

Staring intently at Amy, he lowered his voice. 'You wouldn't be able to get your feet apart, sweetheart.'

She drew her legs back down and mirrored him, a menacing tone in her voice. 'It'd be a two-foot kick, buddy. One for each of your balls.'

Oh, how he missed this.

He shot her a serious look. 'How do you know I've got two?'

'Wait. What?' She drew back, a mixture of confusion and amusement on her face, clearly not knowing whether to believe him or not.

In the end, he had to turn away to hide the smirk on his face.

'Oh, you're such a dick!' She lashed out at him, slapping at his knees and laughing. 'You had me feeling sorry for you.'

'What, you mean you don't normally?' He grinned.

Fuck you, she mouthed at him, shaking her head.

Mmm. It was a much more pleasing offer than his last one, and as much as he really wanted to, he couldn't afford to entertain that thought right now. No, he'd revisit that one later tonight, when he was alone.

'Come on,' he said, rising and pulling her up off the seat as the train pulled into Southern Cross station. 'This is us.'

They exited the station on the corner and crossed the pedestrian bridge to the Esplanade. The rain had eased back to a gentle drizzle, and large puddles filled the pavement. Flynn stepped in one by accident, splashing water up one of Amy's legs. She said nothing but slammed her foot down hard into the next one, causing his jeans to get soaked at the ankle. Grinning, he side-stepped over the next puddle, scooping his back foot across the surface, sending a plane of water directly into Amy's sneakers. She stopped abruptly, head down.

Oh fuck.

But they were only having fun. Gingerly, he pushed the braid off her shoulder so he could see her face properly. 'Ames. You okay?' Surely he hadn't misread her puddle attack? It was a typical-Amy-type retaliation. 'Look, I'm sorry if—'

Amy clamped her hands around his shoulders and hoisted herself up, her legs over his shoulders. He laughed and tried to shake her off, but she held fast until she'd tipped every drop of rainwater from her shoe down the back of his neck. He cringed as the icy trickle met his hot skin. Skin made all the hotter because Amy still had her legs wrapped around him. *Bloody hell.* He knew she was flexible, but she'd never done something like that before.

Springing over his head like a cheerleader, she landed with a cheeky smile, making him race after her. Catching her around the middle, he tickled her for the rest of the way. By the time they reached the Ice Palace, a warm feeling had settled deep in Flynn's chest. He closed the umbrella and dropped an arm around Amy's shoulder, giving her a quick squeeze. 'I've really missed you, Ames.'

'Me too.' She smiled up at him, and he couldn't help but grin back. 'Are we really going ice-skating?' she asked.

'You bet.' He threw on his hoodie and opened the door for her.

'I haven't been skating since I was a little kid,' she squealed, looking around excitedly. 'I'm pretty sure my dad used to take me here.'

He paid for them both, and they made their way over to the rental counter to collect their skates. 'Does that bother you? We can go somewhere else—'

'No.' She cut him off. 'It's perfect.'

—◦✦◦—

Flashback Friday nights at The Ice Palace were clearly popular. Neon LEDs rimmed the barrier, and flashing lights reflected off a disco ball suspended high over the already-crowded rink. A massive TV at one end was screening iconic 1980s movie clips while the speakers belted out modern synth-wave tracks.

'Can you skate?' Amy asked him as they pulled on their skates—black for him, white for her—and clomped their way out onto the ice.

'I've never done it before, but how hard can it be? Can't be that different to skateboarding, can it?'

It turned out that once his feet hit the ice and slid out from under him, causing him to fall flat on his arse, that it was absolutely *nothing at all* like skateboarding.

Amy covered her mouth but failed to silence the snort and giggle that followed. He didn't care. He loved hearing her laugh. It had been way too long since they'd done something fun like this, and if that meant he had to make a fool of himself to amuse her, he'd gladly do it. He pushed himself to his feet, marvelling as she glided effortlessly a few feet from the edge.

'Hey, you said you hadn't skated in years,' he protested.

She spun around to face him, pink-cheeked and happy. 'I haven't. But it's something you don't forget once you start. Like riding a bike. Plus, I have outstanding balance.' She smirked, raising her brows.

Got that right, he mused, his mind flicking back to that moment she'd wrapped her legs around him. Blowing out a breath, he bent his knees and pretended he was pushing his board. *Focus, Flynn.*

His balance wasn't bad either, and he only needed to adjust his centre of gravity a bit differently before he was confidently skating alongside Amy.

The two-hour session was over before he knew it, as the speakers announced that there would be one more speed-skate race before ending with a couples-only skate. He and Amy took up a prime spot near the gate and rested on the barrier, catching their breath as they watched the speed-skaters battle it out.

As soon as the race ended, Amy hauled him back out onto the ice before the others had even exited the rink. 'Come on, couples-skate!'

Her enthusiasm was infectious, and soon he was laughing and dancing on the ice with her. Once the lights went down and the music slowed, Flynn allowed his hand to seek hers. They'd been clutching at each other all night, trying not to fall, but this felt different. Heavy. Loaded.

Then those dickhead speed skaters started weaving around everyone, and Amy lost balance as one of them flew by her, catching her sweater on his ridiculous plastic trophy. She tripped over Flynn's skate, and they both went down. Landing on his arse, legs sprawled out in front, Flynn watched helplessly as Amy slid away from him on her stomach, hands outstretched. The speed skaters were still flying all around them, and he was so worried that she'd get her fingers sliced off. Sliding over to her, he pulled her to him.

'Are you okay?'

But she didn't respond, and that was when he noticed her staring at the exposed skin where his shirt had ridden up. If he were a different guy, he probably would've loved her checking out his abs. But of course she wasn't looking at his six-pack. No.

Amy's eyes were locked on the twenty-seven white ridges that rose like a ladder from his right hip bone to just beneath his ribcage. Self-conscious, he tugged his t-shirt back down.

'Flynn?' Her voice was a whisper, reaching out to him, but he just wanted to get them off the ice. Grasping her wrists, he lifted her to stand with him.

'Not now,' he rasped. 'Please.'

He wasn't ashamed of the scars. They were a part of him. But now, of course, Amy knew. And she'd want to know all about it.

The how?

That was easy. It was called a penknife and a quick hand.

But the why? That was the part he wasn't quite ready to tell her yet.

CHAPTER FIVE

J UST AS SHE'D INSTRUCTED, Amy waited outside the designated café on Flinders Lane at eight o'clock on Saturday night, scanning every face that passed. She was jittery and nervous as hell, drumming her fingers on her thighs and wondering if every passer-by knew what she was planning to do.

Jimmy was the first to turn up. Amy had invited him at the last minute, seeing as he was the one who knew the most about the legend, and could be useful. His family was ex-Army, and he was one of those guys who knew how to do everything. Leona and Kenzie rocked up next, raucous as ever, then last of all, Luka. Amy smiled at him.

'Is Flynn coming?' he asked.

'He should be.'

Flynn had skipped school again, and she secretly worried he wouldn't show. He still hadn't told her about the scars on his body, and she hoped he wasn't deliberately avoiding her.

'Sweet.' Luka dropped a hand on her shoulder. 'So, what have you found? It must be pretty good if Flynn's coming along.'

'Just wait till you hear, man.' Jimmy was bouncing on his toes, hyped up on some kind of highly caffeinated energy drink or something. Amy swallowed. Maybe inviting him was a mistake. She didn't need a loose cannon tonight.

Kenzie spoke up. 'Shouldn't we wait for Flynn, first?'

'Oh, he already knows.'

Luka's hand slipped away from Amy's shoulder. 'Does everyone else know but me?'

'No. Not everything revolves around you,' Leona snapped at him. She turned to Amy. 'How come you didn't tell me first?'

'Will you guys cut it out?' Kenzie looked tired. 'Go on, Ames. Spill.'

She showed them the photo of Boucher's advertisement.

'Holy shit.' Jimmy whistled. 'A legit ghost sign! That's what they're called, you know. Vintage advertisements for businesses that are long dead and then get found decades later.' He smiled, looking pleased with himself.

Leona stared at him. 'Yeah. Thanks for that, nerd-for-brains. So are we going in, or what?'

Amy addressed Jimmy. 'While we're waiting for Flynn, why don't you tell us the story?'

He grinned at her, nodding. 'Okay. Well, back around 1895, I think, there was this French doctor.' He pointed to Amy's screen. 'Doctor Boucher. He was a quack phlebotomist, a blood-letter, who drained hundreds of women, claiming to cure them of madness. Apparently, he spilled so much blood, he became known as the Butcher of Flinders Lane.'

'Rumour has it, he was a vampire who preyed on the mentally ill and harboured a secret fetish for hookers,' Luka added.

Kenzie screwed up her face. 'Ew, gross.'

'I'm not sure about that, but this proves he was an actual person. And he worked out of that very building just over there.' Amy pointed down to the next block.

They all turned to look, but Amy's attention diverted as Flynn rounded the corner. Dressed from head to toe in black, he looked every inch the dark and dangerous bad boy she always thought him to be. She sucked in a shaky breath.

'You came.' She smiled, her heart doing a little flip.

He raised his eyebrows in greeting. 'I'm a man of my word.'

'Hey, where've you been, dude?' Luka locked forearms with Flynn, slapping him on the back.

'Keeping away from you fuckers. So, what's the plan?'

Amy pocketed her phone. 'The plan is, firstly we split up and scope out the best way to get in,' she said, looking at all of them in turn. 'There's a laneway that borders the building on the right. Kenz and Luka, see if you can find a way in there. A door, a window, anything. Jim and Leona can check out the construction site on the other side while Flynn and I scope out the front. Questions?'

'Nope.'

'No probs.'

'Cool.' She nodded. 'Luka, you and Kenz take the lead, and we'll all peel off. And try not to attract too much attention.'

'So, we're really doing this, huh?' Flynn asked, leaning against a nearby vending machine. Its blue light washed over his face, illuminating troubled eyes. She could tell he hadn't wanted to come, and the fact he did filled her heart.

Impulsively, Amy reached for his hand, tugging it free from his pocket and lacing her fingers through his. 'Come on. It'll be fun.'

He gave their linked hands a curious look. 'I promise I won't run away.'

She felt heat creeping into her cheeks. 'Maybe I just want to hold on to my best friend for a while.'

'Best friend now, am I? Don't tell Leona that. I'd like to keep my most prized body part.'

She caught a smile tugging at the corners of his luscious mouth. Squeezing her fingers, he led her out onto the footpath towards the Butcher's House.

The others had already split off in their respective directions. Without letting go of her hand, Flynn stepped out onto the road and peered up at the darkened windows. 'Looks like that top-right window is boarded up. That could be easy to get through, but you know I'm not good with anything higher than the half-pipe. Plus, it's in full view of the street front.'

He was still scanning the windows when something closer to street level caught Amy's eye. She let go of his hand and pressed up against the wrought-iron fence. Beyond that, the ground dropped away to reveal a tiny, sunken courtyard. In the shadows behind a set of glass doors, a tangle of pipes and valves were just visible against the red brick interior. Pulling out her phone, Amy thrust it between the iron rungs as far as she could and snapped a photo without the flash.

The picture was grainy, but on the wall beside the pipes was a small sign. Pointing to the left, the words were obvious: CELLAR.

'Whatcha looking at?' Flynn was by her side, chin on her shoulder.

A grin spread over her face. 'Do you see what I see?' She gestured to the photo.

'The sprinkler system?' he asked with a wry smile.

Rolling her eyes, she thumped him in the solar plexus with her elbow.

'Ow!' he staggered back, rubbing at his chest. 'Remind me again why I came?'

But Amy was already rushing to the laneway. Kenzie and Luka were nowhere to be seen. Pacing up and down the cobblestones, Amy ran her eyes along the bottom of the wall until she found what she was looking for. 'Bingo!' she whispered to herself.

She turned to tell Flynn, but he was tiptoeing up the laneway, back pressed to the brick wall, stealing a look into each alcove and shuttered loading dock. When he was near the end, he stopped and looked back at her with that cheeky lopsided grin, a finger to his lips, beckoning for her to join him. Were Kenzie and Luka making out in one of the secluded recesses?

She huffed out a silent laugh and shook her head. There was no way she could endure watching anyone kiss while Flynn looked on, too. She turned away as heat spread across her cheeks. If tonight proved to be the daring, exhilarating experience she was hoping for, she might just get her blood pumping enough to get a little reckless with him.

Up ahead, Flynn sprang out of the shadows with a yell, and whatever happened next had Luka sprinting after him down the alley towards her.

'Shh!' she hushed at them as they flew past and around the corner, like little boys. Meanwhile, the others joined Amy as she explained what she'd discovered.

'You mean there's a cellar down there?' Kenzie pointed to the small rectangular opening that gaped at street level.

Amy grinned at her. 'I'd stake my life on it.'

'That's rich, considering old man Boucher was supposedly a vampire,' Luka sniggered. 'So then, Buffy. Who's volunteering to go down there?'

They all looked at each other before their eyes collectively fell on Leona.

'Oh no. No way.' She shook her head vehemently.

'Come on, Lee. It's only a foot high, and you're the smallest.' Amy smiled sweetly at her. 'We'll be right here, and we won't let anything happen to you. Promise.' She crossed her heart and hugged her best friend. Whispering in her ear, she added, 'You might just get to see a ghost.'

'Yeah, and I'll haunt you all if I fall to my death,' Leona spat, eyeing the hole with suspicion. Dropping to her knees, she extracted a small penlight from her pocket and shone it into the void. 'I suppose it looks legit,' she sighed, getting to her feet. 'So what am I supposed to do once I get down there?'

All eyes turned to Amy. Behind her, she felt Flynn's warmth, reassuring and close. 'Look for another door that will lead to either the main front door or preferably this side one.' She gestured to the iron door recessed into the wall nearby.

'Yeah, there's zero access points on the other side except for those single glass panels that face the construction site,' Jim added. 'And I don't fancy breaking one of those to get in.'

'You won't need to.' Flynn's voice came from over her head. 'Amy's right. There has to be an internal passage.'

'And if there's not?' Leona asked.

'Then we haul your arse out and call it quits.'

Amy rubbed her hands together. 'All right. Let's do this.'

They formed a tight circle around Leona, shielding her from view while making it appear as if they were just a regular group of teens hanging out in an alley on a Saturday night.

Amy grabbed Leona's arm and pulled her in for a tight hug. 'Be careful. And don't panic. We won't leave without you.'

She held her breath as her best friend dropped to her hands and knees and slipped down into the black hole, feet first. Leona's fingers gripped the concrete for a second, then disappeared from view. Casually backing up to the wall so she could hear what was happening down below, Amy peered into the darkness. She couldn't see a damn thing, but she thought she heard faint cursing and a muffled cough before her phone buzzed.

'Lee,' she breathed. 'You good?'

'Jesus, it smells rank down here.'

'You sound like you're in a tunnel. How big is that space?'

'How about I show you?' The line went dead. Then Amy's phone rang again. Accepting the video call, half of Leona's face appeared, her nose and mouth covered by a black face mask. 'Hi.'

'Hi,' Amy smiled at her, 'show me what you got, babe.'

The camera flicked around as Leona's running commentary accompanied her investigations. 'See what I mean?' She panned the room from floor to ceiling. It certainly looked bigger than Amy expected. 'It's like a long hallway. There are empty shelves along this other wall, and down that end is an enormous door. Can you see it?'

Amy squinted at her screen. The light of Leona's phone might have lit up the rough brick walls and low ceiling, but she couldn't make out what was at the end. It just looked black.

'Not really. Can you get closer to it?'

'I'd rather not. It smells like a bitch down here. But it's padlocked if that's any help.'

'Maybe.' She screwed up her face, thinking. 'Which way are you facing, Lee?'

'Um, towards Flinders Lane.'

'How long do you think the tunnel is?'

'Shit, I don't know. Maybe five or six metres. Does it matter?' Her bestie sounded a little freaked out.

'Probably not. Is there another door anywhere? One that might lead inside?'

'Yeah, but it's locked.' Leona's view swung around and bobbed with her footsteps, coming towards the gap in the wall. 'Here.' A couple of small stone stairs led up to a wooden door, and she rattled the handle.

'Can you kick it in?' Amy asked her. A few dull thuds told her no. 'Hang on a sec. I have an idea.' Walking over to the others, Amy grabbed Jimmy by the arm. 'Hey, did you bring a crowbar?'

'Of course.' He opened his backpack and withdrew a mini-crowbar, and handed it over.

Flynn stood by the wall, waiting for her. 'Let me look at the lock first,' he said, reaching for her phone. Amy handed it to him and dropped the crowbar down to Leona.

'Can you give us a close-up of the lock? I think Flynn's going to walk you through it.'

'What do you reckon, dude? Should I just smash it?' Leona teased.

Flynn scowled and scrutinised the screen. Amy peered over his shoulder at the old-fashioned iron plate and round handle.

'Okay. It looks like a gate hinge. You need to insert the flat end of the crowbar vertically underneath the latch. You won't be able to see it, but it'll be level with the handle.' He waited while she slid the crowbar in place. 'Now whatever you do, don't jimmy it sideways, okay?'

'But what if Jimmy likes it sideways?' Leona snorted a laugh.

'Focus.'

'Fine. Shit, you're uptight, Flynn.'

'Are you done? I need you to lever the bar down with all your weight until the latch pops up. You won't know that it has, but the handle will twist slightly. Keep your eye on it, Leona. When you see it move, grab it with both hands and twist it to the right, as hard as you can. Got it?'

'Got it.' She gave a thumbs up and propped her phone on a step.

Amy sucked in a breath as Flynn's hands performed the actions along with Leona. Then, the crowbar hit the concrete and rolled into view before being replaced with a smiling face. 'That was totes awesome.'

Amy watched as Leona pulled open the door, recognising the sprinkler room she'd glimpsed earlier from the street. Her camera view then turned down a long corridor until it reached another door. Leona's hand flipped the latch, turned the handle, and the screen went black as Leona stepped out into the alleyway.

''Sup, bitches.'

CHAPTER SIX

ONE BY ONE, THEY filed inside the building, with Amy leading the way and Flynn closing the door to the laneway securely behind them.

'Torches stay off, okay?' Amy instructed. Enough light filtered through the window panels facing the construction site to illuminate their way, and they didn't need to be seen lurking inside the derelict building.

'Middle floor, then?' Jimmy asked, glancing at the closed elevator shaft.

'Yeah, I think so. But find some stairs, I don't trust that lift.'

While the others explored the ground floor, Amy made her way to the sprinkler room with the glass door that opened to the courtyard. She tried the handle and was surprised to find it unlocked. Filing that away for later, she turned back to hear Jimmy calling from behind the elevator.

'Over here!'

Amy hurried over. Leona grinned at her like a circus clown. 'I can't believe you actually found it, girl. You go first.' Jimmy was holding open the door to a cold and dark stairwell.

Amy looked around for Flynn. He was hanging at the back; worry etched across his brow. Their eyes met, and he moved toward her. 'You all right?' he asked.

She nodded. 'Can you just, you know, stay with me?'

Those stormy eyes softened. 'Always.'

She took a fortifying breath and led the way up the three flights of stairs, her heart pounding with each step. The door to the second floor was closed, and she paused, suddenly not feeling so brave.

This was it. The real deal. They were about to set foot in a notorious murderer's lair. She turned and glanced around at her friends bunched up in the stairwell behind her. 'Are we all good? There's no shame if anyone wants to turn back.'

Leona glared at her. 'Are you for real, right now? I didn't crawl in that hole for anyone to turn back. Bitch, just open the door.'

'Okay, okay.' She rested her hand on the doorknob and made the mistake of glancing at Flynn. He was staring daggers at her best friend.

Gritting her teeth, she turned the handle. The door stuck slightly, but with a hard shove of Flynn's shoulder, it opened up to a narrow hall. Here, years of accumulated dirt covered tiles strewn with papers and dead leaves, of all things. Amy took a hesitant step before Leona shoved past her, Jimmy on her tail.

Amy moved toward the rear of the building, stopping to poke her head in each room as she passed. The first two were tiny, dark and empty, with a single narrow arched window overlooking the alley and a couple of dark patches on the floorboards where furniture once rested. Bedrooms.

She entered the second one, drawn towards the window. The air shifted with each footstep she took, prickling around her edges and making her palms tingle. In the gloom, the scrapes had almost disappeared.

A footstep sounded behind her, and she turned her head, only to be enveloped by Flynn's familiar scent. A heady blend of soap, sweat, and something undeniably male that made her pelvis ache, deep and low. He was standing so close his breath warmed the back of her neck. Her skin lit up as his arm brushed hers, his hand reaching towards the windowsill. Amy looked down.

Resting on the sill, glinting in the faint light, lay a tiny scalpel. No longer than the length of Flynn's middle finger, it had a pretty handle and an evil-looking blade. Her palms itched as Flynn touched the knife, his fingertip sliding up and down the handle. But the feeling of his body pressed against hers dominated her senses, and she tilted her head back against his hard chest, heat washing over her. His hand dropped from the sill to her waist, his chin falling into the curve of her neck.

'Guys!' Luka burst into the room, causing Amy to blink, and both she and Flynn jerked apart, the scalpel forgotten. 'You've got to see this.'

'What is it?' Flynn asked, pushing her towards the door.

Luka threw them an odd glance as he led them up another flight of stairs. Opening a small door at the very top, he gestured for them to go through. Ever the gentleman, Flynn stood back and let Amy step out into the night.

⸺❖⸺

'Holy shit.'

Amy was standing atop the Butcher's House, beneath the Melbourne city skyline, yet still high enough to make her feel like she was among the stars. The rest of the group had congregated at the street end of the rooftop, where an ancient billboard loomed over Flinders Lane, its advertisement stripped bare, the tin now dull and bent.

'Look!' Kenzie exclaimed. 'If you lean out, you can see right down the street.' She gripped the metal strut of the sign for effect, though it did little to extend her reach.

Amy glanced back to Flynn, who was still standing near the door, chatting to Luka. Feeling the familiar thrill roll through her shoulders, she shook out her hands and legs. Then, before she could change her mind, she started running towards the others. Halfway across the roof, she threw her hands down on the ground and performed a cartwheel, a front handspring, and ended with an aerial walkover behind the sign.

'Woo-hoo, show-off!' Leona hugged her.

They stepped over to the edge of the roof and looked down. Barely any traffic, vehicular or pedestrian, moved below.

Flynn was with her in seconds, dark eyes piercing, his voice deep and concerned. 'I think we should make a move. If someone up there—' he gestured to one of the city buildings beside them, '— sees us down here, we're in deep shit.'

'Yeah, there's only two ways off this roof,' Luka added. 'The way we came up, or—Amy, what the fuck?'

Spiked with adrenaline, she'd gripped the aging billboard and was hauling herself up onto its flimsy ledge to get a better view. 'What, you scared Luka?'

'C'mon Ames.' Flynn was directly below her now, merely two feet from the edge of the roof. 'Don't make me come up there.' He looked shaken. Ruffled around the edges, but still smooth. Like a crow.

'I'm not the one who needs saving,' she whispered. Flynn's body flinched under her gaze.

Leona looked between them. 'Listen, Ames. We found another room on the floor below, but it's completely dead-locked. Even Jim couldn't crack it open. How about you and I go check it out?'

Kenzie gasped. 'You reckon it's *his* room? The one he practiced in?'

'Practiced what? Hooking up with women or bleeding them dry?' Luka asked, amused.

'Probably both. Does it matter?' Jimmy added, an edge to his voice. 'But I agree. We need to get off this damned roof.'

Amy looked out across the skyline. They were right. This wasn't the reason they were here. They should be ghost-hunting, not skylarking.

'Okay, stand clear.' She reached around to the back of the sign. Once she had a firm hold on the strut, she pushed off the ledge, attempting an aerial spin as she jumped down. But the crappy tin beneath her feet gave way, buckling under her weight, and she slipped, tearing a gash in her leggings and up the back of her calf. Crying out, she landed hard on the concrete.

'Off the roof, now,' Flynn growled, scooping her up and striding towards the stairs. He carried her back down to the middle level, the others arguing behind his back as they followed. 'Luka, in here,' he barked, bursting through into the bedroom they'd been in earlier. 'Hold her up for me.'

Transferred into Luka's arms, Amy couldn't help but stare into his worried face as he supported her weight. She couldn't see Flynn, but she felt his strong fingers grip her knee as something cold traced up the bare skin of her leg. Shivering, she pressed closer to Luka, wrapping herself around him like a scarf. Beyond his mop of brown curls, a long-haired girl was standing in the doorway, wearing a grey dress with a white collar and a pinafore splashed with red.

Amy blinked, feeling faint. 'Kenzie?'

Where the hell had she got that dress, and what kind of prank was she trying to pull? Nausea swirled as pain sheared through her leg. Metal clattered against the floorboards, and she visibly jumped, pressing into Luka.

'You're doing good, Ames,' Luka soothed, rubbing her back while Flynn began winding something tightly around her lower leg. Amy closed her eyes against the pressure and focused on her breathing. When her eyelids fluttered open, Kenzie stood directly behind Luka.

Only, it wasn't Kenzie.

Amy froze. Tiny pricks of electricity ran over her skin as the girl pressed the scalpel into her palm. Icy fingers folded around her fist, enclosing the delicate handle. Eyes like silver coins bored into hers. Everything went silent except for two words inside her head.

'He's coming.'

<hr>

'Mate, I think she's going into shock.' Luka slumped to the floor, cradling Amy in his lap. She tried to focus on his face, but it swam before her eyes. Voices came from all directions, making her head spin faster. Someone was tipping water into her mouth.

I think I'm going to throw up.

Rolling sideways, she wrenched out of Luka's hold, her stomach kicking into reverse gear, spilling hot bile onto the filthy floor beside her cheek.

'Amy.' Flynn knelt beside her, his hands warm on her clammy skin, pulling her up out of the mess. 'We have to get out of here, baby. Do you think you can stand?'

She couldn't answer. Her throat burned. Her legs were numb. Shaking her head only made her feel worse. Flynn hauled her up and draped her arm around his neck.

'Keep her leg elevated,' she heard him say, as Luka cradled both her knees and between the two of them, they carried her down the stairs.

Jimmy was stealing a look through each window that overlooked the construction site as they made their way back to the cellar. 'Where did he go?'

'Over there.' Kenzie pointed to the courtyard doors, where the distinct outline of a man was visible up on street level.

'Shut up,' Leona hissed.

'Is it a cop?'

'Security guard,' Jimmy answered. 'You locked the door behind us, right, Flynn?'

Amy caught the thunderous glare Flynn shot him, right before the door to the laneway rattled. Huddled in the shadows behind the elevator shaft, no one dared breathe. After about a minute, Leona motioned to Jimmy. 'Give me the crowbar to prop the door open. I'm going to take a peek through the hole.'

As he passed the tool to Leona, Amy glanced down at her fingers, recalling the press of cold metal in her palm. Her hands were empty. Confusion dizzied her head. Had she imagined it?

Flynn's deep blue eyes rounded on hers. 'We're going to get you out of here, okay? Just sit tight.'

She nodded. At least the nausea had passed. Too bad her leg still wasn't numb, though. It hurt pretty badly, and she gritted her teeth as they waited for Leona to return.

'Okay, dude's gone back towards the construction site. We need to get out, now.' She looked pointedly at Amy. 'And you need sugar and caffeine.'

'Let's go.' Flynn hefted Amy to her feet and supported her to the door. With one arm around his shoulder and the other around Luka, she limped out into the alley. Without so much as a glance behind them, they made a break for Flinders Lane and slipped around the corner, and headed down another laneway. It wasn't until they reached Flinders Street that they all stopped to catch their breath.

'That was intense.' Leona was practically beaming.

Jimmy scrubbed a hand over his crew cut. 'That wasn't intense, Lee. It was too fucking close.'

'And we didn't even see a ghost,' Kenzie added quietly.

'Wait, are you telling me none of you saw *anything?*' Amy looked at each of them. 'Nothing at all? What about a girl? Did anyone see the girl?'

'What girl?' Flynn's voice sounded worried.

'She needs sugar,' Leona said matter-of-factly. 'Let's go to Maccas.'

Luka stretched and patted his stomach. 'Yeah, I'm starved.'

The others ordered food while Flynn eased her into an empty booth. As she slid onto the red vinyl seat, Amy glanced down at her leg for the first time. Flynn had slashed her leggings off at mid-thigh, the missing Lycra wrapped tightly around her cut like a pressure bandage. Dark tracks ran to her ankle. She looked to where he sat across from her, head bowed, fingers clasped on the table in front of him. Fingers that were still streaked with her blood.

Oh, God. All he did was fix her up. First her hands, now this. All she'd wanted was to feel his muscular arms around her, and tonight she had no choice as he supported her weight and helped her walk.

Damn it. She'd really fucked up tonight. Nothing had gone to plan. Cutting her leg, and the creepy security guard... *He's coming.*

The spectral girl's words chased each other around Amy's head. Had she been talking about the guard? Amy's pulse kicked up a notch. Or was she referring to the doctor?

Kenzie dropped a super-sized cola slushie onto the table in front of her. 'Drink this. It'll raise your blood sugar and settle your stomach.'

Amy gave her a weak smile and took a few sips. She didn't feel like drinking anything. She watched as Flynn picked at his fries. Clearly, he wasn't in the mood either.

'I think I should get Amy home,' he said, standing suddenly. 'Clean that wound up properly.'

She nodded wearily.

'Want some help?' Luka asked through a mouthful of cheeseburger.

Flynn shook his head firmly, slipping an arm around her waist. 'I've got her.'

Chapter Seven

GRATEFUL FOR THE EARLIER darkness of the city streets, Flynn was painfully aware of Amy's predicament once in the cold light of the train. She sat next to him with her left foot on the seat opposite, her head on his shoulder. From the softness of her breath, he figured she'd fallen asleep. He kept his gaze fixed on the dark window beside him, his thoughts just as distorted as the reflection that glared back at him.

You fucked this up on a grand level, didn't you? You should have kept her safe.

The gnawing in his right side sharpened its teeth. His fingers, resting on the pocket of his pants, sought the outline of the scalpel. The tiny knife had been the last thing he'd expected to find grasped in Amy's hand as she nearly passed out.

He bit the inside of his cheek, drawing blood. If it weren't for the scalpel's unsanitary state, he'd be pressing in into his flesh right now. He'd only cut with a dirty blade once, and no matter how much he craved the release, it wouldn't be happening again.

Amy woke with a start, her hand gripping his thigh. All his concentration had gone into keeping the urge at bay that he hadn't even realised she'd been clutching him. A blush crept up her neck as she straightened, swiftly pulling her hand back. The corner of his mouth tugged at the sweetness of her discomfort.

'Nearly there,' he told her.

She sucked in a shaky breath and mumbled, 'What am I going to tell Mum?'

Flynn blinked a few times. He'd never had to lie to his own mother. For as long as he could remember, she'd trusted him to look after himself, and when Mick was on the scene, she expected it. Doing as he pleased was both a luxury and a curse.

'Where does she think you went?'

Amy coloured. 'She doesn't.'

'Huh?' Twisting in his seat, he frowned at her.

She pulled her mouth into a grim line, sighing. 'She's the one who went out tonight. I'm supposed to be tucked up at home, eating popcorn and watching crappy old 1930s movies.'

'As I would be.' He nodded.

'I'd like to see that.'

'Don't hold your breath,' he said, checking the time. 'How long do you think she's out for?'

'I don't know. She went to dinner with Pierre. Does it matter?'

He gasped with mock drama. 'She's on a date with her *boss*?'

'Yeah, so?' Amy was squirming, clearly uncomfortable.

'Are you okay with that?'

'Yeah, I suppose. I like Pierre. He's nice. It's just—' She shrugged. 'You know. My *mum*. Dating. It's weird.'

'Well, hopefully they're having a great time. Otherwise, we've got roughly five minutes to get our story straight.' He got up as the train pulled into South Kensington, extending a hand to help her.

'Our story?'

'Yeah. We're in this together, Ames.'

As they cleared the platform, Flynn crouched down and motioned for Amy to climb on his back.

'Are you seriously giving me a piggyback ride?'

'Sure am.' He grinned, grasping her behind the knees and hoisted her up, careful of her injury. 'I figured tonight wasn't nearly as fun as you wanted it to be, so...' He didn't bother finishing. Her sudden and silent embrace around his neck said everything he couldn't.

As he carried her through the park, they debated what to tell her mum.

'Smack my forehead for me, will you? I can't reach.'

She laughed, the sound warming his whole body. 'Why?'

'Because we clearly went to the skate park, and you had an accident. I mean, it's the most logical excuse, right?'

'Duh, you're so right. Why didn't we think of that earlier?'

'Because all the blood had gone from your head to your leg.'

'What's your excuse?'

'You don't want to know,' he mumbled, hitching her higher.

⸻❖⸻

Thankfully, Amy's mum was still out by the time they reached her apartment. Still carrying her, Flynn headed straight for the bathroom, only detouring to drop Amy's backpack into her bedroom on the way.

Before he'd even eased her down to the tile, she'd ripped off her shirt and flung it onto the floor.

'Ew, why didn't you tell me I smell like puke?' She scowled, standing before him in just a sports bra and her uneven leggings.

'Uh...' He saw her in her gym gear every week, and even in a bikini on the rooftop on two exact occasions, but somehow this was feeling far more intimate. 'Where's the first aid kit?'

'Under the sink. God, I can still smell it! Gross.' She sniffed around herself.

'Maybe your hair?'

She grabbed a handful of her ponytail and buried her face in it. Emerged, wrinkling her nose in disgust. 'Yep. Can I *please* have a shower first?'

'Nope. After I fix up your leg, we can cover it with some plastic wrap and then you can wash your hair.' He started pulling out antiseptic, gauze and bandages.

'Plastic wrap? I'm not last night's dinner, Flynn Powell.'

He chuckled, and she thumped him.

'Ugh, fine. But hurry up. I stink. Honestly, I don't know how you could stand it.'

'*Honestly*, I didn't notice.' He rummaged around the box further, looking for butterfly strips.

'Bullshit. I spewed all over myself like a drunken hussy on Cup Day.'

'No, you didn't. You puked on the floor and then collapsed in it.'

'Oh, that makes me feel *so* much better.' She sank onto the edge of the bath, and he knelt before her to slip off her shoes.

'Well, to be fair, you did faint from shock.'

She gazed at the mirror while he removed her thin sneaker socks, the left one stiff and stained with dried blood. Her feet were small and pale in his palms; her toenails painted bright metallic blue. He allowed his hand to linger on her soft skin for a moment, his thumb slowly caressing the arch of her foot. When he raised his head, she was staring at him with something akin to fear in her eyes.

'I think I saw something tonight, Flynn.'

He dropped his hands and manoeuvred her to stand by the sink. 'What do you mean?'

'In the Butcher's House. When you were bandaging me.'

She collapsed a little as he unwound the Lycra band, releasing the pressure on her wound. The gash was long and oozed a bit, but thankfully it appeared to be shallow.

She tried to look over her shoulder. 'Is it bad?'

'No. But it's not good either.' He grabbed the bottle of disinfectant and some gauze and began swabbing the dried blood away. He tried to be gentle, but she gasped as the amber liquid entered the open wound. 'When did you have your last tetanus shot?'

'In school. Like, two years ago, I think.'

'Good.' He nodded. One less thing to worry about—she was already going to have one helluva scar. He hated the idea of her skin being marked permanently like that, but he couldn't change it now. 'So, you were saying you saw something?'

'I think someone else was in the room with us.'

'Yeah, Luka,' he mumbled around the sheet of plaster strips held between his teeth.

'No. Someone else. A girl.' He looked up at her, but she held up a hand. 'I thought it was Kenzie at first, but it wasn't.'

'Are you sure? I mean, you were on the verge of passing out.' He finished closing the wound and cut a length of non-stick dressing to cover it before wrapping almost her entire calf in a cloth bandage.

It would have to do. He stood up, his eyes meeting hers in the mirror.

'She gave me the knife, Flynn.'

What?

He took an involuntary step back, his fingers fumbling in his pocket until they closed around the cold metal handle.

Not possible. After cutting Amy's tights, he'd flung the knife away. Amy must have somehow picked it up when she and Luka hit the floor.

But why would she think someone gave it to her? Was it because she was so desperate to find a ghost in that bloody place? Flynn chewed his lip. He'd have to choose his words carefully to avoid hurting her feelings.

'First, let's get that leg waterproof so you can have a shower. Then you can tell me everything. Sound good?'

He fetched the plastic wrap from the kitchen and returned to find her hacking at her leggings with the scissors.

'What the fuck are you doing?'

'Making them even.'

Her tongue stuck out in concentration as she sliced through the material, holding up a scrap of Lycra in triumph. He blinked and tried not to stare at the expanse of her bare legs. Not only had she evened up the leggings, but she'd also trimmed them *much* shorter. It took all his concentration to wrap her leg in the plastic film while not looking at her tight butt, which was mere inches from his face.

'I'll make you a cup of tea when you're done.'

By the time he left the bathroom, his whole body was vibrating with need. Only after he'd filled the kettle and put it on to boil did he allow his fingers to seek the knife once again.

Pulling it from his pocket, he inspected it in the bright light. It was tiny and smooth, with a hinged blade that folded back into the handle, a bit like the butterfly knife that one of his mum's boyfriends tried pulling on him some years back. It definitely wasn't a modern medical instrument. Impulsively, he opened the lid to the kettle and dropped it in.

While Amy was showering, he sterilised the scalpel five times before emptying the kettle's contents into the sink and refilling it again for her tea.

Hearing the bathroom door open, he quickly retrieved the scorching blade and slipped it back into his pocket. Ignoring the flush of heat it generated through the thin material, he found two mugs and made them a cup of hot, sweet, black tea.

Amy took hers with a grateful smile and limped straight to the sofa. He followed closely behind, nursing his own mug, as she propped herself up on one end of the couch and tucked her good leg up under her. He mirrored her pose at the opposite end and let his eyes run over her. Wearing a pair of sleep shorts and a wrinkled tee that looked like it'd come straight from the wash basket, she looked small. Vulnerable.

He blew across the top of his mug. 'Tell me what happened,' he said, taking a sip.

'You're going to think I'm crazy.' She pinned him with doll-like eyes. Huge. Clear. Incredibly blue.

He shook his head. 'I think you know me better than that.' Putting his tea on the coffee table, he scooted closer to her, their knees touching.

She clutched at her mug with both hands. 'Remember when we first went into that bedroom, before we went to the roof?'

He nodded.

'I think she might have been in the room with us, even then.'

'Did you see her?'

'No. But something, or someone, drew me to that window. I felt... I don't know. I can't even explain it.' She shook her head, frustrated.

'Hey.' He reached over and tipped her chin up to look her in the eye. 'You're not crazy, okay? No matter how ridiculous it sounds, you need to talk about it.'

'Why do you even care? You don't believe in all this, anyway.' She pulled her hand out of his and sat back against the arm of the couch.

She wasn't shutting him out that easily. He leaned forward and removed the tea from her grasp. Then, interlacing their fingers, he waited until hers stopped trembling before he spoke.

'I believe in you, Amy Rose Shipley. If you felt something, I want to hear about it. So, tell me what happened.'

Her eyes glistened for a moment before she closed them and took a deep breath.

'For some reason, I felt drawn into that room like an invisible rope was pulling me. I mean, I had no particular interest in going in there. It was empty.' She paused, swallowing. 'But the air felt weird. Like that feeling you get right before a storm, you know? And then you were there behind me, and I noticed the little knife on the windowsill. As you reached for it, I wanted you... I wanted you to...' Her eyes flicked open.

His whole body stiffened as she held him in her terrified gaze while the blade burned a hole in his pocket. 'What did you want me to do?'

She shook her head. 'Don't make me say it.'

'Amy, talk to me. Please.' His voice cracked on the last word.

She looked down at their clasped hands, her wet hair swinging over her face. She spoke so quietly, he barely heard her. And immediately wished he hadn't.

CHAPTER EIGHT

THE LAST TIME FLYNN cut himself was the day before Amy walked into his life.

Until he met her, he hadn't needed a reason to be strong. He'd put up with Mick's taunting, hid in corners and licked his wounds. But there was something about Amy made him feel like he could stand up to Mick. He didn't want to be anyone's white knight, but she needed protection from the monster next door.

Now he dragged his body away from hers, needing to call on that strength more than ever.

'I wanted you to cut me.'

Her words chased him all the way to the other side of the couch. She continued to stare at him, those blue orbs shining out from behind her curtained hair. A deep part of him ached to reach out and pull his fingers through those damp waves. A part of him that was surfacing with greater frequency. He swallowed; pushed the longing back down. She deserved better.

'You really want to look like this?' he rasped, pulling off his shirt to reveal his scars. 'Because these marks are here forever, Ames. Like a bad tattoo.'

Her eyes dropped, pupils dilating as they fell on his exposed skin. 'No, but—'

Tentatively, she crawled towards him until she was straddling one of his legs, fingers poised above his hip. Lifting her gaze, their eyes locked, hers silently asking permission.

'It's okay,' he whispered.

Laying a hand over hers, he drew it to his side. Amy had touched him plenty of times before, but never like this. Hell, he'd never even been shirtless around her. Luka was the only one who knew about his scars; about what he did to himself. There was no coming back from this now.

Her lips twitched as she counted silently, her fingers lightly tracing each crude line.

'Twenty-seven,' she whispered.

He nodded. Needing to remove her touch, he lifted her hand and laid it against his, palm to palm. He took a deep, shaky breath as Amy interlocked their fingers.

'One for every time I backed down, for every time lost control, or wasn't strong enough to do what was right.'

'Flynn, you are the strongest person I know,' she said, squeezing his palm tight.

He concentrated on her hand in his, unable to look her in the eye.

'No, I'm not. Before I met you, I was a stupid, weak, fuck-up who ran away when things got tough.'

'You're not a fuck-up.' She straightened and pushed a wayward curl behind her ear. 'Look at what you did tonight. You didn't run away when things got tough. You took control, Flynn. It was *you* calling the shots. *You* got us off the roof, and *you* used your smarts to stop my leg from bleeding. If that's not a sign of strength—'

'Then why can't I be strong now?' he muttered, his body leaning towards hers. 'If tonight has proven anything, it's that I'm a bad influence. You need to keep your distance.'

Her eyes filled with tears, causing him to reach out and stroke her cheek.

'Please don't cry.'

'It's not your fault,' she hiccupped. 'I just want to know what it feels like.'

'I will never cut you, Amy. Let's be clear on that, right now.'

He cradled her to his chest, letting her tears flow as he relaxed back against the cushions. Amy stretched out along the entire length of him, her body flush against his, making him hyper-aware of every single place they touched. She nestled her face into the space above his heart. Could she tell how fast it was beating?

Flynn was content to lie like that forever until her hand slipped around to touch his scars again.

'Do you want to tell me about it?' she asked.

Even though her touch was warm, the question was like a bucket of ice. He tightened his arms around her and looked to the ceiling, closed his eyes. After a few deep breaths, he spoke.

'When I was ten, my dad got sucker-punched by a thug outside a club in the city. He was leaving after a work function, and some guy was hassling a couple of girls. Dad stepped in, and... at least it was instant.' He exhaled so hard his breath flipped the hair right off his forehead. 'Mum couldn't cope being on her own, so she started bringing home a string of arseholes who didn't appreciate me being around. So, I started staying out as much as I could. Having lots of sleepovers at friends' houses. Luka's especially. Skipping school. Spent my days at the skate park or up on the roof. Skateboarding made me feel like I was good at something, but it was really an escape. I was just another nobody, going nowhere. Except I was doing it faster.'

Amy pushed herself up on an elbow as a tear slid down her cheek. 'I had no idea, Flynn. You must've felt so lost.'

'Hey, hey, hey,' he whispered, wiping the wetness away with his thumb. 'There's no need to feel sad for me. I mean, sure, it was rough, not gonna lie. But it made me who I am, and—' Now that the words were tumbling out of him, he couldn't make them stop.

'Then one day a few years back, I was blowing off steam after a fight with Mick, and I came off my board. It was in a parking lot, and I got banged up pretty bad. It turned out I'd landed on a broken beer bottle and had a piece of glass stuck in my side.' His fingers drifted down Amy's back to rest on her hip.

'It wasn't in deep or anything, but it was just sticking out—this jagged green shard. The thing was, I couldn't feel it. And I wanted to. I really, really wanted to. So, instead of simply pulling it out, I dragged it across my skin a bit.'

He brushed his finger across her bare skin. Her intake of breath was audible.

'And it felt fantastic. To feel something after years of being numb. And the best thing was, I was in total control of the pain, instead of letting it control me.'

Amy surged forward and wrapped her arms around his neck.

'Pretty fucked up, huh?'

'Did you tell anyone?'

'Only Luka knows. And Mr Jeffries.'

Amy drew back and looked him in the eye. 'The school counsellor?'

He nodded. 'I'd skipped so many days of school that I had to repeat a year. And he got me involved in The Mission, who helped me sort my shit out. Until Mick started coming around more, and I couldn't handle it. Couldn't handle *him*. So I nicked a penknife from the art room at school, and it's not too hard to figure out the rest.' He shrugged.

'Flynn.'

He ignored her pity and cupped her cheek, smiling. 'And then you came along. You're the only one who's made me see I don't need to bleed myself to be strong.'

She leaned into his palm. 'Because you had to carry my shitty suitcase up the stairs?'

'Because when you came up onto the roof that day, you spoke of being invisible, like you didn't have a choice. And yet, you made me notice you without having to try. There you were, wanting to be seen, and me, wishing I could disappear. But, whenever we were together up there, none of that mattered. We could just be *us*.'

Amy sucked in a breath, and his eyes dropped to her mouth. Touching his thumb to her bottom lip, he gently dragged it open; her ragged exhale on his skin, warm and moist. He bent closer until their foreheads were touching.

'When I saw you up on that ledge tonight, I knew you wouldn't fall. But shit, Amy, I felt like I was up there with you.' Their lips were nothing but a breath apart, and a shudder ripped through him. 'And it fucking scared me so much.'

'Flynn.' Her breath swirled over his lips and into his mouth.

He could close the gap. It would be so easy just to lean forward and claim her lips with his. To claim *her*. And she would let him.

Flynn's brain warred with his body. He couldn't. She deserved better. He would not drag her down with him while he fell.

Gently, he pushed her shoulders back and drew her head to his chest once again. Both of them were breathing hard, and as they lay there silent, he tangled a hand in her hair until the pounding of his heart eased.

'What does it feel like, Flynn?' Amy spoke softly, her fingers drawing lazy circles across his chest and twining in his chest hair.

'Your touch? It feels amazing, Ames.' He laughed softly, cuddling her closer. 'That can be your new nickname. Amazing Ames.'

He felt her smile against his skin. 'That's not what I mean.' She feathered her fingertips across his scars, making him shudder. He could barely think, let alone speak.

'Don't romanticise it,' he ground out as her hands explored his body. Unable to get enough of her touch, he grabbed fistfuls of her hair as her lips sought his bare flesh.

'But I want to know—' Her husky voice lit his body on fire, as her tongue flicked across his raised and damaged skin. '—why hurting yourself—' her soft mouth pressed against his hipbone, '—makes you—' she kissed his first scar '—feel—' then kissed his last '—stronger.'

Jesus. How could she be kissing him and causing him such anguish at the same time?

He wanted her so badly, but she was just proving how much of a mistake that would be. She was too good for him. He mustn't give in. He'd only ruin her.

Until the other night, he'd only had the urge to cut again once—the day she and her mum moved away. Channelling everything he had into ignoring the raging need inside, he hauled her up by the arms until she was sitting in his lap.

'It didn't strengthen me. It just made me believe that no one could hurt me, because I could always hurt myself more.'

A key jiggled in the lock. Amy's mum. Shit, where was his shirt? He leapt up from the couch just as Valerie Shipley closed the door behind her.

'Oh, Flynn.' She startled. 'How've you been, love?' Dropping her handbag on the kitchen bench, she went to him, enveloping him in an enormous hug. 'Haven't seen you in ages.'

He rested his chin on top of her head. 'Hi, Val. It's good to see you too.'

She released him, eyeing his shirtless chest. 'Glad to see my girl has such a strapping young man looking out for her.'

He turned and quirked a brow at Amy, who was staring at her mum in horror.

Valerie swayed slightly in her high heels. 'You kids have a good night?'

'Obviously not as good as yours,' Amy quipped, running her hand across the small of his back as she passed.

'Amy!' Valerie gasped, her gaze landing on the bandage covering her daughter's leg. 'What happened?'

'Oh, it's nothing, Mum.' Amy cast him a glance. 'I had a bit of a fall at the skate park and cut my leg on some glass. It looks worse than it is, honestly. Flynn cleaned it up for me with his shirt.' She flashed him a smile. 'I'll wash it and bring it to school on Monday.'

Even though she was covering for him—for them both—he still cocked his head at how easily the lies rolled off her tongue.

'Well,' Valerie said, turning to him. 'Strapping and resourceful, hey? Thank you for looking after Amy, Flynn. I'm so glad she has you.' She dropped a hand to his shoulder and squeezed it.

His eyes sought Amy's. 'Always.'

Valerie yawned. 'Well, since I'm already two sheets to the wind, I'm heading to bed. Goodnight, my loves.'

'Yeah. I should get going too,' he said, walking back to the coffee table to collect their tea mugs. 'Night, Val.'

Amy called out to him. 'Leave that, Flynn. Be back in a sec.'

She disappeared with her mum, leaving him alone and wondering what had happened to his t-shirt. He couldn't see it anywhere. Taking the mugs to the sink, his reflection stared back at him from the black depths of the discarded tea. He considered it a moment before tipping it down the drain. No more secrets. No more lies.

Tracing his steps back to the lounge, he pulled the tiny scalpel from his pocket and left it on the coffee table.

Even though he'd made it out the front door before Amy came back, the cool night air greeting his bare chest was nothing compared to the icy fingers that curled around his heart and squeezed at the tremor in her voice.

'Flynn?'

He stilled. Turned slowly. She stood a few feet from him, confusion clouding her eyes. He studied her for long seconds, his gaze taking in her bandaged leg and the way she was holding herself as if waiting to be hurt. Again. He didn't want to be that guy, but he'd already let her down tonight.

'I spoke to Mum. She said you could crash on the couch if you don't want to go home.'

He said nothing. He just kept his eyes locked on hers. True, he didn't want to go home. But he didn't want to spend the night on her bloody couch, either. He wanted to spend the night with her. In her bed, with her in his arms. His mouth on her skin, kissing *her* wounds. That's how it should've been.

His whole body tensed. 'Amy,' he started. Then stopped. Dragged his eyes across every inch of her body, committing it to memory.

Now, walk away.

Instead, he took a step toward her. Then another. Until he was so close that he could feel her breath on his skin.

You'll only hurt her if you stay.

'I'm no good for you.'

He continued to stare at her, his breath coming short and fast, while she stared back at him. They were standing up on that ledge together, and he was so afraid of falling.

If he reached out to her, would she catch him?

Leaning down toward her, he closed his eyes, whispering, 'Tell me to stop.'

'Never stop,' she whispered, wrapping her arms around him.

Heat seeped throughout his body at her touch. Hot. Burning. Explosive. Burying both his hands in her hair, he closed his mouth over hers and let himself fall.

Months of longing sought comfort in her embrace as he explored her mouth, slowly stroking her lips with his kiss. Once, twice... He kept going until he'd kissed her twenty-seven times.

And each one tasted like salvation.

CHAPTER NINE

A MY WOKE LATE THE next morning, wrapped in Flynn's shirt. She'd found it wedged beneath the couch cushions after he'd left last night.

Oh. My. God. Last. Night.

Surrounding herself in his scent, she lay there for God knew how long—too long, probably—her mind unwilling to let go of the feel of his mouth on hers, the taste of him on her tongue.

She couldn't believe it. She'd finally kissed Flynn. And he'd kissed her back. And those hands—how often had she dreamed of having them all over her? Her injured leg protested in irony as she rolled toward the window. Talk about wish-fulfilment. She missed being in his arms already.

From her bedside table, the scalpel gleamed dully in the sunlight. It was something else she'd found after Flynn left, but the absolute mind-numbing kisses he'd given on her at the front door had left her totally incapable of doing anything about it. Now, she picked it up and rotated the filigreed silver handles, revealing the blade.

Tentatively, she touched it with a finger. It wasn't sharp, but with a bit of pressure, the tip easily pierced her skin.

'Ow!' She watched as a drop of blood welled, bright red and glistening. Putting it quickly to her lips, she sucked, her saliva congealing the flow. The familiar coppery tang sat at the back of her tongue, consuming any lingering thoughts of Flynn. Only one person filled her mind now. A girl with long dark hair and soulful grey eyes. The girl she'd glimpsed in The Butcher's House. Could she really have been a ghost?

Dragging herself out of bed, Amy sat down at her desk and pushed her laptop open. By the time Flynn called, she'd opened every article she could find on Google about the infamous Doctor Boucher and Victorian-era phlebotomy.

'Hey.'

'Hey, yourself,' she almost purred into the phone, her body responding to the sound of his voice.

'How's my favourite patient doing today?'

She crawled back into her bed and curled up on her side. 'A little stiff, but otherwise good.'

'I'd like to come over and have a look at that wound again. You know, make sure it's healing and not infected.'

'Sure.' Her heart beat faster in anticipation. Would he kiss her like that again? And if he did, what would that mean? To prevent getting lost in those thoughts, she glanced at her computer screen, an idea surfacing. 'Do you want to come to the library with me?'

'The library?'

She could picture the disgust on his face.

'Come on, Ames, it's Sunday. Schoolwork can wait.'

'Actually, it can't—' *you moron*, she was going to add, but suddenly it didn't seem funny to call him that. Was their usual banter going to disappear because they'd kissed? 'Leona and I have to choose a new topic, and the whole blood-letting movement has me intrigued. And maybe, I can find out a bit more about Doctor Boucher at the same time.'

Flynn was silent a moment, then Amy was sure she heard him mutter something under his breath.

'What was that? You'd love to come? Oh, thanks, Flynn. That'd be great.'

'I'm fairly sure I'm not allowed to set foot in there,' he said.

'What?' She laughed. 'Why not?'

'I might've um—' he cleared his throat '—skated through there once.'

'You're kidding! No way you've skated through the Library of Melbourne.'

'True story. I was being chased. It was a shortcut.'

'Did you get caught?'

'Of course. Why do you think I can't go back?'

She rolled onto her back and adopted her best dreamy-teen voice, 'Oh my God, Flynn Powell. You're such a bad boy. I love it.'

He snorted, and they both burst out laughing.

After one in the afternoon, he finally arrived at her place, and Amy had tried on no less than fifteen different outfits. This was stupid. It was just Flynn. She'd never cared about clothes before. *Just be yourself. Things won't change just because he kissed you.*

Oh, but they did.

She opened the door to find him lounging against the frame, skateboard tucked under his arm, hair gloriously wind-tousled and wearing that sexy lopsided grin she loved so much. He lifted a brow as his eyes ran over her.

'Is that my shirt?'

'Yeah, about that.' Her face grew hot as she remembered throwing it back on with her jeans at the last minute.

He leant down and kissed her softly on the lips before shifting his mouth across her jaw, his breath hot against her ear. 'Keep it. It looks good on you.'

His voice sent shivers of anticipation down the back of her neck. How on earth was she going to stop herself from melting into a puddle on the bathroom floor while Flynn redressed her wound?

'You should become a paramedic,' she told him once he was finished cleaning up the cut.

He grunted. 'I'm not smart enough to study medicine. But I do know basic first aid. It comes with the territory, you know? Anyway, that cut is going to heal nicely, and you should be able to take the plasters off tomorrow.' He stood up. 'So what have you found regarding the not-so-good doctor?'

'What makes you think I've been looking?'

He crossed his arms and regarded her in the mirror. 'Come on, Ames. This is you we're talking about.'

She couldn't deny that.

'Well,' she grinned, leading him to her bedroom, 'virtually nothing on Boucher himself. That's what I need to go to the library for. Check out some old newspapers.' She sat at her desk and opened a tab on her laptop. 'But I did find a lot of stuff on antiquated medicine and blood-letting instruments. It's actually quite fascinating.'

She glanced at him. He was sitting on the end of her bed, his elbows resting on his knees in typical Flynn-pose, yet he looked anything but relaxed. 'You okay?' she asked.

His response was an intense gaze from those dark blue eyes that made her want to stop talking and push him down onto her bed. Instead, she picked up the knife from her desk and flicked it back and forth between her fingers. He watched her but remained silent.

'This scalpel, for instance, is called a lancet. The handles were traditionally made of tortoiseshell, but some French ones had ivory or beautifully crafted silver handles, like this one.' She flashed it at him. 'There's a surprising number of them for sale on eBay, as well as these little brass boxes called scarificators that hold twelve rotating blades attached to a spring mechanism, causing multiple shallow cuts at once. Oh, and then there's this grotesque beauty.' She pointed to the screen. 'The spring lancet. The practitioner would cock this thing like a mini pistol against the patient's inner elbow and, once triggered, snapped a blade into the vein at the required depth.'

'Jesus,' Flynn muttered, looking away.

'Oh, crap! I didn't think. I'm so sorry. I know I can get carried away about stuff, sometimes.'

Flynn scrubbed his face with both hands. 'S'okay.'

'No, it really isn't.'

She crawled into his lap, and he lay back against her pillows, gathering her into his shoulder with one arm.

'You're pretty amazing to watch when you're passionate about something, you know,' he murmured into her hair, causing a flush of goosebumps down her neck.

She smiled, sliding a hand up the inside of his t-shirt. 'Really? I can give you a much more personal demonstration if you'd like.'

'Yes. I think that would be the right thing to do in this situation.'

His breath hitched as her fingers toyed with the dark hair on his chest, making her smile.

'Are you sure you won't come to the library with me?' She teased, dropping little kisses across the column of his throat. 'I can be very persuasive, you know.'

'I know,' he chuckled, 'but I should get home. I still have a media assignment to do. Come on. I'll walk you to the train.' But he didn't make a move, except to roll her over and cover her mouth with his.

As much as she wanted to stay wrapped up with him for the entire afternoon, Amy needed to get access to the newspaper archives before school tomorrow. Reluctantly, she pushed herself up on an elbow. 'Fine, let's go then.'

They parted ways at the station with another lingering kiss. Flynn had cruised alongside her on his board the whole way, holding her hand as if it were the most natural thing in the world. As she sat on the train and waved goodbye, she hoped Flynn would make good on his promise to be at school the next day while also dreading how to announce their relationship to the group. Was it even a relationship yet? Just because they'd kissed a few times (okay, the number was more in the thirties), did that automatically mean they were now official? Oh God, high school was the worst.

Amy's nerves jangled as she bounded up the library steps and checked her backpack in at the front desk. Having slipped the lancet in at the last minute, she was terrified of setting off the security scanner or being accused of having a knife in her possession. Thankfully neither occurred, and she headed straight for the newspaper reading room, grinning at the idea of Flynn riding his skateboard through the foyer and wondering how on earth he got past the guards.

Amy's previous Google searches hadn't given her any information on Doctor Boucher, other than he was most likely one of many quacks practicing at the end of the nineteenth century. Phlebotomy wasn't popular in Australia and was already being discredited around the globe by then.

The National Library's online newspaper archives turned up nothing more than the same article on many barber surgeons practicing during that time. Identified by their iconic red and white striped poles, these particular practitioners used razors for more than just shaving. But Amy was fairly certain Boucher wasn't among that cohort. It classified them as being of "a most respectable class of men", and Luka's quip about the doctor favouring prostitutes didn't make him sound very respectable at all.

That he had only female clientele seemed at home with his location in Flinders Lane—or Little Flinders Street, as they called it back then. She'd discovered that Boucher's address was in the heart of the rag district—crowded with milliners, seamstresses and clothing factories—providing an almost wholly female working trade. Perhaps the ghostly girl she'd seen was one of his clients?

After an hour of trawling through microfilm, looking for advertisements in the Herald and The Age, she still found no mention of the doctor or his practice. The Australian Medical Society Registry held no record of him either, but that meant nothing. The man was a charlatan. He likely had zero medical training and relied solely on his French charm.

She switched to the library's online catalogue and searched ship manifests, hoping to find his arrival in Australia. A few Messrs Boucher were recorded as entering Port Melbourne in 1895, but she couldn't verify anything further without paying money to an ancestral search site. *No thanks.*

Printing out what she needed for her school assignment, Amy packed up, disappointed. There was absolutely no information on the man anywhere, other than a sketchy urban legend and a faded ghost sign. Still, that sign was proof that he existed. As for the urban legend, it remained to be proved false or otherwise.

So who was the girl in Boucher's residence, and what was her role in all of this? Amy knew the factories were notorious for using child workers. They'd studied the Industrial Revolution in history class years ago. And the girl looked far too young to be a nurse. So that meant she had to be a client, right?

None of this changed the fact that only Amy could see her, nor answered the question of why she was so intent on giving Amy the lancet.

Determined more than ever to find out who—or what—she'd seen, Amy opened up another search tab. With shaking fingers, she typed the word "haunted" into the search engine and sat back.

It took a while to wade through all the crap, but eventually, she found some accounts of spirit manifestation. Of ghostly entities moving objects and touching the living. Of poltergeists and restless souls locked into repeating patterns, unable to move on.

It was terrifying and thrilling all at once. But the presence she'd encountered at Boucher's hadn't felt threatening. Instead, something was compelling, yet oddly calming, about the girl. Amy turned off the computer and stared at the blank screen, her mind back to the moment she and Flynn were alone in that room. Back to where it all began.

His hand dropped to her hip. Flynn...

Her palms itched. She turned her left one over and held it out to him.

Flynn. Please.

Her eyelids fluttered, her pulse thrummed, and desire built deep and hot in her belly. It was beyond disturbing that she'd even wanted him to cut her, but knowing how much it excited her was far, far worse.

Chapter Ten

Having jumped aboard the first available city tram, it was only a matter of minutes before Amy was strolling down Flinders Lane towards the Butcher's House.

A chilly blast of wind laced with icy droplets tore at her bare arms as she reached the laneway and rattled the door they'd exited from last night. Of course, it was locked. Dodging puddles, she headed around to the front and peered up through the drizzle at the iron fence. Sure, it was about nine feet high and topped with sharp spikes, but she knew the glass door would be unlocked. Small mercies, right?

Thanking her mum for encouraging her gym classes, she fished out her parkour gloves and tugged them on while casting a paranoid scan over the construction site for security guards. When there were no pedestrians in sight, Amy grabbed the iron bars and hoisted herself up, wedging her foot into the decorative scrollwork. She swung her legs over the top and dropped to the other side. Landing on the wet, mouldy tile, Amy's shoes slipped, sending her sprawling awkwardly and pain shearing through her injured calf. She scrambled through the door as quickly as she could and stood up, brushed her hands on her jeans, then grinned. It shouldn't have been that easy.

In the daylight, the interior of the Butcher's House looked different, and she took her time, relishing the opportunity to have a good poke around. The exposed walls of the basement level were red brick, and the floor tiles were classic black-and-white marble. Her sneakers squeaked across the floor, the smell of rain and wet bitumen following her to the stairs behind the elevator shaft. Pushing open the door, Amy was greeted with darkness, the only light coming from the glass panelled doors on each level.

Exiting on the first floor, she stuck her head out and peered down the long and narrow hallway. Delicate arches and the remnants of an impressive chandelier adorned the high ceiling. She froze as someone passed by the art déco front door, their silhouette triggering second-hand panic from last night's security scare and her own personal warning.

He's coming.

Heart pounding, she continued down the hall, exploring what appeared to be a tiny reception room at the front of the building. It was empty; the shutters half-drawn on the windows. She shivered at the thought of standing in Boucher's waiting room. Despite its purpose, the building must have been beautiful in its day. Clearly, the man was wealthy, or maybe there was lots of money to be made in being a quack. Then again, his ghost sign proclaimed his practice was on the middle floor, so perhaps he wasn't the only tenant in this building.

Amy pondered this as she continued her exploration up to the next floor. She paused at the entrance of the second bedroom, noting the mess of leaves and papers in the hall again but feeling nothing of the thrill of the previous night. The room was icy, but she was already shivering well before she sat cross-legged on the dirty floor, staying well away from the stain that still smelled faintly of her vomit.

Now that she was here, Amy was at a loss for what to do. She couldn't summon the ghostly girl like they had Elodie—she didn't know her name. Nor the doctor's first name. So he was also out of the question. She sighed. What a stupid idea—sitting on the floor of a haunted room waiting for a ghost to make contact. It was hardly her finest moment. In fact, it was borderline crazy.

But if the rumours about Boucher were true, she ought to be surrounded by the ghosts of hundreds of butchered women. Amy didn't know what to believe, but surely those numbers were blown out of proportion. *Hundreds* of missing women couldn't have just slipped unnoticed through the history books. Could they?

Determined to find out the truth, there was only one ghost she was interested in raising right now. Closing her eyes, she relaxed and went over everything she knew so far.

Boucher was a phlebotomist, a blood-letter who removed blood to improve a patient's health and well-being. Her leg had been bleeding heavily when the ghostly girl first visited her. And then, this morning, when she pricked her finger with the lancet and tasted her own blood, she had that weird flashback. Surely this young woman was reaching out to her, and Amy felt powerless to resist.

Digging through her bag, she pulled the blood-letting knife out. Its silver handle almost glowed in the darkened room. It couldn't be that easy, could it?

Unfolding the blade, she pressed the tip to her finger and held her breath. Did she really want to cut herself? Her thoughts snapped to Flynn. Unlike him, she didn't have a reason to do this. She was doing it for fun, and that was all kinds of crazy. Not realising she'd dug the blade in, she gasped out loud as it bit into her tender flesh.

And something happened.

The air in the room thickened, cold and heavy. What weak light suffused the room flickered like lightning. Then insubstantial at first, and devoid of colour, the girl Amy had seen last night manifested, not three feet away. Ice seeped into her bones. But her eyes remained glued to the apparition.

The girl pointed to the lancet and made a cutting motion on her open palm. Understanding forced Amy to push the tip of the knife into her index finger. She didn't feel any pain. She pushed harder and dragged. Blood bloomed from the open cut and trickled down her skin. A single red drop splashed onto the floor. And the girl smiled.

Blood. The very essence of life.

Blood was the key.

⸺❖⸺

'Bonjour.'

Amy dropped the lancet with a clatter and stared. A real flesh and blood girl stood before her. A beautiful girl. Petite, with dark brown hair that shone like liquid chocolate and luminous, silvery grey eyes. She wore a heavily starched nurse's outfit, the apron pristine except for a tiny splash of red across the bottom. Blood.

Amy swallowed. 'W-w-who are you?'

The girl's skirts rustled as she bent to the floor and retrieved the lancet. 'Valentina Boucher,' she said, holding it in her outstretched palm. 'Et toi?'

Recognising the French accent, Amy wracked her memory for the simple phrases Pierre had taught her, but her brain refused to function. She should know this.

'And you?' Valentina prompted in English.

'Amy. Amy Shipley.'

She couldn't tear her gaze from the lancet. Its blade was still wet, glistening with tiny beads of blood. *Hers.* Holy crap, what had she done?

Valentina took a step forward. 'Take it.'

'No!' Amy scrambled backwards and to her feet.

'But you must.' The girl's wide grey eyes implored hers. 'Or you cannot come back.'

Come back—what did that even mean? Her voice shook. 'Where am I?'

Valentina tilted her head like a sparrow. 'In my quarters, of course.'

Feet leaden, Amy turned around slowly, taking in the room's contents. It was now full of things that certainly weren't there a moment ago. A small iron bed, dressed in crisp white linen, was pushed against the wall beneath the window; a simple wooden chair and washbasin beside it. And a curved dresser, adorned with a mirror, sat against the opposite wall. Amy looked at the two reflections staring back at her. She must've hit her head when she slipped over earlier.

But no. Only her butt was feeling the effects of that ill-timed landing. Her parkour coach would be livid.

Valentina gently grasped Amy's wrist, and she flinched, expecting the same frozen grip from the night before. But the girl's touch was warm. Solid. *Living.* So much had happened since last night. It felt like a lifetime ago. And just like she had then, Amy felt the folded blade being pushed into her hand. Absently, she slid it into the pocket of her jeans.

Turning away from the mirror, she faced Valentina. 'How old are you?'

'Quatorze.'

Only fourteen? Amy reeled. That made Valentina three years younger than herself.

'Why are you dressed like a nurse?'

'I assist my brother. Marcel is a blood doctor.' *Marcel.* With her accent, the name dripped off Valentina's tongue like something forbidden.

Amy felt a rush of warmth fizzing up from her toes that settled in her belly for a moment before lurching the words from her throat. 'Is Marcel here?'

Valentina straightened her pinafore and looked her over with a clinical eye. 'Do you require his services?'

Amy was positive she didn't *require* being bled to death, but Valentina's well-rehearsed question raised about a million more. Her heart began thudding in her chest. Swallowing her fear, she asked, 'What services does he provide?'

'Sanguination. Do you suffer melancholy, folly, dementia, rage?'

A sudden muffled thump sounded from the floor above, causing Amy to flinch and gasp out loud. Valentina's eyes narrowed.

'Excusez moi.'

She exited the room, leaving Amy standing cold. For all of about two seconds. Slinking out behind Valentina, Amy stared in shock at the floor. Gone were the dead leaves and detritus. The same black-and-white tiles that graced the floors downstairs lay in front of her, completely swept clean.

Keeping her distance, she followed Valentina up to the next floor, pausing in the hall as the girl disappeared through a massive door painted in the glossiest black. She didn't remember seeing this door last night as they made their way to the roof, but she recalled Leona mentioning something about a door on the third floor that wouldn't open. This must be it.

Valentina had left the door ajar, and Amy crept towards the narrow opening. She could barely see anything beyond, save for a glimpse of dark red patterned wallpaper and the soft flicker of candlelight.

She pulled out her phone and tried to ignore the inner voice of reason that was begging her to run, to turn and leave, and never come back. Instead, she focused on the voice that argued this wasn't—couldn't—be real. That this was all a dream, and therefore she could do whatever the hell she pleased. And right now, it pleased her to find out what was happening beyond the black door.

Hushed voices drew her closer. Valentina's soothing French lilt combined with an intense masculine cadence that almost rendered her heartbroken. By the sound of it, a man who had lost control of his emotions openly cried like a small boy. Was this Marcel Boucher?

'Mon Dieu,' he wailed. 'What have I done?'

The pain lacing his voice was a visceral thing, and Amy's heart ached. She started a video recording on her phone and sidled up to the door. She didn't dare push it open anymore, no matter how much she wanted to. Angling the phone's camera around the edge of the door, she kept her eyes on the screen, hoping to see something. Anything.

Footsteps moved toward her, and she jerked the phone back as something crashed to the ground just beyond the door. Amy leapt back as a forearm landed on the floor and remained still. Her eyes widened in fear, her breath coming in sharp gasps.

It wasn't the graceful hand that lay unfurled, not a foot away that made her flight instinct kick in. Nor was it the long tapered fingers that look like they belonged to a pianist. No, that response was completely and utterly a reaction to the sight of the blood that seeped across the pale wrist.

Oh crap. This is not happening. Crapcrapcrapcrapcrap.

Pocketing her phone, Amy bolted for the stairwell, not caring about how much noise she made. Flinging the door open, she hurled herself down the stairs, vaulting over the railings, pulse thundering in her ears.

The door to the laneway was her closest escape, and she scratched at the latch, desperate to be free. Sobbing with frustration and fear, it took several attempts before her shaking fingers fumbled it open, and she burst through, not daring to look back.

Rain fell in sheets outside, pushed by a strong wind that tore through her wet clothes and chilled her to the bone. Everything hurt. Her legs, her lungs, her broken and bloodied nails. Ignoring the phone buzzing in her back pocket, Amy didn't stop running.

Flynn. She needed Flynn. Her desperate need to be in his arms was the only thing that stopped her from screaming.

CHAPTER ELEVEN

TAKING A HUGE BITE of the shiny red apple in his hand, Flynn flopped back onto his bed, music pumping loudly through his headphones, and tried once again to focus on his stupid media homework.

It wasn't his fault the movie was so boring that he fell asleep in class. And there was no way he was going to spend his Sunday afternoon watching it again. Surely there was an internet page that analysed the whole sibling dynamic for him somewhere?

A simple online search yielded *pages* of results. Tens of pages, actually. He groaned, his head spinning after just looking over the first few.

Maybe he should just blow school off again tomorrow, but he'd promised Amy he'd turn up. As he scrolled through the results, the lead character kept reminding him of her and the fun they had ice-skating on Friday night. He'd surprised himself with how much he actually enjoyed it, even though he knew it had more to do with being with Amy than with the actual activity. Still, he ached to take her skateboarding. Guess that would have to go on hold now.

Everything was going so well until that bloody Butcher's House visit.

Even though he never wanted to repeat that night, if he hadn't ended up back at Amy's place, cleaning her up and listening to her ghost stories, would he still have kissed her? It was something he'd been thinking about doing for a long time. And right now, he really wanted to do it again.

'Fuck,' he muttered, slamming the laptop shut in frustration. Concentration was useless. Luka had a little sister. Maybe she could explain it all to him. The movie thing that is. Not the kissing thing. He pulled out his phone and dialled Luka's number.

An hour later, he and his best mate were playing eight-ball on the battered ex-pub table that graced the Marinellis' back patio, while Luka's younger sister, Sofia, sat on a nearby barstool making moon eyes at him.

'I think she likes you,' Luka whispered as Flynn walked behind him and sunk the number seven ball, followed by the two.

Flynn snickered. 'If you're trying to put me off my game, mate, you've gotta do better than that.'

Luka grunted a response as Flynn turned to Sofia.

'So, you know all about movies, hey?'

He shot her his most dazzling smile, and he was sure the girl melted just a little. He then told her about the movie he was supposed to analyse and begged her help.

'I just didn't get it.' He shrugged in the most helpless way he could and deliberately missed the next ball so that he could sidle up beside her.

'You're such a dick.' Luka chuckled and cleared the table while Flynn got a very in-depth explanation of not only the sibling dynamic but the entire movie.

'Wow,' he enthused when Sofia finally ran out of breath. 'Thank you, that was very... thorough. Now, how about we team up and kick your big bro's arse?'

Sofia's eyes lit up. 'I'm not very good, though.'

'That's okay. I'll teach you.' He winked at Luka, who rolled his eyes and simultaneously tried to make himself gag.

'Vom.'

'You're just jealous 'cos she likes me better than you.'

Luka gave him a strange look. 'You're right,' he growled, flinging the balls from the pockets and across the table.

'Whoa, dude. What's wrong?' Flynn paused in his demonstration of how to hold the pool cue and considered his friend.

Luka rattled the balls into the triangle. 'Nothing. Forget it. Your break, sis?'

Flynn stood over Sofia and guided her elbow until she'd perfected the smooth motion required to hit the ball. She was tiny, like all the Marinellis, so he leaned on the edge of the table and rested the cue tip between his knuckles. 'Fire away.'

Sofia's arm wobbled, and she completely missed the white ball. Her face fell.

'Hey,' he came around to her, 'you can do this. Girl power, and all that. Isn't that what we were just talking about?'

She shrugged. 'More like sister power. I wish I had a big sister.' Turning on Luka like an angry parent, she blurted, 'You need to get a girlfriend so I can have a sister.'

'What's this about?' Flynn chuckled while Luka gave Sofia a death stare.

She ignored her brother and turned to him. 'Do you have a girlfriend?' she asked, lining up the white for another shot. 'I bet you do.'

Was Amy his girlfriend now? They'd only kissed a few times, but he liked the idea.

'Yeah, kinda.'

Luka sniggered. 'Mate, you either do, or you don't. There's no in-between. Believe me.'

'Ooh.' Sofia's eyes took on a dreamy look as she punched the pool cue. 'Do you love her?'

'That's none of your business, Sof,' Luka warned.

'Fine,' she said, handing Flynn back the cue. 'You're on your own. I'm making nachos.'

After she'd gone inside, Luka turned to him. 'So what's going on with you and Amy, anyway?'

Flynn sunk a few balls before he answered. It was definitely something, but it was so fragile, he didn't want to jinx it. He shrugged. 'Something. Maybe nothing.'

'Have you kissed her yet?'

Luka was lining up a hard shot, yet underneath his golden Mediterranean complexion, his ears were flushing red. Flynn blinked. *Well, fuck me.* He waited for a beat. Two. Luka drew back the cue, and—

'Yeah.'

Luka fumbled, the cue skittering off the white and leaving him half-lying on the table.

Flynn crossed his arms, smirking. 'Do you like her, Luka?' He watched his best mate stand up and retreat to the far side of the table.

'Amy? She's amazing. What's not to like?'

'I don't mean as a friend.'

Luka kept his eyes averted. 'You taking your shot, or what?'

'You do.' It was so obvious now. 'Why haven't you said anything?'

Luka twisted his hair up into a man-bun—a sure sign he was flustered. 'Mate, I've liked her since the first day of school, okay? But it's chill. We all know you staked a claim long before she met the rest of us.'

'I never staked a claim.'

'You did, and maybe it was unintentional. But she likes *you*, Flynn. So don't worry about it.'

'Luka—'

'It's chill, bro.'

'Yeah, looks like it.' He rammed the next four balls into the corner pockets.

'I'm down with it. Just don't fuck it up, okay?'

'Or what, you're going to be waiting in the wings?'

'For fuck's sake. It's not like that, and you know it.'

'I know it? You've had a crush on Amy all this time, and yet you never said one word about it. Not one, Luka.' His voice was straining in an effort not to yell.

Luka eyeballed him, breathing hard. 'Seems to me, I'm not the only one. People in glass houses and all that.'

Flynn lined up the black. It was a short backward cut shot into the middle pocket—his specialty. Not even bothering to watch the ball fall, he dropped the cue onto the table and walked away. 'Fuck you.'

'Come on, man.'

He flipped his middle finger up behind his head and pulled out his phone. He sent a quick text to Amy, wondering if she was still chasing ghosts at the library.

how's the research going?
want some help?

He hit send, then paused—no more secrets.

miss u

His messages remained unread, so he assumed she had her phone turned off and stalked inside to grab his board.

'Who wants nachos?' Sofia called from the kitchen as he passed through.

Luka followed him in, ruffling Sofia's hair. 'Thanks, but I'm not hungry anymore.'

'Same. Thanks for your help, Sofia, but I'm going to head off. It's going to piss rain any minute.'

'Come on, boys. Don't let all those repressed feelings get the better of you,' Sofia said.

Luka's eyes flashed. 'What's that supposed to mean?'

'It's another motif from the movie.'

Flynn caught the smug glance she threw him and frowned.

'It's why Elsa destroys everything, of course. You know what I mean. You keep something bottled up for too long, and one day the pressure gets too much and—' She made an explosion gesture with her hands.

Flynn and Luka exchanged a wary glance before Flynn cleared his throat. 'Um, how old are you again?'

'She's twelve,' Luka deadpanned.

Sofia gave him a withering look. 'And a half, thank you very much.'

Flynn shook his head. 'I'm out of here.'

'You coming to school tomorrow?' Luka's voice was tinged with hope.

Flynn halted and turned back to his best friend. 'Sure. Why not.'

'That's the way!' Sofia beamed. 'Bros before ho—' Luka clamped a hand over her mouth before she could finish.

Flynn suppressed a grin as he grabbed his board from the porch and rolled down Luka's drive to the street. Above him, thunder cracked, and the sky split open, dumping a torrent of rain that instantly soaked him to the bone. As he pushed on through the downpour, his phone began buzzing in his back pocket. It was probably Amy returning his texts, but he couldn't check it in this weather. Finding a nearby bus shelter, he stopped undercover to read her message.

Where are you?

just left luka's.
wanna come over?

I'm already at your place.
Will you be long?

5 mins. u ok? is mick there?

A flash of violent anger spiked through him at the thought of his mum's boyfriend leering at Amy. If that bastard laid so much as an eyeball on her...

I'm alone. Hurry. I need you

He grinned, the anger quickly fanning to desire as he guessed at the hidden meaning in her words. The rain eased to a gentle shower, so he started skating again, texting at the same time.

need u 2
on my way

Good. I'm wet and cold

huge fan of that but not the cold bit

You do know it's raining, right?

Yeah. Of course .... *Wait.* Flynn halted, his entire body heating at the thought of her wearing his t-shirt. As if that wasn't enough... Now it was *wet.*

r u still wearing my shirt?

She slept in it last night?

'Fuck,' he breathed, trying not to imagine her clad in his tee, the fabric concealing her curves and warm from her body. He failed dismally and adjusted his suddenly too-tight jeans.

Need pushed him onwards, and he raced up the stairs to his flat to find her sitting wet and bedraggled on the dirty concrete. Her knees were drawn up, and her back slumped against his front door.

'Ames.'

She lifted her head, her red-rimmed eyes meeting his. Flynn's desire morphed to anger, then fear, as she propelled herself at him, burying her face in his chest. His arms caught her, enfolded her, held her tight as she sobbed and sobbed, clutching at his back like he was her lifeline.

What the fuck had happened? Who did this to her? His body was tense with so many unanswered questions, yet he pressed his cheek on top of her head and asked the most important one of all.

'Are you hurt?'

She clutched him harder but shook her head. *Thank fuck.*

He let out a pent-up breath; the tension still wound tight in his body. Even though he wanted nothing more than to pour his warmth and love into her right there, he had to get her inside. She shivered in his arms. With cold or fear, he couldn't tell.

Still holding her tight, he got the front door unlocked and scooped her up, carrying her to his bedroom. Kicking the door closed, he slid the bolt across and sat down on his bed, cradling her in his lap.

Her breathing was uneven. Her face was blotchy from crying. And yet, she was still the most beautiful girl he'd ever laid eyes on. He brushed the dishevelled hair from her face and tilted her chin so he could look into those denim blue eyes he loved so much.

'Tell me everything.'

Chapter Twelve

FLYNN CRADLED AMY IN complete silence as she recounted the events of her afternoon. The rage that overcame him at the start soon settled like a stone, deep in the pit of his stomach. Just what the fuck was she thinking, going back there alone? If someone was squatting in that place, she could've been seriously hurt. She could've even... He clenched his jaw so hard he swore he heard something crack.

'You don't believe me, do you?' Her face was pale and drawn. 'To be honest, I don't blame you. If I hadn't seen it with my own eyes, I wouldn't believe me, either.'

'I didn't say that.'

'You didn't have to.' She crawled off his lap to pull her phone from her jeans, holding it out to him with trembling fingers. 'But, I got some video.'

Reluctantly, he took the phone from her and scrolled through the recording. The screen remained completely black.

'What am I supposed to be looking at?' He wandered over to the window and closed the curtain, eliminating any glare.

'The gap in the doorway. You can see a man's hand on the floor. It's right there.'

He squinted at the screen again, pausing it and zooming in. There were varying degrees of darkness, but nothing was distinct. If he really stretched his imagination, he could make out a doorframe. Lowering his eyes, he handed her phone back.

She stared at the screen. 'Wait. What? No. No. No!'

'Amy.'

'But it was right there!'

'Amy.'

'I didn't imagine it. I swear.'

He cupped her face in his hands and leaned in. Pressed his lips to hers. Kissed her until she softened under his touch. Then he pulled away and searched his drawers for a clean pair of sweats and a hoodie.

'Here, put these on while I make you something to eat.'

'I'm not hungry,' she protested, but she took the clothes. Leaving her to change, he fixed her a cup of chicken noodle soup in his favourite tin camping mug that reminded him of happier times. Like those when his dad was still alive. His fingers absently reached for the crucifix around his neck, rubbing the thin metal until it warmed between his fingertips. God, what he wouldn't give to have some fatherly advice right now. He was flying blind without a safety net and wouldn't be the only one to get hurt if he fell.

When he fell, somehow, it seemed inevitable.

Flynn took the soup back to his room, grateful that Mick wasn't around. He didn't need that prick adding to the clusterfuck this weekend had already become. Amy was sitting cross-legged on his bed, looking tiny and cute in his clothes. She'd rolled the track pants up and had pulled the hood over her damp hair. Her wet clothes lay discarded on the floor. He handed her the soup and gathered up her jeans and his tee.

'I'm just going to run these down to the laundry and put them through the dryer for you, okay? I'll be right back.' She looked so defeated, and it was utterly lost on him how to fix it. 'Hey. Eat your soup. You don't want me to come back and spoon-feed you. It could get messy.'

The corner of her mouth turned up a little as she raised the cup to her lips.

The laundry room was on the ground floor of the block of flats, and thankfully no one else was using it. Not that it would have mattered. He would have hauled out their washing just to put Amy's in. She was his number one priority. And yet, he'd let her down again.

He slammed the door of the dryer and resisted smashing his fist into it. Instead, he let out a string of curse words that would've put Mick to shame. He was so wired; he almost wished the old prick was around so he'd have an excuse to smash his smug face to a bloody pulp.

God help anyone who looked at him wrong tonight.

Right now, he didn't care about repressed feelings or destroying everything around him. He just needed to get the rage out, and *for once*, he didn't feel like cutting. Which was pretty fucked when he thought about it because at least the relief would've been instant.

He returned to find Amy lying on her stomach on his bed, doodling in his media notebook, of all things. The tin cup on the floor was empty.

'Shouldn't take too long.' He dropped onto his back beside her, grunting. 'If I knew you'd get that bored while I was gone, I'd have given you my homework to do.'

She gave him a weak smile, and he was happy to see a flicker of the old fire back in her eyes. 'Thanks for the soup. And I'm not bored, just wondering about something.'

'I don't think there's anything that chicken soup can't fix.' He turned on his side as she tapped the pen on the paper. She'd drawn little hearts in the margins. Cute.

'Why is there no record of him anywhere? If the urban legend is true, why can't I find anything about it?'

'*Because* it's an urban legend. It isn't true. Someone clearly made it up. He was probably just some ordinary blood-letter going about his job.'

'But what reason would someone have to make up something like that?'

'I don't know. Maybe one of his patients had a bad experience. Maybe some creepy Victorian-era kids wanted to scare each other. Who knows?'

'Is that what you really think?'

He reached out and rubbed one of her wavy locks between his fingers to separate the strands. 'Does it really matter?'

She frowned at him and looked away.

Flynn sighed and reached for her, pulling her against him. He needed to get her mind off where she'd been and what she'd seen (or thought she had). Her fascination with that fucking leech confused him. What she needed was a good dose of reality. To see what was right in front of her instead of chasing the past. And for what, exactly? He doubted she even knew.

'Hey, I think it's stopped raining. I want to show you something.' He took her hand and led her outside, where they climbed the iron stairwell to the rooftop.

'Oh my God,' she exclaimed, grinning madly as the wind pushed the hood from her head, whipping her hair around her face. 'I haven't been up here in forever.'

'I know.'

She pulled him over to the ledge, where they stood with knees pressed against the brick surrounding, and looked out over the suburbs. The sun was breaking through a bank of low clouds in the west, turning everything golden, and yet, he couldn't stop looking at Amy.

The light had caught in her eyes, turning them from their usual blue to mini galaxies, complete with black holes, and exploded supernovas. There was so much going on underneath her surface, and he wanted in. He wanted in so badly.

'I miss coming up here,' she said.

'I've been hoping you'd come back sometime,' he ventured. 'So I got you something, you know, just in case.'

He retreated to the far corner where the shadows concealed the old broom he used to sweep away the pigeon shit and occasional puddle. Nudging it out of the way, he planted his foot on top of the small pink plastic skateboard and scooted it over to her.

'What's this?' she squealed.

He chuckled, totally chuffed at her surprise. 'It's your very own Penny board.' It was only a replica; he couldn't afford the real thing, but he knew she wouldn't care.

'Seriously, for me?'

'Well, pink's not really my colour,' he scoffed, walking over to put his arms around her waist. 'Besides, I don't think my size thirteen feet will fit. Do you like it?'

'I love it.'

Wrapping her arms around the back of his neck, she smiled up at him and pulled him down for a kiss. He elicited a deep groan as her lips melted against his. Ever since the day they'd met, he'd longed to kiss her up here. Her hair whipped around his face like a caress, and he moved his hand against her nape, pulling her closer. He didn't want the moment to end, but there was something else he wanted to do up here, too.

'Come on.' He reluctantly pulled away, knowing it was getting late, and she'd have to leave soon. 'I'll give you your first skate lesson. Just watch your bare toes. If you catch one in the wheel, you'll rip one of those pretty toenails right off.'

First, he showed her how to walk with the board under one foot, and then the other, to determine if she was goofy-footed or not. (She wasn't). Then he walked beside her and held her hand as he taught her to cruise. The joins in the concrete roof didn't help, and she kept wobbling and stalling, but she wasn't bad for a beginner. Most of all—she had the hugest smile on her face the entire time. And that? *That* was everything.

'You have a go!' She jumped off and perched herself on the ledge, the lowering sun at her back turning her hair into a halo of molten gold.

He shook his head. 'I'm too heavy for that board.' That was a load of crap, but she didn't know that.

'I call bullshit,' she said. *Well, fuck.* 'You just don't want to be seen on a pink ride, am I right? Come on, Flynn. I won't tell anyone. I can't even take photos because my phone's still on your bed. Please? I just love watching you skate.'

His heart did a little ollie at that.

'Come on. You know you want to,' she teased, biting down on her lower lip.

How was he going to deny that? There was nothing like skating to loosen him up, release all that tension from his body. Grinning, he sauntered over and toe-flipped the board up into his waiting hand and planted a kiss on her cheek.

'Okay, one kickback flip coming up.'

He cruised the board to the end of the roof, turned around and pushed off until he was about two-thirds of the way across. Then, planting all his weight on his back toe, he flipped the board up, kicking it forward as he jumped, sending it spinning three-sixty degrees before he landed back on the deck.

But, just as he predicted, his feet really were too long for the narrow board, and he misjudged the landing. Rolling an ankle, he fell in a spectacular barrel roll, stopping right at Amy's blue-painted toes.

She dropped to her knees. 'Holy crap, are you okay?'

'Yeah. I just figured I should show you how to fall properly. It's all in the way you roll,' he said, laughing.

'You are such a dick.'

He lifted a brow. 'That's the second time I've heard that today,' he said. But she spoke at the same time, and it sounded a lot like *Lucky I love you, though.*

Flynn didn't move. He just sat there on the wet ground staring up at her while she stared back at him, chewing on her lip. Silence descended around them, thick and black, like the shadows creeping across the rooftop. Was she waiting for him to say something? Did he even hear her correctly? And if he did—had she meant it?

Hauling himself to his feet, he picked up the Penny board and handed it to her. His heart thumped so hard in his chest it was about to burst right out onto the ground in front of him. 'You'd best get going before it gets too dark.'

'Sure.' Her eyes were downcast as she took the board from him and hooked it under her arm.

He let her back into the flat while he fetched her clothes from the dryer. It didn't bother him if she went home wearing his sweats, but Amy thought her mum might get the wrong idea.

After she changed, he threaded her board through the straps of her backpack and his fingers through hers and walked her back to her place. They mostly stuck to small talk—his media homework and the small tornado of sass that was Luka's little sister.

'Oh yeah, I've met her a few times at their house. Seems like a sweet kid.'

'I didn't know you'd been to Luka's place.' Flynn felt his hackles rise.

Amy gave him an odd look. 'Really? I thought you two told each other everything.'

Clearly not.

The trees were still dripping as they walked hand in hand through the park. Leaves were strewn all over the dark, dampened concrete. He stopped to pick one up, Luka's words ringing loud in his head. Had he really staked a claim on Amy?

Maybe it wasn't intentional. But she likes you.

Either way, he was staking one now.

He handed Amy the leaf. It was in the throes of changing colour —yellow and green and orange. And shaped perfectly, like a heart.

CHAPTER THIRTEEN

AMY WAITED ALL MORNING for Flynn. But by the time history class rolled around in fourth period and he still hadn't turned up, it was clear he wasn't going to. Flynn skipping school wasn't something new, but he'd never broken a promise to her before.

Even Luka looked pissed off. 'Has anyone heard from Flynn?' He dropped into their regular seat at lunch and sucked on his iced coffee in agitation. 'He said he'd be here today.'

Amy gave him a rueful smile and nibbled at her sandwich.

'What's up?' His brow furrowed.

She sighed. 'I just thought he'd show today, you know?'

Luka leaned across the table, lowering his voice to a whisper. 'Um. Did you guys—' He cleared his throat. 'You know ... hook up yesterday?'

'WHAT? NO!'

'Okay, okay.' He sat back quickly, palms raised in front of him.

She frowned at him, crossing her arms tightly. 'Why the hell would you think that?'

'No reason.' A red flush began at Luka's neck and quickly engulfed his entire face. 'Shit. Quit looking at me like that.'

Flynn had been with Luka yesterday. Had he been talking about sleeping with her? She didn't think he would do that, but had to admit the idea of him wanting to kind of excited her. She sat back with a huff and rolled her eyes, unable to keep the smile out of her voice. 'What the fuck, Luka.'

Pulling out her phone, she checked it yet again. Still no word from Flynn. She considered texting him but knew it wouldn't achieve anything. The boy knew how to disappear when he wanted to. She just hoped her confession wasn't the reason.

It had just sort of slipped out, unbidden. But shouldn't that be a good thing? Like she hadn't been consciously thinking of saying it? It certainly hadn't happened the way she'd rehearsed in her head. If it were, she'd have timed it better instead of talking right over the top of him. She hadn't even thought he'd heard her at first. He'd been so silent.

She had no choice but to sit tight and be patient. Flynn wasn't a man of many words. His unspoken gesture with the leaf was testament to that.

Oh, and what a gesture. Bent on one knee, offering her his heart. Swoon, honestly.

⋯⟡⋯

The rest of the day dragged on. When she finally set foot in the patisserie after school, her mum was the last person she expected to see.

'Oh, hi Mum.' She glanced around. 'Where's Pierre?' Stepping behind the counter, Amy hugged her mother, noting the dark circles under her eyes. This wasn't unusual considering she'd been up since some ungodly hour doing the late-night baking shift. 'You haven't been here all day, have you?'

'Not all day, no. But long enough. Pierre had to take care of something, and I offered to cover him for a bit.' She ruffled Amy's hair. 'Do you think you could take over for me till closing? I'm dead on my feet.'

'Of course.'

It wasn't the first time Amy had done a bit of work for Pierre—hence the obligatory French lessons—and the next couple of hours flew by in a blur of hazelnut strawberry crepes, macarons, and family-sized quiche. Pierre finally arrived to close the shop and offered to drive her to gym class, but she politely declined. The walk wasn't far, and it would also serve as a pre-class warmup. Besides, for some completely screwed-up reason, she wanted to get another look at the Butcher's House on the way.

—◈✦◈—

Slowing her footsteps as she approached the cream Victorian, Amy slipped into the laneway and stopped. At least from there, she could have a good look and not have to worry about tripping over sandbags or impeding pedestrians. Her eyes drifted up to the third floor and across to the right, trying to find the room that Valentina had disappeared into yesterday. All the windows looked the same. Narrow, double-hung, arched at the top. All uniform-distance apart. Absolutely unremarkable from the outside.

Feeling slightly miffed, she turned back towards Flinders Lane, pausing as she drew level with the hole in the wall. Leona's access point. Dropping to her knees, Amy thrust her phone as far as she could inside and snapped a couple of photos, praying that this time she'd capture something. Maybe even the padlocked doors Leona had seen. Amy's mind spun as she got to her feet. Why on earth would there be a locked room under the street?

Wait. Maybe it wasn't a locked room at all. Her phone's camera lens wasn't strong enough to show any detail, but the photos she took showed something. Something that she discovered yesterday. Something that Melbourne was notoriously famous for—and was rumoured to be *everywhere* under the CBD. There was a reason they built the city like a grid.

As above, so below.

Her feet moved of their own accord, propelling her down the laneway and towards the building across the road. The golden stucco Art Nouveau structure now housed a dingy café and a barber shop, of all things. She knew from her research that the building was formerly a hotel, built in 1890. Making it a very new establishment around the time of Boucher's arrival and perhaps a rather seedy one at that.

By the time she'd jogged to the YMCA, she'd concluded that those doors were concealing a tunnel that ran beneath Flinders Lane, connecting Marcel's rooms and possibly a hotel brothel across the street. The only question was, why?

Gym class was beyond punishing. It probably didn't help that she'd skipped last Wednesday to go ghost-hunting. Plus, her calf was still hurting. Even though the wound looked good on the surface, it was clearly still healing from the inside. To make matters worse, she kept looking up every two seconds to see if Flynn walked through the doors.

He didn't. Which meant he hadn't gone to The Mission either.

She scrolled through her messages while waiting for the train home. Luka asked if she'd heard from Flynn. She hadn't. Her mum asked if she wanted to go out for gelato later. She didn't. Leona wanted to know if she was game to go back to the Butcher's House sometime. To see if they could unlock that door. Did she? Her fingers hovered over the screen. More than anything, she wanted to be with Flynn. And she thought that's what he wanted too. But then, maybe she was wrong.

Damn, maybe she had scared him off with her confession. Things weren't turning out the way she'd planned. If only she hadn't gone chasing Elodie's ghost, then she wouldn't have lied to him. And she would've confessed to him properly, on the swings in the park, that night. Instead, she blurted it out on the rooftop, her words getting snatched away on the wind and mixed up in his.

The silence was killing her. Opening up his last message, her fingers flew across the screen.

> **You can't give me your ❤ and then disappear.**
> **Meet me at the swings tonight?**
> **If you can't, or don't want to, pls just tell me**

He still hadn't responded by the time she got home, but she was so surprised to find Pierre having dinner with her mum when she walked in, she momentarily forgot all about it. They were standing at the kitchen bench, eating out of noodle boxes. Amy sighed. At least her mum's relationship was escalating nicely.

Pierre looked up from his steaming Pho Ga. 'Bonsoir Amy. How was your class?'

She dropped her backpack and stared at him. He looked so out of place in their small kitchen that her brain refused to function. Beside him, her mum raised an eyebrow.

Oh, right. Manners. 'It was tough, Pierre. Thanks for asking.'

'Ah.' He pointed at her with his chopsticks. 'C'était difficile.'

'Oui, whatever.' She sounded like Valentina—all jumbled French and English. What was it called? Frenglish? No, Franglais. That was it. She wondered how Valentina managed the language. Surely nineteenth-century Australian women didn't speak any French. It must have been hard for her.

'Is there any food for me?' She rummaged through the takeaway bag by the sink.

'It's in your room, love.' Amy didn't miss the loaded glance her mum shot Pierre.

Since when did her mum let her eat in her bedroom? 'Okay. This isn't weird.'

'I just want to have a few words with your mum for a bit, Amy. You don't mind, do you?'

Amy hesitated. Although Pierre had always been very formal with Valerie, it was hard to take him seriously. Amy snorted, but the air was tense. Oh my God, he wasn't about to propose to her, was he?

She looked at her mum. 'You guys good?'

'Yes, love.' She smiled. 'Have some dinner. You must be starving.'

Amy's stomach grumbled although she didn't feel hungry. She checked her phone one more time. Still no message from Flynn, but she could see that he'd at least read hers. Her heart jumped.

'Thanks, Mum.' Giving her mother a quick peck on the cheek, she raced upstairs to her bedroom, suddenly ravenous.

Pushing open her door, her heart hit the carpet along with her appetite. Flynn was sitting in the middle of her bed, a bowl of laksa perched on his knee. And even under the glow of her neon pink LED strip lighting, she could tell something was wrong with his face.

'Flynn?'

He raised his head but didn't look at her.

Resisting the urge to fling herself at him, she shifted the soup to her bedside table and knelt on the mattress. With trembling fingers, she cupped his face with both hands to inspect the damage. A bruise covered his left cheek. His upper lip was cut and swollen. One eyebrow was split; the eye beneath it, bloodshot. And his knuckles were absolutely ravaged. Panic rose, bubbling in her throat. 'What happened?'

His eyes slid to hers with a mirthless chuckle. 'You should see the other guy.' Cracking his neck, he exhaled loudly. 'Mick tried to smack Mum around.'

Oh, Flynn. Her hands slid into his, pressing her lips against his broken skin. His blood had dried, but it still tasted coppery against her tongue, making her want to curl into his lap like a puppy and lick his wounds.

'When I got home yesterday, he had her bailed up against the stove. Talking shit about me. Saying I had no right to be living there anymore. He reckons I cost too much to feed. That she should be done providing for me. Shit like that. As if the fucking prick doesn't spend all her money on booze and smokes. He's the one who's bleeding her dry, for fuck's sake.' He shook his head. 'There was a boiling pot of water, right there on the stove. She should've thrown it at him. But no, she let him spit in her face and then he... He shoved her, and she hit her head on the rangehood and then—' Flynn looked at Amy, a feral glint in his eye. 'Then it was on. I've never understood it when people say they see red. But fuck, you do, Ames. You really do.'

He told her that a neighbour called in a domestic disturbance after the fight spilled out onto the balcony, and the cops turned up not long after. They both got hauled away and spent the night in the lockup. Sadly, his mum wasn't pressing charges against Mick, and the bastard promised he'd come back for Flynn. Not knowing what to do and not wanting to worry anyone, Flynn called the only adult he trusted. Pierre had picked him up, cleaned him up, fed him, and brought him here. To her.

Amy pushed herself up to lock her arms around his neck, holding on tight. His arms came around her. 'I could've killed him, Ames.' His whole body shook as he buried his face in her neck. 'I really wanted to kill him.'

'But you wouldn't, Flynn. That's not you. That's not you.' She kept whispering it like a mantra as they rocked in each other's arms until Flynn eased her back onto the bed with him.

'I know I broke a promise to you today.'

'Don't even.'

'But—'

'Flynn, do I have to kiss you to shut you up?'

He rolled her over, wincing as his mouth curved into a lopsided smile. Even more lopsided since he split it. God, even though he looked like hell, he was still hot.

She peppered his face with tiny soft kisses until he dropped his head and murmured into her hair, almost too quiet to be heard.

'I want to forget. Please make me forget.'

She wrapped her legs around his and raked her fingertips up and down his back beneath his tee. His skin was warm and hard under her touch, igniting heat through her veins. Flynn's mouth traced her collarbone, his tongue flicking across the hollow at her throat, driving her wild. She moaned and arched into him, feeling the loss of his lips on her skin as he slipped lower, reaching under her singlet. Lifting it to reveal her stomach, he kissed every inch of her exposed flesh, making her shudder every time his ruined lip scratched across her skin. Closing her eyes, she sank into his touch. When he finally pulled his mouth back to hers, her bones were liquid, having completely dissolved in his intoxicating scent of blood, sweat, and lust.

'Amy.' His lips whispered against hers. 'Amy.'

'Amy?' A loud knock on her door had them reluctantly pulling apart. Flynn rolled off her and pulled her into his lap. She quickly shoved her top back down and sat up, hoping she didn't look too flushed. 'Come in.'

Pierre appeared in her doorway, addressing Flynn. 'Time to go.'

Flynn nodded but didn't move. Pierre appeared to suppress a smile. 'I'll give you a minute, mate, but then we really have to leave.'

Chapter Fourteen

L UKA ROUNDED ON HER at the school gates the next morning. 'Is it true?'

Amy hefted her backpack onto her other shoulder and pinned him with an exasperated glare. 'What are you talking about?'

'Jim said Flynn got arrested for assaulting his mum's de facto.'

Crap on a stick. 'Great to see the grapevine still works.'

'So it is true,' Luka grumbled through a clenched jaw.

'Of course it's not.'

Knowing Luka wouldn't drop it, she stormed ahead, looking for a quiet place to talk. The entire school didn't need to hear about this.

He was by her side in an instant. 'Are you saying he didn't beat up the arsehole?'

She skidded to a halt and pulled him against the back wall of the cafeteria, his eyes widening in surprise.

'Just how well do you know your best mate, Luka?' she whispered in his face, but all he did was stare at her with those melted chocolate eyes. Gah, boys. They were so dumb sometimes. 'Put it this way, genius. *He didn't get arrested.* You with me?'

A beat of silence. 'Fuck.'

'Right? Come on,' she said, dragging him by the arm, but he refused to move.

'He hasn't returned my calls.'

'Luka, you know what he's like. For what it's worth, he hasn't contacted me either.' She turned to go.

'You don't understand. I have to see him.'

She lifted a brow. 'Are you two dating or something? Should I be jealous?'

But Luka ignored her joke. In fact, he looked downright miserable. It wasn't like him at all.

Looking around, she lowered her voice. 'He's okay. He's staying with a family friend under direction to lie low for a while. I think he'd appreciate it if we all did the same.'

He shook his head. 'I can't, Ames.'

'Why not?'

He looked away. 'We had a fight.'

'Really?' This surprised her. Flynn and Luka never argued. 'You want to talk about it?'

He was still leaning against the cafeteria wall, his face stricken. She reached out and laid a hand on his forearm. 'Look, he'll be alright. This is Flynn, remember. Whatever went down with the two of you... He'll be fine.'

As Amy walked to class, she wasn't sure who she was trying to convince—Luka or herself.

Still, she spent the rest of the morning trying to distract herself from thinking about Flynn, worrying about Flynn, or imagining what might have happened if Pierre hadn't knocked on her door last night. Her whole body flushed with the memory. *Jesus, girl. Get it together.*

So when Leona caught her doodling hearts on her Math folder and accused her of trying to seduce Mr Grayson for extra credit, Amy caved and confided in her about breaking back into Boucher's residence. Leona was a captive audience, and by the time Amy had whispered her entire Sunday afternoon escapades (sans everything Flynn), she was eager to test her theory regarding the tunnels.

'You're kidding, right?' Leona gaped, 'So, either some squatter's living in that room, or—'

'Leona. No squatter would have hands that manicured. This guy would put Kenzie to shame.'

'Could be a starving artist.'

Amy gave her a withering look.

'Well then, girl, it sounds to me like you might've just seen your first ghost.' Leona grinned. 'I am so fucking jealous right now.' She tapped one of the heart drawings. 'Why's this one bleeding?'

'Huh?'

'You've drawn this one dripping blood,' Leona said, grabbing her books as the bell rang. 'That bloodletter murdered a lot of women, Ames. Maybe Luka was right all along, and he really was a vampire.'

'With a fetish for hookers.'

'Hence the secret tunnel to the brothel.'

Grinning wickedly, Leona linked her arm through Amy's and led her to the cafeteria for lunch. Amy had barely sat down before Leona pulled her back to her feet beside her and draped an arm around her shoulders.

'We're going back to the Butcher's House tonight. Who's coming?'

'Hell yeah!' Jimmy shot to his feet, fist-pumping the air, but Kenzie shook her head.

'Are you two mad? Tell me you're not going down that hole again, Lee.'

'I won't need to, Kenz,' Leona chirped, beaming at Amy. 'Our little monkey here scaled the fence.'

Luka's eyes met Amy's, and she dropped her head, feeling his scrutiny. 'Does Flynn know?' he asked quietly.

'That I scaled the fence?' She toed the ground, then looked at him defiantly. 'Yeah.'

He pursed his lips. 'About you going back?'

She held his gaze. Truthfully, she didn't even know why she wanted to go back after everything she'd witnessed. She just needed to prove to herself that it wasn't all in her head.

'No, he doesn't. Flynn has enough going on at the moment, Luka. And I wouldn't want to cause him more worry. Would you?' Her challenge hung in the air between them like an icicle. Cold and hard.

She didn't want to hurt Luka, but a part of her was resenting the fact that Flynn was so against her seeking Boucher's ghost. Marcel was still there, in that building. She'd seen his bloodied hand, his blood. Her heart beat faster as she blinked away the memory of that pale wrist, dripping crimson.

At that moment, she knew she had to go back. She had to find out what happened to him and find out if the rumours were true. She just had to.

Except that night, Amy's mum declared they were having dinner at Pierre's, and everyone was under strict instructions to "dress nicely". Amy had rolled her eyes, having been texting with Flynn back and forth all day. He was staying with Pierre for a few days in case Mick came back for him, and had been told the same thing—but it was no ripped jeans in his case.

Amy didn't do dresses and had finally opted for a long maxi skirt to hide her cropped leggings underneath, ready for exploring later with Leona. She matched it with a knotted white t-shirt and ballet flats, throwing her denim jacket over the top. She added a slick of lip gloss and piled her hair up into a loose ponytail.

When they reached Pierre's boutique townhouse, Flynn opened the door with that sexy lopsided grin and stood back, waiting for them to enter. 'Valerie. Amy.' He hugged them both, letting his hand linger on Amy's waist. Dropping his mouth to her ear, he whispered, 'You look incredible.'

She blushed, drinking in his muscular form, wrapped in not ripped but distressed dark denim jeans and a navy collared shirt that matched his eyes. He'd rolled the sleeves to the elbow and left the top few buttons undone. With his healing facial cuts and purple eye, he looked every bit the smooth bad-boy she always knew him to be. Heat pooled between her legs. How on earth was she going to concentrate at dinner with him looking like that?

'Ladies!' Pierre interrupted, exiting the kitchen wearing an ice-breaker of an apron emblazoned with *"embrassez le cuisinier"*, the French equivalent of "Kiss the Cook" on the front. He greeted Valerie with a glass of Pinot Noir and a little too much PDA for Amy's comfort. She turned to Flynn, who had both eyebrows raised in a horrified expression, making her laugh out loud.

'Why don't you kids make yourselves scarce for a bit.' Pierre ushered them towards the living area.

'Kids?' Flynn muttered, grabbing a beer from the fridge and lemonade for Amy. 'Babe, why don't you choose some music, and please, not the crap that Frenchie plays all day.'

'Hey,' Pierre shot back. 'I have great taste in music.'

'Yeah, if it was 1920.'

Amy giggled, glad that her two favourite men were getting along so well, while she scrolled through her phone, settling on a playlist of French house and electro-swing. A deep bass erupted from Pierre's wireless speakers, and Amy let her shoulders move to the beat as she sank into the plush leather lounge. Flynn remained standing, taking a deep pull on his beer.

She cocked her head and put on her best Joker voice. 'Why so serious?'

He shrugged, those dark eyes never straying from hers.

Standing, she went to him, slipping off her jacket. 'Well, maybe I can help with that.' She plucked the bottle from his fingers and left it on the windowsill. 'Dance with me.' Leading him out into the middle of the room, she draped her arms around his neck as his hands came to rest on her hips. As they swayed to the music, Flynn stepped forward, pressing his body against her and dropped his head to that space between her neck and shoulder. He smelled good. Like soap, and boy, and—wait—not boy. Man. Clean *and* dirty.

'Hey, knock it off, you two,' Pierre called from the kitchen. 'Some of us have to eat. Dinner's ready,' he added with a twinkle in his eye.

Pierre's cooking was divine. Amy watched as Flynn helped himself to three servings of the thinly sliced bistro steak, opting to forgo the simple side salad in favour of Pierre's famous buttermilk onion rings. The conversation was light until Flynn announced that a mate of Pierre's had offered him a job working at a local pub, unloading kegs of beer and boxes of booze.

'Yeah, we thought it was about time I started paying my own way. Hopefully, it'll keep Mick off Mum's back for a while.' His grim smile tilted at one corner as he sat back and patted his rock-hard stomach. 'And it'll keep me fit. All this French food isn't good for my waistline.'

Everyone laughed, and Amy's heart swelled. Flynn needed someone good like Pierre in his life.

After they'd finished eating and had cleared the table, the four of them settled in for a few rounds of Whiskey Poker. Pierre was a card shark from way back and didn't play soft. He and Flynn looked so much like a couple of old friends; Amy was half-expecting them to crack out some cigars.

Meanwhile, she and her mum escaped to the living room, pushing furniture out of the way to make room for a dancefloor. Holding hands, they twirled and laughed as the music pumped out of Pierre's impressive sound system. Both men watched them dance for a couple of songs before joining them.

Amy watched Flynn shamelessly, her eyes hungry, as his body rocked and swung in front of her. Not only had she never seen him so loose and carefree—but the guy had *moves*.

Valerie and Pierre left them to retire with a nightcap on the front patio, but when Flynn took her hand and led her to the spare room he was crashing in, Amy didn't protest.

Her whole body buzzed with anticipation as she collapsed backwards onto the bed. Flynn hovered over her, his eyes like dark pools behind his scrappy black fringe. The next thing she knew, he'd scooped her up, leaving her breathless and millimetres from his lips.

'Flynn—'

'God help me, I'm trying my fucking hardest to be a gentleman tonight,' he growled. 'But I can't do that if you're lying in my bed.'

Reaching behind her, he snatched up the quilt in one hand and led her outside with the other. In the darkness of Pierre's tiny rear courtyard, Flynn spread the quilt out on the ground and lay down on his back, motioning for her to join him. Stretching out, she nestled into his side, her head on his shoulder.

Wrapped up in his arms, she gazed at the stars. It was such a beautiful night, and she could happily stay like this forever. Flynn caressed a gentle hand down her back and over her hips before swirling around her thigh and back up again. A lazy figure eight. But with every sweep of his hand, her skirt crept higher and higher until his fingers brushed the Lycra of her leggings, then stilled.

'Are you wearing your gym gear under this thing?'

No. Nope. No way. Definitely not.

'Mmm-hmm.' Amy closed her eyes, waiting for the inevitable. If he asked her why, she knew she couldn't lie to him again, so she jumped in first. 'Icona wants to have another look for Boucher tonight.' She held her breath.

Flynn's body tensed. 'What. The. Fuck?' His voice was deathly quiet.

The sounds of her mother and Pierre clattering around inside broke the silence. 'I think we might have to make a move.' She tried to sit up, but Flynn's grip around her arms tightened.

'Please don't.'

She smiled down at him. 'I don't exactly want to leave either, but somehow I don't think either of those two would let us—'

'You know what I mean.' He let out a long exhale.

Of course she did. But she didn't know how to respond, except to brush her lips to his in the dark.

⸙

Leona had called after she got home, unable to make good on her promise to go to Boucher's. Jimmy was still keen, but Leona suggested they postpone their late-night rendezvous until dawn the following morning, as Amy would need to get over the fence before the construction workers were on site, and they couldn't risk being seen exiting, either.

Falsely telling her mum that she was heading to the gym for a before-school workout, Amy met Leona and Jimmy at the same café as last time, just after sunrise. The street was empty, and Amy slipped in without drama, opening the laneway door for the others.

Jimmy had brought bolt cutters, and they made their way back through the cellar to the tunnel, propping the door open with the mini crowbar again. Aided by Leona's flashlight, they paused in front of the padlocked doors. Jimmy easily snapped the aging iron lock, and it hit the cobbled ground with a dull clank. Amy took a deep breath as he pushed the doors open.

The first thing she noticed was the cold, dank air seeping up through the cobblestones at her feet, chilling her bare legs. The second thing was the chair.

'You guys see this too, right?'

She shone her phone on what appeared to be an old dining chair, attached to four rusted wheels. Something shifted in her stomach as she spied a set of handles on the back. It was a wheelchair—crudely made from what she could tell—the upholstery now rotted and stained.

Jimmy appeared behind her, his voice floating over her shoulder in the cavernous hall. 'That's nasty.'

'I don't even want to think about what that was used for,' Leona added, hugging herself.

Amy snapped a couple of photos. 'This was your idea, girlfriend. Remember that.'

'Yeah, but—'

'I thought you wanted to do this.' Amy stared at her. 'Stay here if you want, but I'm going.' She turned and began walking down the tunnel toward the hotel across the street.

Behind her, she heard Jimmy say, 'I'll keep watch. You go ahead.'

'Ames, wait up.'

She waited for Leona to catch up and light the way with her torch. The GPS on Amy's phone worked well underground, and soon they had gone way past the hotel without seeing so much as another door or opening in the bricked walls.

'Do you think we missed something?' Amy asked.

Leona flicked the torch onto high beam. Before them, the tunnel stretched away into a blackness that seemed infinite. 'I don't know. How much longer do you think this goes on?'

'According to the map, if we continue in a straight line, we'll reach the Yarra.'

'The Yarra? You know, I've heard more than once that there's a tunnel that runs between the casino and the river that's used to eliminate bodies because of their high suicide rate.'

Amy glanced at her friend. 'What did you just say?'

'I said that—'

'Look, I actually heard what you said, Lee. I just can't believe that you said it.' Out loud. Down here, of all places. Dead bodies? This tunnel was giving her the creeps.

'Shouldn't we get going? I don't want to be late for school.'

Amy raised her eyebrows, even though she was aware Leona couldn't see them in the darkness. 'Sure, Jim's probably bored out of his arse by now, anyway.'

As they reached the daylight of the tunnel entrance, Amy had an idea.

'Hey Jim, can we quickly try the bolt cutters on that door upstairs?'

They followed her back up to the third floor, where the black-painted door remained firmly closed, even after she rattled the handle.

'Amy.' Jimmy put a hand on her arm. 'There's no lock to break. This one needs a key.' He pointed to the iron lock plate. 'Or Flynn,' he added with a cheeky grin and a shrug.

'Yep.' Amy let her lips pop on the 'p' in exasperation. 'You guys can go. I'm going to poke around a bit more. Thanks for your help.' She hugged them both warmly, then pulled the lancet from her skirt pocket.

'See you at school, then. Whoa, what the hell is that for?' Leona was staring at the blade now held in Amy's palm. 'Are you going to pick the lock?'

'I thought I might try it,' she said out loud.

But not the lock you're thinking of, she thought to herself. This time, the lock is *me.*

CHAPTER FIFTEEN

THE LANCET WORKED JUST like an actual key.

Although she really shouldn't have pulled it out in Jim and Leona's presence, she covered her mistake by tapping the open blade on her palm a few times, in an increasingly agitated fashion, like she was impatient to get moving. Which, of course, she was.

When they left, Amy headed straight to the tunnel and dragged the blade down across her palm. In hindsight, it was a stupid place to cut. It was going to hurt like a bitch every time she flexed her hand, but the scar would be next to invisible alongside the myriad creases in her palm, and much easier to explain.

The blood rose like a thin red river breaking its banks, overflowing, running faster until it spilled over the side of her hand and dripped to the ground. The pain followed just a half-second behind. 'Holy crap!'

Her knees faltered as her pulse throbbed in her hand and temples, making her vision distort. Bracing a hand on the icy wall, she closed her eyes as a whooshing sound filled her ears. Just like in the train tunnel with Elodie, a great rush of air pushed toward her, like a dark, oppressive cloud.

⚫◆⚫

'Bonjour Amy.'

Valentina's pale face appeared out of the shadows in front of her, dainty hands resting on the back of the wheelchair. Amy took in the dark circles that sat beneath her grey eyes, making her appear even more forlorn than last time.

'Bonjour Valentina. Comment ca va?'

'I have been better.'

Valentina gave her a tired smile as she pushed the chair past and up the step to the cellar, with an ease that suggested she'd done it many times before.

'Can I ask what you were doing just now?' Amy gestured to the chair, now a rich golden brocade in the morning sunlight streaming in from outside.

Valentina's lips pressed together. 'Helping my brother.'

Uh-huh. Suddenly, Leona's tale of the casino sluicing bodies into the river didn't seem so far-fetched. Amy's pulse raced. 'May I speak with him?'

Valentina's grip tightened on the back of the wheelchair before a mask of indifference covered her delicate features. 'He is, how do you say, momentarily indisposed.'

Amy arched a brow. 'Is he with a patient?'

'Non. Excusez-moi, s'il vous plaît.'

Amy walked with her while she stowed the chair in an alcove near the sprinkler room. 'Could I perhaps stay and talk to you, then?'

Valentina faced her, a spark flickering in her grey eyes. 'Oui. I would like that.'

They climbed the stairs to the third floor, with Amy's heartbeat speeding up all the way. Would she see him this time? Valentina lifted a key from around her neck as they approached the black door and fitted it into the lock. The door swung open, and Amy gasped.

Sweet, cloying smoke hung in the centre of the large room, above a man sprawled out on a plush chaise longue, a couple of half-naked women by his side. He held a thin brown cigarette in one hand and a glass of rich coloured liquor in the other, his head rolled back in ecstasy. The women draped over him, caressing his chest through his open shirt, and smelling his skin. All that was needed was some thumping deep bass, and Amy could have believed she'd walked into a private nightclub. Except, of course, for the twin rivers of blood that poured down his lily-white forearms.

'Marcel,' Valentina hissed.

The man's head lifted, his gaze sharpening for a moment as they drew closer before he buried his face between one woman's breasts. Then, pushing her aside, he rose and staggered towards Valentina. Bending to kiss both her cheeks, he whispered something to her in French, then turned the full force of his handsome face on Amy.

'Well, who do we have here?'

He carelessly disposed of his drink and the sickly cigarette on a nearby table before taking a swaggering step towards her.

Oh, crap.

Amy's pulse ratcheted up as he took both her hands in his bloodied ones and pressed burning lips to her knuckles. He then turned her left hand over and ran a delicate finger over the slash in her palm, his shoulder-length brown hair swinging forward to cover his expression. When he finally lifted his head, his silvery eyes shone with mischief. A hint of a smile played across full lips, the candlelight catching a dimple in his chin.

'You... you can see me?' Her voice shook with disbelief.

He chuckled, and warmth bled through her fingertips, coursing through her veins, making her entire body tingle.

'Of course I can see you. Feel you, too. What is your name, child?'

His English was impeccable, a soft timbre with a lilt that shamed Pierre's. But who was he calling a child? He couldn't be over twenty years old himself. He was tall and lean, dressed impeccably in slim black trousers and a crisp white shirt—if it weren't for the blood, he could've passed for a model. There was absolutely no way this man was a doctor.

She wet her lips. 'Amy. My name is Amy.'

'Ah, the pleasure is all mine, mon cherie.' He was still clutching her fingers in his. 'You must forgive me—' He gestured to the women behind him, 'As you can tell, I was not expecting company.'

Throwing an irritated look over his shoulder, he barked at them to leave. Hastily throwing on shawls, both women cast her curious glances before shuffling out the door.

Like a puppet, Amy allowed Marcel to lead her to the chaise, where he pulled her down to sit beside him. She was still trying to wrap her head around the fact that this man—this ghost—was physically touching her. Valentina locked the door behind the women and returned with a basin of water and some bandages. Kneeling before him, she cleaned and dressed his wounds. 'Mon Dieu,' she muttered, shaking her head.

My God, indeed, Amy thought, echoing Valentina's sentiment as she watched her wash off the blood, revealing a legacy of thin, white scars down the inside of Marcel's forearms. *He looks just like Flynn.*

She shook her head. He might look like Flynn, but he was nothing like him. For all his charm and good looks and ... *Oh, God... his gentle touch—DO. NOT. LET. HIM. FOOL. YOU. This man is a murderer.*

A murderer. Who more than likely just had his little sister dump a dead body in the Yarra River. A murderer who was holding her hand while his little sister cleaned up his self-inflicted wounds—a murderer who was openly weeping. Soft tremors shook Marcel's body as Valentina rolled his shirtsleeves down over his bandaged arms. Amy pulled her fingers from his grasp, startled.

Marcel's eyes fixed on his sister, his cheeks stained wet with tears.

'C'est ma faute,' he whispered, his voice thick with emotion.

Valentina took his elegant hands in her small ones, pressing them to her lips. 'Marcel, c'est pas ta faute.'

He shook his head. 'Oui c'est.'

'Non.'

'It is my fault!' he roared, causing Amy to flinch. She jumped up and stood several feet back from Valentina, who was pulling Marcel to his feet.

'Please help me with him.'

Mirroring Valentina, Amy warily wrapped one of Marcel's arms around her neck and the two girls half-dragged him down the stairs to the second floor and into the other bedroom. Valentina pulled back the covers on the simple iron bed, and he crawled in like a little boy.

'Amy.' He gestured for her to come closer, his eyes dulling like pewter in the dim room. 'Je suis navré.' He looked completely miserable, and against her better judgment, Amy's heart ached just a little as he shifted to face away from her. 'Je suis navré.'

Amy turned to ask Valentina what had happened when she felt dizzy. Forcing her eyes closed against the pressure in her head, she opened them to find herself in an empty room.

⟿◈⟾

Her palm instantly throbbed. Inspecting her hand, she found it smeared with dried blood where Marcel's fingers had laid in hers. The cut was no longer bleeding, but it looked angry and raw. She'd have to visit the first aid nurse at school.

What time was it? How long had she been here? Amy took out her phone, surprised to see she'd lost almost an hour. Crap, she was going to be late, and she was feeling sick. Her stomach was empty and growling.

Grabbing her backpack, she raced down the stairs and exploded out of the laneway door, her feet propelling her all the way to Pierre's Patisserie.

'Bonjour Amy, mon amie,' Pierre greeted her with his usual enthusiasm. 'To what do I owe this pleasure? You know your mum's shift has finished, right?'

Despite her agitation, she smiled. 'Of course. Actually, I wanted to grab a pastry and ask you something in French.'

'By all means. Ask away.' He took out a blackberry danish, handing it to her on a black-and-white checked napkin.

'What does *je suis navré* mean?'

The normally smiling Frenchman stared down at her, a frown darkening his features. 'Did someone say this to you?'

Yes. 'No, but I overheard the man next to me on the train saying it repeatedly into his phone. He sounded pretty upset, and I wondered what it meant, that's all.'

My God, she was becoming too adept at lying to people.

'It's a strong apology. Like I'm really sorry, or I'm terribly sorry.'

Marcel was telling her he was sorry? But why? He hadn't done anything to hurt her.

'Couldn't he have just said *désolé*, then?'

'Unlike *désolé, navré* isn't a word to be said lightly. It means to be deeply sorrowful for cutting someone.'

'Cutting someone? You mean physically?' Amy's heart began pounding.

'No, metaphorically. It translates to wounding someone deeply and being just as regretful. Does that help?'

More than you realise.

'Thanks, Pierre.' She bit into the danish and flew out the door, knowing she'd never make it to school before the bell.

CHAPTER SIXTEEN

I T WAS JUST HIS luck. The first day that Flynn went back to school after his fight with Mick, and Amy didn't show. She wasn't answering any of his messages, either.

He waited at the front gate for Leona, ready to give her a piece of his mind. She didn't need to be encouraging Amy with all this ghost bullshit, and neither of them should've been thinking of breaking and entering last night. The moment he spotted her and Jimmy crossing the road behind the bus stop, he propelled himself at them, laser-focused like a missile.

'Whoa, dude.' Jimmy put up his hands and stepped protectively in front of Leona. Flynn stifled a smirk. The guy might've been built like a brick shithouse, but Leona had more balls. He'd back her in a fight any day.

'Where is she?' he ground out.

Leona glanced at Jimmy. 'She's not here yet? She was only going to hang back for a bit and look around some more.'

'You just left her there on her own, at night?' Flynn's throat constricted so much he could barely breathe.

'Nah, dude. We went this morning. All three of us.' Jimmy grinned. Flynn didn't appreciate his honesty and was fixing to wipe that arsey smile off his face.

'Maybe she just lost track of time.' Leona had the audacity to put her hand on his arm, but he shook it off, glaring at her. He knew Amy didn't wear a watch, and maybe the lack of messages meant her phone was dead, but still. Anger and fear flared hot in his chest.

'And neither of you thought it'd be a good idea to... I don't know, maybe *stay with her?*' Flynn bellowed. 'Fucking unbelievable.'

Behind them, the second bell rang, and Leona looked around anxiously. 'I really need to get to class, Flynn.'

'Leona. She's your best friend.'

Jimmy shrugged. 'Look, dude, if it's any consolation—'

'It's not.' Flynn cut him off with a death glare.

He waited until they were both out of sight before turning around and booting the shit out of the chain-wire fence. Fuck! He should've known she'd go back. Should've noticed it last night when he'd practically begged her not to. But what else could he have done? He couldn't control what she did and sure as hell didn't want to. He wasn't Mick.

Ignoring the sudden tingle in his side, his fingers sought the crucifix through his shirt. Crushing it in his fist, he squeezed his eyes shut. *I don't want to lose her, Dad. What should I do?*

He paced in a circle for a bit before heading towards the train station. Breaking into a run, he rounded the bend and recognised a familiar pair of legs. The rest of her was in shadow from the trees lining the footpath. He let out a huge breath and pushed down the lump that had risen in his throat.

Wanting nothing more than to crush her in an enormous hug, he forced himself to walk steadily towards her. Even from this distance, he could see the smile break out on her face when she raised her head and locked eyes with his.

'Hey,' she said when they were face to face.

He reached down and wiped a smear of blackberry jam off the corner of her lip. 'Hey.'

'You're here.'

'I am.' He nodded. Sliding his hand around the back of her head, he drew her mouth up to meet his. Whispering against her lips, he added, 'Should we skip school today?'

'What?' She exhaled breathily.

'It's almost first break. Let's do something fun instead.'

She drew back and looked at him for a long moment. 'You're serious, aren't you?'

He shrugged. *Come on, say yes.* His eyes held hers, unable to believe she was actually hesitating. She'd happily blown off her morning to chase that *fucking* ghost, yet here she was deliberating about spending time with him? He reached down and grabbed her hand, but she snatched it away as if he'd hurt her.

'I... I can't, Flynn.'

She tried to step around him, but he shot an arm out to block her. 'Wait. What's the matter? Talk to me.'

She kept her head down. 'I have to go. I need to see the nurse.' She turned away.

'What the fuck for, are you hurt?' His eyes roamed over her quickly. *Her hand.* She was flexing it gently over and over. Like a snake, he reached out and snagged her wrist before she reacted.

Turning her hand over, he pried her fingers out of the fist she'd formed, revealing a two-inch cut that intersected her life line.

Clamping his mouth shut, he looked away, nostrils flaring as he tried to regain composure. 'Did you do this?' he asked, his voice somewhere between a whisper and a growl.

She didn't answer. Didn't need to. Her silence was all the confirmation he needed.

'For fuck's sake, Amy. You're coming back to my place. I'll take care of it.'

'No, Flynn.' She wrenched out of his hold, folding her arms around herself. 'Let me go to the nurse. You're always fixing me up! It's not your job to fix me. I did this. Let me deal with it.'

'You can't go to the school nurse. She'll be able to tell it's self-inflicted—' He took a quick breath as need erupted in his side, '—or that you got knifed in a fight. They're not stupid. They'll write up a report, and it'll go on your permanent record. You're about to finish your senior year, Ames. Is this how you want things to end?'

'But you're just the same!'

'The hell I am.'

'Don't be such a hypocrite. How is this any different from when you cut? Would you want me to fix you up afterwards?' Her face twisted as she looked up at him.

'You don't get to pass judgement on me.' Wounded, his voice shook. 'I'm not about rescuing anyone.' He took a step closer. 'But I'm also not about to let someone I love just throw everything on the line for a fucking dead guy. Not when there's one that's very much alive and standing right-the-fuck in front of her. Who'd do anything for her.' He reached out and ran his thumb across her cheek, his voice softening. 'Did you hear me, Ames? *Anything.*'

'What—' She swallowed, her eyes shimmering, '—are you saying?'

'You heard me.'

He slid his thumb across her jaw and down her neck, along the curve of her shoulder and ever so slowly, down her arm, letting it drift across the back of her hand until he felt her fingers clasp onto his. A gentle tug and she pressed against him. His heart might have been jackhammering in his chest, but it was the calmest he'd felt in a long while.

Sliding an arm around her shoulders, he pressed his lips to the top of her head. 'Come on,' he said into her hair, smoothly leading her away. 'Let me love you.'

⸺⸱❖⸱⸺

Twenty minutes later, he was pushing open the door to his flat. Thankfully, he no longer had to worry about Mick turning up because his mum had put a temporary restraining order out on the bastard, and she'd be at work until late tonight, anyway.

The place smelled clean for the first time in months. Flynn took a cursory glance around as he pushed through. The kitchen was tidy. No dirty dishes stacked in the sink. No filthy ashtray overflowing on the coffee table. He breathed easily for the first time in ages. Fetching the first aid kit from the pantry, he led Amy straight to his bedroom and pushed her softly to his bed.

Kneeling on the carpet before her, he inspected her outstretched palm. Her skin felt so soft in his hands. He drew the cut to his lips and gently kissed it better. Her chest rose and fell rapidly before him. Letting go of her hand, he pulled out the antiseptic and swabbed the whole of her palm, ever-so-slowly in an infinity pattern. Then he drew her hand back to his mouth and blew softly across her skin to dry it, keeping his gaze firmly on hers. Her lips parted as his breath caressed her flesh.

'Did you use the lancet?' he asked, cutting a thin strip of gauze to cover the cut.

She nodded, silent.

He finished the dressing with a short length of sports tape and considered the small pair of scissors in his hand.

'Why, Amy?' he whispered. 'Tell me why you felt the need to hurt yourself.' He pushed himself to his feet, kicking off his shoes as he crawled onto the bed, eyes locked on hers. She scooted backwards, licking her lips and shaking her head. 'I don't know.'

'I think you do.' He dropped his voice, low and sultry. 'You know. I just wish you'd talk to me.'

He pulled off his shirt and stretched out on his side, facing her, so his scars were visible. Her pupils dilated as her gaze skated across his bare chest, over his hipbones, and then finally, they dipped lower. He allowed himself the pleasure of watching her check him out before bringing the scissors in front of her face to redirect her attention.

'Do you want to cut me, Amy? I'll let you if that's what you want. Spill my blood instead of yours.'

'No,' she gasped. 'I don't want that.'

'What if I bled for you?' He'd do it willingly—anything to stop her from harming herself further.

'No.' She lurched forward and snatched the scissors out of his hand, but he just as quickly locked his fingers around her wrist, holding firm.

'You don't want me to hurt myself, and yet—' Leaning his head close to hers, he bore all his frustration into her worried gaze.

'What makes you think it's okay for you to do it?'

She shrank from him as he ripped the scissors from her grasp and flung them to the floor.

'You're bleeding yourself dry for a dead man.' He rolled on top of her, pinning her to the bed with his chest, forearms on either side of her head. 'For fuck's sake, Ames. I'm *right here.*' His voice cracked as he thrust against her, making her gasp out loud. 'Aren't I enough?'

Her chest rose and fell rapidly against his, but he was done waiting. Closing his mouth over hers, she rose to meet him, her fingers grasping at his back as he rocked his hips against her pelvis. She moaned as he dragged his lips down her throat. Beneath his tongue, her pulse throbbed, turning him on even more. Sliding lower, he straddled her thighs, caging her. Her sudden intake of breath dared him to push up her top, exposing perfect breasts encased in white lace.

'Do you want me?' he rasped, running his finger from the hollow of her throat down the centre of her cleavage.

She nodded.

Fuck, she was killing him. He could barely hold it together. She was giving him all the right signs, but he had to hear her say it first. He had to know that it was him she wanted.

'Tell me. Who do you want?'

He exhaled softly over the swell of her breasts, watching his breath raise goosebumps across her skin. *Let me love you. Love me back.*

'You,' she panted, arching her chest up to meet his waiting lips. 'I want you, Flynn.'

Oh, how he wanted to believe her. Wanted nothing more than to bury himself in her and forget that anything else existed.

She was practically begging him to fuck her—grinding her pelvis against his—and as much as he wanted to, he wouldn't let her get off just yet. Pushing himself up onto his elbows, he cradled her face as he looked down into her eyes. They were electric. He touched his thumb to her bottom lip and dragged it open.

Her breath was ragged under his touch. 'Flynn.'

'Shh...' he whispered, closing her mouth with a press of his thumb. He couldn't afford to be distracted by her gasping his name. 'Can you see me right here in front of you, Ames? I'll always be right here. In front of you. Behind you. Beside you. Always. But if we're going to make this work, I need you to be here for me, too. But I'm not sure you're ready to do that.' He grasped her bandaged palm and held it in front of her face. 'Are you?'

Amy closed her eyes as tears leaked from each corner, coursing down across her temples and soaking into his sheets. Flynn pressed his lips gently to hers, then sat up and pulled her shirt back down, smoothing it over her stomach.

By the time she finally opened her eyes, he had dressed and stood with his hand outstretched. Waiting.

Chapter Seventeen

FLYNN COULDN'T GET AMY off his mind. Ever since they'd left his flat, she'd occupied his head. And his body.

He'd been ready to make love to her this morning. And while her body was willing, and probably her heart, her head just wasn't in the game. It was still with that fucking leech. And so he held back —even though he felt like complete shit, for leading them both on the way he did. But he didn't just want her body. He wanted her all, her *everything*. And she clearly wasn't ready to give it to him.

But he couldn't dwell on that right now. Being his first shift at the Terrace Hotel, he needed to make a good impression. And a quiet, mid-week shift meant he had time to think. To get distracted.

He'd busied himself hauling dozens of kegs through to the bottle shop and had started on the wine crates when he heard a female voice call out behind him.

'Well, look what the dog threw up. If it isn't Flynn Powell.'

He looked over his shoulder to see a tall and willowy, brown-skinned young woman, arms crossed, smiling at him. Stacking the crates on the floor, he turned and walked toward her, not needing to see the cigarette burns on the backs of her hands to recognise whose smart mouth that quip had fallen out of. He hadn't heard it in almost six years.

'Stacy Peters. It looks like we're hanging out in the same bowl again then, huh?'

She laughed as they hugged, then she pushed him to arm's length, giving him an appraising once-over. 'You certainly turned out for the better. Are you working here, too?'

'Just started tonight. What about you? You look great, by the way.'

She took her hands from his arms, her wide mouth grinning with pride. 'Been here a couple of years now.'

'That's so good. I'm glad to hear things are finally working out for you.' And he meant it. Stacy had been one of the regular street kids he hung with after he lost his dad. A few of them used to haunt the skate bowl, and they became firm friends, sticking up for each other when needed. Getting help when they needed it, too. Even though Stacy was a couple of years older than him, he'd helped her out of more than one situation when her lily-arsed drunken prick of a father was punishing her. His eyes flicked to the light-coloured circular scars, and his jaw clenched.

'Hey, you want to grab a drink with me when you finish up?' she asked, moving behind the bottle shop counter to serve a customer.

'Sure.' He smiled. 'I'd really like that.'

He filled the next hour with more unloading before filling out some paperwork with the hotel manager. Pierre had promised to pick him up around nine, but Stacy's shift didn't finish till then, so he grabbed a couple of takeaway coffees from the hotel's bistro and joined her on a stool by the counter for the last half hour.

'Here,' he handed her a cup and dumped a handful of sugar packets and little jugs of long-life milk onto the counter. 'I didn't know how you liked it, so...'

She emptied three sugars into her cup and gave it a vigorous stir. 'Hot, black and sweet. Just like me.'

Flynn practically spat his coffee everywhere with laughter. 'Jesus, Stace. Only you could get away with saying that.'

'I know, right? Some things never change.' Her cheeky grin cranked up his nostalgia. 'What made you choose coffee, by the way?'

'Because I know you'd never touch a drop of alcohol.'

'Hmm.' Golden-green eyes regarded him, sparkling with mischief.

He took a moment to admire his old friend. Those eyes were the only good thing she inherited from her father. Her hair was still a mess of short, wiry brown curls, and she now sported a silver nose ring. She'd really blossomed into the proud Indigenous woman he'd always hoped she would. Fuck. Back then, he'd just hoped she'd survive.

She nudged him with an elbow. 'What are you thinking about? You're still so serious, you know.'

He rolled his eyes. 'Me, serious? Fuck off.'

She laughed, and the sound warmed his core. They'd never had much to laugh about growing up.

'Well, you're still fighting, I see.' She pointed to his face.

He frowned. She never could let anything slide. 'Well, you know what they say. You can take the boy out of the hood...'

'Somehow, I doubt there's much that's boyish about you anymore.'

She left him to help another customer, and Flynn sat up, squaring his shoulders. Something about the tone of her voice awakened a long-buried feeling inside him. It brought out that survival instinct again. But this time, it made him feel like a man.

Sauntering back over, she stood before him, arms crossed, a knowing look on her face. 'So, have you been fighting over a girl, or what?'

He looked away, drumming his fingers on his thigh. It was just like Mick to butt in and mess with everything good in his life. Well, not tonight, arsehole.

'Not in the way you're thinking.'

'You sure?' she pressed. 'You always were quite the little heartbreaker.'

He glanced back at her, amused. 'What's that supposed to mean?'

'Don't act like you don't know.' She shook her head. 'Every girl in a five-k radius had a crush on you. Those lips always were pretty irresistible.'

She laughed as he pouted, heat creeping into his face.

'Still know how to use them too, I see.'

He'd kissed his fair share of girls over the years, but one particular day, he'd been skating with the other kids in the bowl when Stacy had appeared by the big gum tree. Her round cheeks were dirty and tear-stained, and she'd sat against the trunk, cradling her skinny arms around her long brown legs.

He'd gone to her immediately, forcing her to show him the newest burn on the back of her hand. The raw skin underneath had been visible, and the thought of it now made his stomach twist. He couldn't believe that someone would hurt their own daughter like that, and at the time, he'd wanted to smash the fucker's head in. Instead, he'd punched the tree behind her, telling her he'd give her something to protect her for next time. Even then, at the tender age of twelve, he'd recognised that there would *always* be a next time.

Kneeling in the dry grass, he'd taken her face in his hands and softly touched his lips to hers. Still cradling her cheeks, he'd told her that whenever she felt unsafe, to remember that kiss and know that someone cared for her because knowing that someone cared for you made you stronger.

His thoughts flashed to Amy. He knew she cared for him, but he wasn't feeling strong right now. His mouth twisted into a wry grimace. 'I don't know about that.'

'See, I knew you were having girl trouble.' She shoved his knee with her hip. 'Wanna talk about it? I'm a good listener, you know.'

Flynn's mouth twitched. 'I don't doubt that. It's just—' His phone buzzed with a message from Pierre. 'Look, I gotta go. My ride's here.' He got up, drained the rest of his coffee, and tossed his paper cup in the bin under the counter. 'Maybe another time. It's so good to see you, Stacy. I really mean that.' He gave her another hug just as Pierre walked into the bottle shop, not missing the sharp gaze he gave them.

'When are you working next?' Stacy asked.

'Friday night.'

'Me too. Maybe I can give you a lift home?'

Flynn nodded, shunning Pierre's gaze. 'Yeah, that'd be great.'

⤙❖⤚

The drive back to Pierre's wasn't anywhere near as quiet as Flynn had hoped. Seeing Stacy again brought back a lot of feelings he'd long buried. That, coupled with Amy's hesitation, had him doubting who he was—who he'd tried to become as he grew up. No matter how much he'd tried to become a man, when it all boiled down, he was still just a rejected boy with a dead father and an absent mother.

'How was your first night?' Pierre asked, breaking through his thoughts.

Flynn yawned. 'That place sure goes through a shitload of beer.'

Pierre chuckled. 'That's footy season for you. Listen, Patrick called on my way here. He's more than happy with your output tonight. If you continue to impress him, he might just let you do some bar work.'

'Really?' Flynn sat up straighter. 'That'd be cool.'

'He's a good bloke. Likes to give people a second chance, you know what I mean?'

Like Stacy. *Like me.* Flynn's face hardened. 'I'm not a charity case.'

'I didn't say you were, mate.'

'I know. Look, thanks for the opportunity, but you don't need to worry, Frenchie. I won't let you down.'

He could tell Pierre was psycho-analysing him, so he turned away to the window, watching the lights fly by. He'd always loved the nighttime. It was dangerous and perfect for taking risks.

'Want me to drop you at the gym?'

'No thanks.'

'You're not seeing Amy tonight?'

He shook his head. 'Nope. She doesn't want to see me.'

'What happened?' Pierre was looking at him so hard, Flynn thought they'd have a crash if he didn't look back at the road soon.

'Nothing *happened*, Frenchie. That's the problem.' He ran a hand through his hair. 'She made it pretty clear.'

'That can't be right.'

'Yeah, well, it is.'

'Does this have something to do with the young woman you were just embracing?'

'Stacy? Hell, no.'

'What brought this on, then?'

'Dunno. That's something you'd have to ask Amy.'

'I wouldn't need to ask her. She doesn't stop talking about you. Ever.'

Flynn's jaw clenched. 'Yeah, well. As I've discovered, what Amy says, and what she does, are not the same thing.'

'Be careful what you say, mate.'

'Look, I'm not dissing your woman's daughter, okay? Amy's my friend, too, remember. And regardless of what she thinks she wants, believe me, her actions speak otherwise.'

'You want to talk about it?'

Now he'd done it. He'd opened his fucking mouth when he shouldn't have. 'No. Just forget about it.' He wasn't about to spill Amy's dirty little secrets.

'No, I'm not going to "forget about it". Not when I care about the both of you.'

'Yeah, well, I understand you have a duty of care to Amy, but you don't need to look after me. I'll be out of your life by the weekend. It's not like I asked you to care.'

Pierre braked hard at a red light, making the seatbelt cut into Flynn's shoulder. 'Actually, you did. When you called me from the bloody police station.'

The light turned green, but the Frenchman was clearly on a roll. Flynn sat there, staring blankly ahead, waiting for him to shut the hell up.

'Look, I know I probably wasn't your first choice, but I don't for one minute regret taking you in.'

'Well, maybe you should've.'

The light turned amber and then red again. Flynn ground his teeth. Considered getting out of the car.

'Why, because you don't think you're worth it?'

'I'm not!'

'Just because you're a kid who was dealt a bad hand early in life, you don't think you can turn your luck around?'

'This has nothing to do with luck.'

The light turned green, and Pierre sped off, squealing the tyres of his precious Peugeot. 'Ta gueule.'

'What did you say to me?' Flynn's voice was low and laced with venom.

Pierre sighed. 'I said, shut the fuck up.'

'Oh, so you too, huh? That's just great, Frenchie. Thanks for giving a fuck, not. Or should that be *pas?*' He spat the French word, crossing his arms and turning his head to the window for the rest of the trip home.

Flynn didn't even wait until the car had pulled to a stop in the drive before he shot out. Unlocking the front door, he ignored Pierre as he followed him inside.

'That's not what I meant, son. And you know it. I want to hear what you have to say. Really, I do. But you've got to stop talking shit about yourself. You're better than that.'

'Don't call me son. You're not my dad.' He stormed straight to his room, slamming the door closed behind him. Flynn didn't care that this wasn't his home. He was about to tear some shit apart.

The door flung open. 'I'm not trying to be your father, mate. You're a grown man.'

'You're right, I am. It's about time I started acting like one. I'm heading out.'

'Je m'en fous.'

Flynn rounded the bed, and before he knew it, was up in Pierre's face. 'Will you stop speaking in fucking French? I can't understand a fucking word you're saying.'

'I'm not speaking in French. I'm swearing in it. And I just told you, I don't give a fuck. If you want to go out, go out. But I'm having a beer.'

Pierre disappeared and came back with two bottles of Peroni. He held one out. Flynn eyed the beer. Pierre put his hand on Flynn's shoulder. 'Seriously, mate. I'm here if you need me. And I think perhaps right now, you just might.'

Flynn didn't feel like drinking but understood that Pierre's gesture meant more than just that. 'You got anything stronger, then?'

<h1 style="text-align:center">CHAPTER EIGHTEEN</h1>

'WHAT HAPPENED TO YOU yesterday?' Leona hissed when Amy sat beside her in Maths class.

Amy's face grew hot. 'Nothing.'

'Bullshit! Flynn ripped shreds off me when you didn't turn up.'

Amy winced. 'Sorry. My bad. I had a headache, so I went home and slept.'

Her best friend's eyes narrowed. 'Is that all? Because Flynn never came back to school.'

Amy did her best to appear unfazed. 'Flynn's always ditching, Lee. That shouldn't be news to you.'

'I suppose not. So, did you find out anything else?' A wicked grin spread across Leona's face.

Like... Flynn is honestly the best kisser in the history of the universe and we nearly had sex but I think I stuffed everything up and now I'm not sure if it will ever be the same again. That sort of thing?

Leona's fingers were snapping in front of her face. 'Are you okay, Ames? You look like you've seen a ghost. Oh my God. You saw him, didn't you?'

'Who?' Amy's heart was like a caged bird, beating frantically against her ribs.

'Boucher.'

Amy shook her head. She didn't know why she felt compelled to lie to Leona. After all—she was the only one of her friends who were truly interested in the blood-letter's ghost. But meeting Marcel seemed precious. And she realised with alarming certainty that she didn't want to share him with anyone. Not even Leona. He would remain her indulgent secret.

'As I said—my head was pounding, and I felt dizzy. So I ended up going home.'

It wasn't a complete lie. She *had* felt dizzy upon leaving Marcel, and she went home after being with Flynn. But she hadn't spent the afternoon sleeping.

Instead, she'd grabbed her gym gear and gone back to the Butcher's House. She must've been mad, going back there again, but Marcel had her entranced. She hadn't been able to forget the sheer depth of his apology and knew there was more to his sorrow than what she'd witnessed earlier that day. Despite the prostitutes, she didn't think there was any truth to the rumours. Marcel wasn't a vampire preying on the mentally ill. He suffered by his own hand. And that was something she understood all too well. And so, it wasn't Marcel that she went to see. It was Valentina.

'Why did you come to me that night?' Amy demanded, after coming face to face with her in the bedroom once again.

Valentina had been folding laundry when she'd appeared and motioned for Amy to follow her upstairs onto the roof, where they could talk privately. The rooftop looked nothing like it had the night they'd all been up there. Not only was the ancient billboard missing, so were all the towering city buildings. Someone had strung a crude washing line up between two thin timber poles, where a few linen sheets flapped in the breeze.

'You gave me the lancet for a reason, Valentina. Why?'

'You wanted it,' Valentina said, stooping before a bucket of bloodied water. Amy's stomach clenched, and she looked away, not wanting to know what the girl had been washing. Or why.

'I don't understand.'

'The boy touched it first, but you wanted it just as terribly.' Baleful eyes pinned her to the spot. 'You cannot deny it.'

Amy swallowed. Even though she'd wanted Flynn to cut her, she hadn't taken the lancet willingly. This couldn't all be her fault. 'But you put it in my hand, Valentina. You're the one who showed me to cut. How to come to you. Why would you do something like that?'

Valentina finished prodding whatever was in the bucket and stood to look her in the eye. 'Because you are different to all the others, Amy.'

Amy's pulse thrummed in her temple. 'How so?'

'Marcel finds women easy to understand, but he could not do that with you. He recognises something of himself in you and is wary in your presence.'

'Wait, a minute.' Amy's head reeled. 'Marcel was there that night?'

'Oui.'

Of course. *He's coming.* He had been coming for them all along. For her. It was never a warning, but a statement.

But Marcel hadn't succeeded, so his little sister had taken it upon herself to make Amy come to him, instead.

Finding herself standing on the roof of the Butcher's House in the middle of the afternoon wasn't nearly as disturbing as what Amy had discovered. She'd pulled herself together and gone to the gym early. She needed time to process, and the best way to do that was to work out.

Once again, Flynn hadn't shown up after her class. She was aware he was starting his new job at the hotel, and even though they'd left things kind of awkward between them, she really thought he might have dropped in. Or at least called. Texted. Something. But no. All she'd got was radio silence.

'Too bad.' Leona huffed and opened her notebook.

Amy scowled before realising that her friend was still referring to Marcel.

'So, are you going to go back again?'

'Probably not.' Amy breezed through the lie. 'Doesn't seem to be much point, really.'

'What if Flynn picked the lock on that door for you?'

Amy stilled. Flynn wouldn't do that for her. Not now. 'Nah. If there were ghosts there, they'd have shown yesterday, locked door or not.'

'Yeah, fair point,' Leona conceded, shivering theatrically. 'Besides, if there is some creep squatting in that house, who knows what could happen.'

There was no chance Leona would call Marcel a creep if she'd seen him. Amy hid a grin. 'True.'

Leona ducked her head as Mr Grayson passed. 'So, is Flynn ditching today too? I haven't seen him.'

'Probably.'

'Will he even be able to graduate?'

'Dunno.'

Mr Grayson turned around, pausing beside their desk. 'You won't be graduating, Miss Liu, if you don't pass this semester's exam.'

Leona smiled sweetly up at him. When he moved on, she flipped the bird behind his back. A few seconds later, she shoved her notebook over to Amy, with a note scribbled in the margin.

Do you have a dress yet?

Amy's head snapped up. Oh crap. Graduation.

Their small community college didn't even do uniforms, let alone senior formals. They did, however, do an end-of-year grad dance. It wasn't a big deal, but they were expected to frock up.

No. Have you? She wrote back.

I can't decide. Want to help me choose on Saturday?

Amy took a shuddering breath. Her initial reaction was to answer—*not really*—but she supposed it couldn't hurt to have a look. Some girl-time would do her good. Maybe she could find a cute playsuit or something other than a dress to wear.

Sure.

Sweet! I'll tell Kenz.

Amy turned to Leona and gave her an enthusiastic thumbs up. Crap-tastic.

⬩◈⬩

Thankfully, most of Amy's lessons were now just revising for the final VSC exams because she couldn't focus for the rest of the day. She was still trying to fathom why the Boucher siblings had reached out to her specifically; she hadn't heard from Flynn at all, and now

Leona had her stressing out about the stupid graduation dance. Flynn hadn't asked her to be his date yet, and she wondered if he was even going to show up.

She'd love the chance to dance with him again, but more slowly this time. Thinking about their dance the other night had heat flowing through her limbs, making her feel like the inside of a roasted marshmallow. God, now she was craving marshmallows, and that got her thinking about Flynn's lips and how they'd kissed her yesterday. So soft. Her fingers were still touching her own lips when she pushed through the door of the patisserie.

'Salut, mon amie,' Pierre greeted her as she crossed the floor, and she closed her eyes, sinking into his warm hug.

'Salut, Pierre.' Stepping back, she noticed Flynn leaning in the baking room doorway.

His dark eyes were on her. 'Coucou.'

'What?'

Pierre squeezed her shoulder. 'Francais, Amy! The word is *pardon*.' She ignored him, totally focused on Flynn.

'Coucou. It means *hey*.' A blush rose to his cheeks. 'Did I say it wrong?'

Amy cocked her head to the side and smiled. 'No. I'm just surprised, that's all.'

He shrugged. 'Frenchie's been teaching me.'

'Has he now?'

Amy turned back to Pierre, who was busy wiping down the glass counter and doing a terrible job at pretending not to eavesdrop.

'Thought it might come in handy,' he mumbled.

Amy turned back to Flynn. 'You heading to The Mission?'

'Yep. You going to gym class?' His brow quirked sceptically.

'Of course.'

'Let's go, then.' They bundled up the day's left-over provisions for The Mission's kitchen and stepped out into the afternoon sun.

'I missed you at school today.' She shoved him lightly with her elbow. 'You might not graduate if you keep skipping, you know.'

'Nah, Mr Jeffries said I've been putting in the work, and as long as I sit the final exams, I'm good.'

'Well, that's a relief.' She held her breath lightly, hoping he might bring up the dance. He didn't. 'So what happened to you today? Were you that wiped out from work last night?'

'Not really. They kept me busy, though.' He sounded like he was about to say more but didn't.

'I think it's really great that you're doing something for yourself.' Even Amy cringed inwardly at how forced the conversation sounded.

'Thanks, I guess.' Flynn glanced at her, concern pulling at his brows. 'You okay?'

No, she wasn't okay. Trust him to notice. 'Look, can we talk about yesterday?'

They had reached the corner of Spencer Street and stopped at the crossing. He sighed audibly. 'How about we wait until I meet you after gym class? I'd better get these to Roger in the kitchen.' He lifted the large bag Pierre had given him.

Amy nodded. At least it meant he'd be walking her home again. 'Yeah, sure. See you then.' Resisting the urge to turn and watch him go, she crossed the road towards the YMCA, leaving Flynn to walk in the opposite direction.

Throughout her class, Amy's head spun with what she wanted to tell Flynn. He'd all but told her he loved her yesterday. Both of them had said it but also not said it. They hadn't properly declared those three little words.

Yesterday, he'd held her as she dried her tears. Whispered into her hair that he would always wait for her, but she had to be clear about what she wanted. She knew he was referring to Marcel, but Amy wasn't ready to sacrifice one for the other. She wanted Flynn. That was an easy decision. She'd loved him from the day she met him. From the moment he'd looked her in the eyes and told her she wasn't invisible, Flynn had always seen her. He'd always only had eyes for her, and she for him.

But Marcel? He saw her completely differently. Here was a ghost to whom she was not only visible; she unnerved him. And that both terrified and fascinated her. She needed to find out why. What made her so special? Why couldn't the others see him? And until she figured all that out, she wasn't prepared to let him go.

But how was she going to tell Flynn all of that without pushing him away? He didn't believe in ghosts, and she didn't want to lie to him again. She'd done too much of that lately. Lying to her mum, to her best friends. Her mind was cartwheeling so much she felt dizzy. She closed her eyes and put her fingers to her temples.

'Are you feeling alright, Amy?' Her coach frowned from the other side of the mat area.

'Yeah,' she lied. *Again*. 'I think I just need some water.'

Amy pushed open the gate to the spectators' arena and went to the bubbler. Taking a long drink, she let the cold water go straight to her head. Nothing like a good old brain freeze to clear out the cotton wool feeling. As she straightened up, she saw Flynn walk in through the main doors and immediately got the usual flutter in her chest. Wiping her mouth, she waved at him, waiting for that lopsided grin that made her clench her thighs together. Only he didn't smile at her like that. Nor had he when they were making out on his bed yesterday. He'd been *different*.

Intense. Determined. Certain. *Hurt*.

It hit her suddenly, along with the realisation that she was the cause. At that moment, it became painfully clear what she had to do. The iced water in her stomach tossed around like a stormy sea, and guilt was a tiny boat riding the waves. Racing for the bathroom, she flung open the door and hung over the toilet bowl, expecting to be sick, but the nausea soon abated. A few deep breaths later, she went to the basin and splashed some water on her face, knowing she couldn't tell Flynn how much she loved him and then waltz straight on over to Marcel and Valentina. There was only one thing left to do.

She'd already lied to him once. As much as she couldn't bear to hurt him again, she had no choice but to do it one more time.

CHAPTER NINETEEN

FLYNN WAS SITTING IN his usual seat (front row, third from the end) when Amy joined him after her warm down. Her stomach was still roiling, and the thought of whatever sweet treat he'd brought with him from The Mission had her almost gagging. Maybe she should get it over with and tell him already. Once absolved of her guilt and anxiety, she might actually be able to swallow something.

Unless the whole thing went pear-shaped. Ugh. If it did, she would seriously vomit onto her shoes, for sure.

Flynn handed her a white paper packet. 'I got these for you. I know they're your favourite.'

Peeking inside, she spied a couple of Pierre's strawberry macarons. 'Thanks.'

Amy winced at the false chirpiness in her tone and blew a heavy breath out through her nose. The macarons' delectably sweet smell was turning her stomach. Or maybe it wasn't the macarons at all. She'd never felt this way around Flynn before. Sure, she'd been plenty nervous—he had that effect on people—but never this.

She realised it was fear. Fear that she'd mess everything up. Fear that things would change and never go back to the way they were. Afraid that he would stop wanting her.

'So,' she said as they began walking to the train station, 'are you going to tell me about the new job?' She was tempted to add *because you still haven't spoken to me / I thought you'd want to talk about it / insert hurt phrase-of-choice here*, but she kept her mouth firmly shut. Otherwise, she'd most likely shove a macaron in it just to keep herself quiet, and then she really would be sick.

Flynn gave her an amused glance. 'You're really interested enough to ask me twice about it?'

'Yeah, of course. A job's a big deal, Flynn.' She forced a laugh. This was feeling all kinds of wrong.

'There's not much to tell,' he replied, shoving an entire pistachio macaron into his mouth. 'I just did a lot of grunt work. But Frenchie said there might be an opportunity to shift into the bar down the track, so we'll see.'

'That's great. I'm thrilled for you.'

Again, Flynn shot a frown at her unopened macarons. 'What's up?'

'Nothing.'

'Bullshit. I know when something's not right with you. Just spit it out.'

Hah, he had no idea how close she was to spilling her guts right now. And not in the metaphorical sense.

She looked sideways at him. Those navy eyes were almost pleading with her. God, she'd never been able to deny him anything.

'It's about yesterday,'

He lifted his brows. 'Mm-hm?'

She dropped her head, unable to look at him. 'I'm sorry.'

'You've already told me that. Multiple times. Do you want me to forgive you again?'

'Yes. No. It's really not about that. I just don't think I can do this right now.'

She didn't want to push him away, but what else could she do? She was in too deep, hurting too many people. It was for his own good. She had to make him think she needed space. It was the only way to protect him.

'Do what?' His voice was quiet.

She felt sick. 'This.' She gestured between them.

'You mean us?' Flynn turned to her, his question hanging in the air as their train pulled into the station.

He was still staring at her as the doors opened and people began shifting around them. At the last second, he grabbed her hand and pulled her onto the train just as the doors started to close. Leading her to a seat, he sat down next to her. He kept her hand in his and didn't say a word or push her to speak until they'd got off the train at her stop. Once they were making their way through the park, Flynn squeezed her hand and slowed his steps.

'I'm sorry if I moved too fast for you yesterday.'

'That's not it.' She took a shuddering breath. 'I'm just so confused right now. I don't know what I want.'

'I thought you wanted me.'

She looked up at him through eyes blurred with tears. 'You've no idea how long I've wanted you.'

Flynn looked at the ground, running his free hand through his hair. 'I don't understand.'

The hurt in his voice broke her heart, but she had to stay strong. 'I want you, Flynn. But there's still so much that I need to figure out. About myself and about Marcel. And I really need you to let me do that.'

'I'll never stop you from doing anything you want. Even if I disagree, I hope you don't think I'll control you, Amy.'

She squeezed his hand. 'No! That's not what I mean.' Dropping onto the swing, she added, 'I know you're only trying to look out for me. And it's not that I'm ungrateful, or anything—'

'Hey.' Flynn crouched down on the ground in front of her, taking both of her hands in his big, warm ones. 'Have I ever told you the story of why I first started volunteering at The Mission?'

She shook her head. 'Only that Mr Jeffries helped you with it.'

'Right. Because I'd lost so many days skipping school, but you don't know the reason I was MIA so much.'

He sank forward onto his knees, and Amy bit her lip. She was so attuned to his body language; she could tell this would not be a light conversation.

'My story began a few years ago when Mick was staying over regularly. I couldn't handle listening to him banging Mum all night, so I looked around the neighbourhood for other places to sleep. I thought about camping out on the roof, but that's my space, and I didn't want him ruining it for me. Plus, there's zero shelter up there.

'So, one night, I found this tiny, abandoned shopfront on a nearby side street and picked the lock. It was safe in there for a while until the owners found me in there one morning. Naturally, they called the police and tried to detain me. But I fought like hell and ended up smashing the front window to get out.

'Instead of getting free, I got a free ride to the station, and they took my statement with a social worker present. The social worker, I found out later, volunteered at The Mission. After my release, she took me down there to give me a meal. The shop owners were actually pretty chill and didn't press charges, so long as I got some help because they were concerned for my well-being. The Mission set me up in a diversion program aimed at teaching me to make better choices and help in the community. Over the length of my public service, I actually enjoyed the work, and when it officially finished, I kept it up.

'I guess the reason I'm telling you this, Ames, is because I don't want you to get into the kind of trouble I did. I was lucky. Because if you get caught in that building or hurt again, I don't know what I'll fucking do.' He dropped her hands and rubbed his jaw. 'I won't stop you from going back in there. But I will ask you not to. Please.' His last word was barely a whisper.

The tears that were brimming in her eyes spilled over onto her cheeks as she looked at the guy she loved, knowing she couldn't do as he asked. Trembling, she stood up from the swing and cradled his head in her hands. His arms came around the backs of her legs, holding on tightly like he didn't want to let her go.

'I'm sorry, Flynn, but I need to do this. Please trust me.'

His eyes snapped to hers. Hurt bloomed in those stormy depths like a shadow cast over the ocean. Slowly, his arms dropped from her body and his gaze levelled out over the park. Bending to kiss the top of his head, Amy stepped away from him and fled to her apartment. It wasn't until she reached the door that she let herself turn around.

The park was in darkness, and Flynn was gone.

CHAPTER TWENTY

FOR THE FIRST TIME since he began walking Amy home after her gym class, Flynn didn't wait to see her inside safely. He just needed to get away. Away from the hurt. Away from himself.

The moment she walked away from him, he rose to his feet and clutched at his side. It wasn't tingling this time. It full-on fucking ached with a need to be satisfied.

Every step he took was agony. His skull felt too small, and his heart was being squeezed with an iron fist. Saliva pooled in his mouth. Flynn spat on the ground and picked up his pace. He needed to get home. Not to Pierre's, but back home to his own bedroom, to the roof, to somewhere familiar and comforting.

The porch light was on at his place when he arrived. *Fuck.* Was Mick inside, waiting for him to come back? The tightness in his chest intensified. It'd be just like Mick to break the restraining order, and he was a complication Flynn didn't need tonight. Not bothering to listen at the door this time, he keyed the lock and pushed it open. The kitchen light was on, but no one was home.

Good. He didn't feel like company. All he wanted was to release the pain.

Taking the half-empty bottle of vodka from the freezer, he locked himself in the bathroom and stepped into the shower, fully clothed. Sitting cross-legged on the tile, he let the hot water cascade down over his head, taking great gulps of vodka. It hit his throat like icy fire, warming the back of his tongue. He didn't intend to write himself off; he just needed a few mouthfuls to soften the edge. The last person he wanted to become was someone like Mick. Or Stacy's father.

Stacy.

God, he wished he'd got her number last night. He could really do with a sympathetic ear right now.

When the water ran cold, Flynn wrenched off the taps, stripping out of his wet clothes and leaving them on the floor. He wrapped a towel around his waist and wiped the mirror clear. His skin was flushed red from the hot water, his scars prominent. They still tingled. Picking up the vodka from the floor, he pressed the still-cold bottle to his side, like an icepack, the temperature change making him flinch. At least he wasn't numb.

He snatched the tumbler from next to the sink and sloshed in a good measure of the alcohol. Next, he picked up his disposable razor. He already knew that a good crack against the sink would break the flimsy plastic, leaving him with a nice, single-edged blade. It was the reason he deliberately shied away from using an electric razor. He wanted to prove that he could resist the temptation.

But now.

Bracing his arms on either side of the sink, he gritted his teeth at the guy staring back at him from the mirror. Last night's conversation with Pierre had been illuminating. He'd expected Frenchie to tell him to cut Amy some slack. But he hadn't. Instead, he'd urged him to do that to himself. Flynn had laughed out loud. If there was anything he was good at doing to himself, it was cutting. His eyes flicked to the razor again.

You're so much stronger than this. His mind protested, but his body was on auto-pilot, falling into the old habit like it was as regular as breathing. The razor sank into the tumbler of vodka, tiny bubbles of dried up shaving cream clinging to the steel blades. A few seconds later, he was rotating the handle through his fingers like a magician twirling a playing card.

But this wasn't some magic trick, and Flynn was under no illusion about how broken he was. He'd fought long and hard against being the guy Amy wanted. She deserved better.

Someone stronger. Someone who could give her whatever had her chasing the dead.

Someone living.

Someone whole.

But he couldn't ignore the feelings he had for her. He didn't just want her; he fucking needed her. And that lack of control almost brought him to his knees. He crashed his fist down on the porcelain. The razor shattered, sending splinters of plastic flying into the sink and the blade digging into his palm.

Flynn squeezed his fist tight, watching as his blood dripped red onto the white benchtop. The relief wasn't the same as when he cut, but the tingling in his side eased somewhat. Ten months had passed since he'd watched himself bleed. Ten months of not intentionally slicing his skin. But *fuck,* he'd come close tonight.

Still loathing his reflection, he dumped the tumbler of vodka over the cut and cleaned it up.

Retreating to the darkness of his bedroom, he fell back onto his bed. Jesus, his sheets still smelled like Amy. Even when she wasn't with him, she was a part of him. A part that ached more than the constant pain in his side. Would he bleed his own heart for her if she asked him to? Hell yes. He thought that's what she'd wanted yesterday, but clearly, he'd been wrong. He had no idea how to get through to her. *Fuck this.*

Dragging himself to his feet, he climbed up to the roof to clear his head. He always could breathe better up there.

The night sky was darker than usual, the moon high and barely a sliver. A warm breeze kissed his skin, reminding him of the last time he was up here—with Amy just a few days ago—when he'd taught her to skate on the pink Penny board.

When she'd told him she loved him.

Was that just a lie, too?

She'd run to him that day like she needed him. But now? Now she was running *from* him to that bloody ghost. Was that love? He didn't think so. But he wasn't about to let her go without a fight.

Sitting down on the dirty concrete, he closed his eyes and let his mind drift back to the first day they met. When she'd climbed up onto the roof and asked his name. This girl, who was so desperately afraid of being invisible, was the brightest thing he'd ever seen.

He only wished that she'd let him inside her heart, so he could make her see otherwise. He'd trusted her with his deepest secret, and vulnerability didn't come easy to him. It hurt that she didn't feel the same. He'd never given her any reason not to trust him. It wasn't as if he was about to up and leave, for fuck's sake. Couldn't she see that?

Frustrated, he got up and kicked the wall. Everything ached like something was trying to crawl out of his chest via his throat. Surely he wasn't jealous?

He didn't care if she was hellbent on finding out about some dead guy. People did that sort of shit every day. They called it research. No, he cared that she was harming herself intentionally to feed that obsession. It was messing with her head. And that messed with his.

He didn't think he'd be strong enough to save her, and that scared the absolute hell out of him.

⁓⊰✦⊱⁓

Flynn didn't bother heading to school the next day. He had study to do and didn't really feel like seeing Amy. Pierre was at work, and he had the whole place to himself for the last time. He was moving back into his mum's flat the next day and needed a plan if Mick decided to show his ugly face.

Flynn grimaced. He'd left that bastard's nose broken in at least three places. You'd think that would be enough of a deterrent. But even with the restraining order, if his mum wanted Mick to come around, there wasn't anything he could do to stop her, short of reporting the breach. He'd all but given up on trying to get her any help. The quicker he could afford to move out and get his own place, the better.

Working at the Terrace Hotel was his saving grace. The physical work was demanding, but he liked the way his muscles burned afterwards. And he was looking forward to seeing Stacy again.

Charity case or not, he had Frenchie to thank for that and for letting him crash at his pad for the past week. To show his appreciation, Flynn tidied up the place and prepared some dinner. Then he alphabetised Pierre's music collection, just for kicks. He doubted the Frenchman even used his CD player anymore, but it would be a surprise when he did.

After doing some more study, he had a quick bite to eat and got ready for work. Not wanting to rely on Pierre to drop him off, he took the train into Richmond, hoping that Stacy's offer for a lift home was still on the cards.

When he arrived, the sun was still high, making unloading the trucks harder in the heat, but he didn't mind the sweat. Friday nights were hectic, and he was soon wheeling crates of booze from the cold rooms to the bar and even helping to stack the glass washers. He caught Stacy's eye a few times as he passed through the bottle shop, and she gave him her wide, bright smile. But neither of them had a moment to stop and chat.

When his shift finally ended at nine, Flynn freshened up in the bathroom and met Stacy in the bottle shop.

'Hello, you,' she said as he approached. 'What did you think of your first Friday night? Pretty crazy, huh?' She undid her apron and hung it on a hook under the counter.

'At least no fights broke out.'

Walking up to him, she slung a slender arm around his shoulder, pulling his ear closer. 'But the night is still young.'

He lifted a brow. 'Do they happen often?'

'Oh, you have no idea.' She laughed, leading him through to the public bar. 'Let's stay and have a drink. I want to hear all your goss.'

Flynn insisted on buying the drinks, and they made their way to a table outside, where it was quiet enough to talk. The Terrace beer garden was in a sunken courtyard lined with trees and overhanging fairy lights. Amy would love it.

'So, what's been going down in Flynn Town?' Stacy asked, sipping her coffee.

Flynn took a long pull on his beer and sighed. 'Nothing exciting. School. Work. Skating. I'm still pretty boring.'

She gave him a look that said she knew better. 'You were never boring. And boring doesn't give you a face like that.'

'What's wrong with my face?'

'You know what I mean.'

He shrugged, shifting in his seat. 'Family issues.'

'Wanna talk about them?'

'Nope.'

'Okay, so what about your girlfriend?'

He shot her a look.

'Come on. We never finished that conversation the other night.'

'We never started one because there's nothing to tell.' He levelled his gaze at her.

Those yellow-green eyes narrowed knowingly. 'Bullshit. And don't tell me it's complicated.'

'What if it is?'

'Fuck,' she muttered. 'You still try to avoid talking, don't you?'

'Came with the territory, remember?' Flynn glared into his beer before finishing it in one go, slamming the empty glass down on the table.

Stacy reached out and placed her hand on top of his. 'I'm really sorry, dog-spew. I didn't mean to bring all that up.' She started making exaggerated gagging noises.

He flicked his eyes to hers. They were sparkling. 'Get fucked,' he said with a smile.

'That's more like it.' She punched his arm playfully. 'So?'

Flynn shook his head. He didn't want to dump his sorry-ass problems onto her, no matter how much he felt like doing so the other night. But if Stacy was anything, it was tenacious. He knew she wouldn't let it go, not because she was nosy but because she genuinely cared. He took a deep breath. 'I really don't want to talk about it tonight, Stace.'

'Yeah, don't I know it.' She grinned. 'That's okay. I know you'll open up when you're ready. And it doesn't have to be with me, Flynn. But don't leave it too late, you know what I mean?'

He nodded, regarding her with an appreciative smile. 'So, did you really have a crush on me when we were kids?'

'Absolutely. And that was even before you kissed me.' She laughed out loud shamelessly, and the warm sound filled his veins with happiness. She touched his forearm. 'I'm so glad we ran into each other again.'

'Yeah, me too,' he said and meant it. Being with someone who actually wanted to be in his company made him feel really good.

She made him feel good.

CHAPTER TWENTY-ONE

AMY RELUCTANTLY MET LEONA outside Brunswick Station on Saturday morning. She'd almost pulled out of the whole dress shopping expedition, but her mum wasn't having any of it.

'Is Pierre coming over or something?' Amy had grumbled as her mum practically shoved her out the front door.

'Something like that.'

Ugh. She didn't know which was the lesser of two evils— spending four hours being dragged around and dressed up by the likes of Leona and Kenzie or being at home while her mum and Pierre made out. The dress shopping won, *obviously.*

'Come on, already.' Her best friend looped her elbow through Amy's and dragged her along the platform towards their destination. 'It'll be fun.'

Fun, my arse.

Amy gritted her teeth and put on her best plastic smile. Fake it till you make it, right?

They met Kenzie at the first store that made up the formalwear district, and Amy was glad she'd worn her sneakers. It was going to be a loooooooong day.

Leona had already picked out a long red playsuit and a short black dress and spent approximately half an hour in each, twirling in front of the mirrors, unable to decide. She looked equally gorgeous in both and still hadn't made up her mind by the time Kenzie insisted they stop for cake and chocolate milkshakes.

'I won't fit into either of them after eating all this!' Leona lamented when the waitress brought over their orders. It didn't stop her from digging into her thick slice of mud cake, though, Amy noted with a smirk. The little café was brimming with hungry shoppers and some other girls from their school were at the counter, too. Amy recognised them as the art students but didn't know any of their names. She sipped her milkshake thoughtfully.

'Hey Kenz, isn't that one of your friends over there?' she asked.

Kenzie lifted her head from her phone and glanced in the girls' direction. 'Oh yeah. Nina, hi!' She waved enthusiastically. A girl turned and smiled, approaching their table.

'Hi, Kenzie. You girls out getting your grad dresses too, huh?'

Nina had a warm, friendly face, and Amy liked her immediately.

'Trying to.' Kenzie laughed. 'You having better luck than us?'

'Oh, I'm just here for moral support.' She motioned to the rest of her friends. 'I'm going to make my dress. Piece it together from some thrifted pieces. You know, like in that eighties movie, *Pretty in Pink.*'

'Oh my God, I love that idea!' Kenzie gushed.

Amy tapped her chin thoughtfully. 'Me too. I think we should have an eighties movie marathon before graduation.'

'That would be awesome,' Kenzie said. 'We should invite the boys.'

Amy grinned back, knowing how Kenzie felt about Luka. 'Let's set it up.'

'Speaking of pink, Ames, with your hair, you'd look so hot in soft pink. What do you reckon, girls? Flynn won't be able to keep his hands off you.' Leona winked, causing Amy's mouth to drop open.

'Ah. So you and Flynn are together?' Nina asked.

Amy felt the intensity of the girl's gaze, and her cheeks instantly heated. 'Um.'

'Yes, they are.'

Amy swung her head to glare at Leona. 'We're just—'

'Don't you dare say friends,' Leona interrupted, rolling her eyes. 'You're not fooling anyone, Ames. You two have been hot for each other forever. I'm surprised you haven't started an inferno, with the looks that pass between you.' She flapped a hand and slurped on her shake. 'Everyone knows.'

Nina chewed her lip and bent to Kenzie. 'Can I talk to you for a minute?'

'Sure.'

When Kenzie wasn't budging, Nina grasped her elbow, glancing at Amy. 'Not here.'

'Aw, but I have a food baby,' Kenzie protested as Nina pulled her away near the door.

As they whispered together, bent over their phones, Amy fidgeted with her straw. What the hell was going on?

'What was that about?' Leona asked when Kenzie re-joined their table.

Kenzie chewed her lip. 'Nina was at the Terrace Hotel last night.' Her gaze flicked to Amy's and held. 'A family birthday or something, and she saw Flynn there.'

Amy nodded sheepishly. 'Yeah, I forgot to tell you guys. He's working there now.' She tried to smile, but something about Kenzie's expression was off.

'I don't know how to say this, Ames.' Kenzie shook her head and took a deep breath.

'Dramatic much, Kenz? Just spit it out.' Leona rolled her eyes, despite clearly hanging on Kenzie's every word.

But Kenzie said nothing. Instead, she pushed her phone toward Amy. Amy glanced down at it.

Right there, on the plus-sized screen, was a photo of Flynn sitting with a girl. A beautiful girl. A beautiful girl who had her hand on his bare forearm and her head bent close to his. They were laughing.

The milkshake congealed like blood in Amy's stomach.

Leona sat back and huffed out loud. 'Why did she take a photo of them?'

'Nina's not a troublemaker. She only spotted them in the background of a family photo when she was going through them later. This is zoomed in, but the quality is fantastic, so...' Kenzie shrugged.

Amy swallowed and found her voice. 'Did she see them kiss or anything?'

'She didn't say, just that they looked pretty close.' Kenzie's voice was apologetically soft.

'That's fine.' Amy stood, suddenly needing to get out of there. 'He's allowed to have female friends, right?' Grabbing her bag, she added, 'Come on, I still need to find a dress.' God, she would never have guessed she'd hear herself say that in a million years.

'Fuck yes,' Leona grinned. 'Let's show that boy what he's missing out on.'

Amy led the way outside, not bothering to mention that *the boy* still hadn't asked her to be his date yet. Not that it mattered, she decided. She would have fun at her graduation, whether or not he showed up. Even if he brought someone else.

Who was that girl, anyway? Jealousy bloomed in her chest, hot and hard. An alien thing, taking root inside her ribcage—its tentacles wrapped around her bones and holding on tight.

Storming across the road, she shook her head, trying to get away from her thoughts. A dress in a shop window caught her eye, and she darted inside, the other girls hot on her sneakered heels. Skimming through the racks, she found what she was looking for and disappeared into one of the massive, mirrored change rooms.

'Oh. My. God. Amy. What. The. Actual. Fuck.'

'Language,' Kenzie hissed at Leona. Both girls and a couple of random mothers in the store were staring as Amy stepped out of the dressing room.

'Sorry, not sorry. Flynn is going to cream his jeans.'

Kenzie shook her head at Leona and sighed. 'You look amazing, Ames.'

Amy's breath hitched at her friend's words. Amazing Ames. It was the nickname Flynn had given her the first time they kissed. The night she cut her leg. Her scar was still fresh, but the wound had practically healed already. And the long skirt would cover it up, anyway.

Amy looked down at the swathes of blush chiffon that fell to the floor. The skirt whispered understated elegance, but most of all, it was skin coloured. Which meant that when paired with the cropped white lace top she'd chosen, she practically disappeared.

⬦

On the train home, Amy toyed with her phone and thought about calling Flynn. She'd asked Kenzie to delete the photo of him and the mystery girl, hovering over her until she was sure it had disappeared forever. She never wanted to see it again, but the thought that it might get circulated around school worried her. Flynn didn't use social media and wouldn't be able to defend himself.

If he had any legitimate reason to, of course.

Still, she punched in his number, wanting to hear his voice.

'Hey,' he answered.

Amy smiled despite her misgivings. The way his voice dropped low and soft when he spoke to her like that always did crazy things to her body.

'Hey yourself.' It was their standard greeting. 'Want to come over and watch crappy eighties prom-coms with me?'

There was a beat of silence. 'I'm not doing a Molly Ringwald marathon, Ames.'

Her grin grew wider. She loved that he was a film student. Not too many eighteen-year-old guys would even know what a prom-com was, let alone be able to name a lead actress from thirty years ago.

'Oh, come on, it'll be fun.'

'Yeah, but why prom movies? They're so cringe. I'm not watching *The Kissing Booth*, either. Make it *Carrie*, and I'm there.'

She rolled her eyes and poked out her tongue, forgetting that he couldn't see her. 'We have our grad dance in a couple of weeks. I thought it'd be fun.'

'Oh. So you want a bucket of pig's blood tossed all over your pretty head, then? That's fucked up, Ames.'

'No! You're the one who brought up the gory horror movie, not me.'

Their banter made her feel almost normal enough to forgive him for not taking the bait and asking her to the dance. Almost, but not quite.

'Okay, we'll compromise. Eighties high school movies without proms. Sound good?' She rattled off a few of their iconic favourites.

He didn't answer, and Amy felt her heart dropping with each pounding beat. Right into that little green monster's grasp. 'I'll make that salted caramel popcorn you like.'

Crap. She'd never resorted to bribing him with food before, and she closed her eyes, hating herself for grovelling.

He exhaled loudly. 'Now there's an offer I can't refuse. Okay. See you at eight.'

Amy ended the call, feeling elated. Things weren't the same. Not by a long shot, but at least he was talking to her again.

Flynn arrived at eight o'clock on the dot. When he knocked on her door, Amy was busy stirring melted caramel, ready to pour over the hot popcorn. She'd opened the door earlier to eliminate the smell of burning oil that still lingered in the kitchen and turned, her breath catching at the sight of him. He looked just like a modern-day version of her favourite eighties heroes, in mid-blue tight jeans, sneakers, and a white vee-neck tee. She felt her knees go weak. He brought chocolate.

And tonight, he's all mine.

He helped her mix the popcorn and then broke up the block of Dairy Milk into irregular pieces, leaving his fingerprints ingrained all over the softening squares. He motioned to the bowl of chocolate as he fell on the couch and propped his feet on the coffee table. 'I touched them all, so they're mine.'

'Hmm. Is this a version of I-licked-it-so-it's-mine? Because that's a game I could definitely get on board with.' She smiled wickedly at him.

He stared at her. Then squeezed her thigh and reached for the remote. 'So, what are we watching?'

She decided on one of Flynn's favourites because she was desperate to make him happy. They mucked around quoting all their favourite lines and threw popcorn at each other, just like old times. Like the times before they kissed. And if they had to start as friends again, then she could do that. She craved him pretty hard, and it would be torture, but she would do it for him.

Midway through the movie, Flynn's phone buzzed on the coffee table. Amy's eyes flashed automatically to the screen as it lit up, and her body froze. On his screen was a picture of a girl. *That girl.* The pretty one with the gorgeous skin in the photo Nina took. The girl that had been laughing with Flynn. Touching him.

Amy's vision blurred, but her brain registered the caller ID: STACY.

They looked pretty close, Nina said.

Flynn grabbed the remote and hit pause. 'Sorry, I have to take this.' To his credit, he didn't leave the lounge, just stared ahead at the TV, frowning.

Amy got up and banged around in the kitchen, unable to stop herself from listening in on his conversation.

'Okay,' he said. 'Thanks for the heads up, Stace. Yeah. I'll see you soon, then. Barf you later.'

Barf you later? What sort of sick joke was that? But it was the size of Flynn's smile as he finished the call that had Amy's stomach caving in like he'd just punched her. She gripped the kitchen bench for support.

'Want a coffee?' she offered, trying to stop her voice from shaking and desperately hoping he'd decline because she didn't think she'd be able to hold the mug without dropping it.

He put his hands in his pockets and shook his head. 'Sorry, but I have to head into work.'

'What, you mean like right now?' Her voice turned hard.

He pinned her with those dark blue eyes and dragged his teeth over his bottom lip. 'Yeah, my boss is about to call. He needs me to work the bottle shop tonight till closing.'

'Can't someone else do it?' Desperation made her voice shrill, and she hated how it sounded.

He threw her a helpless look as his phone rang. This time he put the phone on loudspeaker, so Amy had no choice but to listen.

'Patrick! What's up?'

'Sorry to call on you last-minute, mate, but Stacy said you might be up for some more shifts?'

'Yeah, absolutely.'

'Great. There's a footy game on tonight, and she's getting swamped in the bottle-o. Some patrons have been rough, and I'd rather we had some muscle in there, you know what I'm saying?'

Flynn winked at Amy, flexing his biceps. She turned away. She didn't want his muscles anywhere near *Stacy*.

'No problem, Patrick. I can be there in forty minutes.'

'Thanks, mate. You're a lifesaver.'

Flynn ended the call.

'I'd better go.'

Amy kept her back to him. 'Sure. You do that. Go.' The monster was expanding in her chest, filling the entire cavity with its poison.

'Amy—'

'Just leave, Flynn. Save Stacy, or whatever her name is. And before you do—' She half-turned, keeping her eyes trained on the floor. 'Just remember that you're not about being anyone's saviour.'

She could feel him watching her, hear his chest heaving with each breath.

'You're right,' he said finally. 'I'm not.' Then he turned around and walked out.

Amy burst into tears.

Fuck him. Fuck her. Fuck them both.

Chapter Twenty-Two

'ARE YOU SURE THIS is the right place?' Luka called out. He was a few metres behind Amy as they picked their way along the northern docks of the Yarra River.

'I really don't know,' she answered, feeling more stupid by the second. Why had she thought that Marcel's tunnel would lead all this way? She and Leona hadn't ventured far enough the other day to determine if it turned left or right anywhere.

In front of them, the Banana Alley Vaults stretched over sixty-five metres all the way back to Flinders Street. Now that they were actually pacing out the distance, Marcel's house was almost twice that far away again. Crap, she really hadn't thought this through.

Of course, she hadn't—images of Flynn being with Stacy kept invading her thoughts, leaving little room for anything else. After he'd walked out last night, she'd almost run to Marcel—her desire to be seen obliterating all rational thought.

Instead, she'd called Luka. They'd talked for hours. Flynn hadn't told him anything about Stacy, and as Amy wanted to change the subject, they'd ended up spending way too much time discussing her theory about the underground tunnels.

Luka said there were sites all over the web dedicated to "draining" and "urbexing". That he wanted to help her with this instead of telling her to forget about it filled her chest with warmth. And then to have him turn up on her doorstep in the morning, suggesting they scope it out together? Well, it wasn't the first time she'd wished Flynn was more like him.

She waited for him to catch up. 'Do you think we'd have a better view from the bridge?'

Luka peered around her. 'That would make sense. See, I knew we brought you along for a reason.' Amusement danced in his eyes.

She punched his arm, then grabbed his sleeve and pulled him onto Queens Bridge with her. They'd barely walked a couple of metres before she spied it: a square opening, half-submerged in the river. *A large opening.* Bigger than any stormwater drain she'd ever seen.

Adrenaline thrummed throughout her body, momentarily rendering her mute. 'That has to be it,' she said finally, pointing at the darkened square.

Luka cocked his head. 'We won't get in that way, though.'

He was right. They could end up drowning. Or worse. Sewer-dwelling clowns popped into her head, and she shuddered. How else were they going to get in there? Neither of them would fit through the hole that Leona used, and scaling the fence again was completely out of the question until much later in the day.

'Come on,' she said to him. 'Let's get something to eat and work out what to do.'

Her feet naturally led them to Pierre's, and as they walked, Amy relaxed. Being around Luka always did that to her. He was so easygoing. Maybe that's why he and Flynn were such good friends. He balanced out Flynn's intensity.

'So, you think nothing's going on between Flynn and that girl?' she asked, trusting Luka would be perfectly honest with her.

He reached down and took her hand in his. 'Look, just because he had a drink with a co-worker doesn't mean anything, Ames. I'm here with you now, aren't I? And we're just friends. If Flynn saw us right now, scoffing our faces with waffles, do you think he would read anything into it?' Hope sparked in those warm brown eyes.

'I guess not.' She squeezed his palm. 'Waffles, hey? Well, I suppose you did save my life.'

'Yeah, about that. I think I deserve much more than mere waffles.' He tugged her close enough for his breath to tickle her nose. His eyes flicked to her lips. 'I also want one of those huge iced coffees. With a double helping of whipped cream.'

Laughing, she pushed him away. 'I will not be responsible for clogging your arteries. You're not having a heart attack on my watch, buddy.'

He pushed open the door for her, his other hand on his heart in mock reverence. 'Ah, but at least I'll die a happy man.'

'Salut Pierre,' she called, squeezing past the counter and into the baking room beyond. Luka clung to her back like a shadow.

Pierre winked at them as he flipped some crepes. 'To what do I owe the pleasure of this weekend visit?'

'Luka's craving waffles, and I told him he just had to try your legendary French toast variety. Any chance we could get some, *s'il vous plaît*?'

'And have I met Luka?' Pierre raised his eyebrows.

Luka stepped forward and introduced himself. 'This room smells amazing. It's like my mum's kitchen, only better.' He turned to Amy and whispered, 'Don't tell her I said that.'

'Your mother isn't French, then?' Pierre asked with a wry smile.

Luka grinned. 'No, she is one-hundred per cent Italian. And would skin me alive if she knew I was eating someone else's food. This could be my last meal.'

Pierre chuckled. 'I don't know about legendary, but they've fast become Flynn's favourite too.'

'Have they?' Amy tried her best to sound unaffected. Clearly, she failed because Pierre asked her what was going on between them as he shovelled the crepes onto some trays.

She didn't know how to answer that, so she said nothing. He passed the crepes through to the front counter and began whisking together milk and eggs. Luka seemed entranced.

'Talk to me, mon amie.'

'Why? Has Flynn said something to you?'

'He doesn't have to.' She waited for him to elaborate while he dumped a generous slug of maple syrup and vanilla essence into the bowl and continued whisking. 'That kid has been as miserable as hell since he left work the other night.'

'I doubt that,' she scoffed. 'Last night, he could barely wait to get back there.'

'He's just trying his best to put in a good impression.'

'Yeah, I'll bet.' She crossed her arms to squash the green monster in her chest.

Pierre's eyes narrowed. 'It's not what you think.'

'And what would I be thinking?'

Pierre frowned, cutting some thick slices of brioche and dipping them in the mixture. 'That's not for me to say, cherie. But I can tell you he's going through some tough stuff at the moment, and when he comes out the other side of it, you can either be there for him or not. That's your choice to make.'

'What, you think I'm going to abandon him? I might be jealous, but I'm not irrational.'

'I don't mean to sound disrespectful, mon amie. But sometimes, things are less complex than they appear. Especially with men.' He dropped the soaked bread onto the waffle plate and closed the lid. 'Maybe you just need to tell Flynn exactly how you feel.'

'What if I tried that already?'

Pierre approached her and wiped a hand on his apron before laying it on her shoulder. 'Look inside your heart, mon cherie. It knows exactly what you want.'

He was right about that, at least. Inside that pounding organ in her chest was blood. Lots and lots of blood. Blood that she couldn't wait to spill so that she could see Marcel again.

⸻◆⸻

Amy and Luka finished their waffles in awkward silence. He'd been acting super weird since the conversation with Pierre.

'What do you think I should do?' she asked him, chasing a blueberry around her plate with a fork.

He stopped slurping on his iced coffee. 'I think the Frenchman is right,' he said slowly before raising his eyes to meet hers. 'There's no doubt that Flynn adores you. You know that, right?'

She shoved the blueberry into her mouth and grimaced. It was tart, or maybe her mood had turned it sour. Flynn might adore her, but it did nothing to convince her of his belief regarding Marcel.

'Hey.' She tapped Luka's fingers where they rested on the table. 'Do you want to come with me to the Butcher's House?'

Luka coughed, snatching his hand back. 'Like, *inside*?'

'Yeah.'

'I thought we were just checking out the tunnels.'

'We were.'

'But?'

She shrugged.

'Look, Ames. I don't have the fondest memories from the last time we were there, you know? You getting hurt, and that we almost got caught. I'm happy to help you prove your tunnel theory, but I'm not setting foot in there again. And I don't think you should, either.'

'Oh. So *you* don't think I should.' Well, that was just great. Yet another man trying to tell her what to do. 'Fine. Let's crawl into the sewers then. Maybe we'll come across Pennywise, and you won't have to worry about ghosts because we'll have a demon clown trying to kill us, instead.' She shook her head. 'You're no better than Flynn.'

Luka eyed her, wary. 'What do you mean?'

'Trying to get me to drop all of this. Not wanting me to pursue this one thing that I find interesting. I thought you were different, Luka. One of the good ones. But now I see you've only been trying to sweet-talk me out of it all along. Just how far were you willing to go today?'

'It's not like that, Ames. Shit.' Luka pushed out of his chair.

'Just forget it, Luka. Go home. I don't need a babysitter.' She brushed past him and out of the patisserie before she could change her mind.

Luka followed her out and grabbed her arm, yanking her to face him. 'You're right. I don't want to see you get hurt. And neither does Flynn.'

She gave him her best gloating smile. 'Like I said. You're just like him.' Then, turning on her heel, she stalked towards Flinders Lane.

'You don't get it, do you?'

'Apparently not,' she called over her shoulder.

'Ames.'

She ignored him and kept on walking, even though her heart was breaking. This gentle boy, who had already saved her life once before, was only looking out for her. But damn it, she was going to find out the truth behind this urban legend, with or without anyone's help.

'Please, Amy, don't do this.'

Something in the way he said *please* made her slow and turn around.

'What?' She crossed her arms, waiting.

'I don't regret saving your life for one minute, okay. Not even for a millionth of a second, and I'd do it again. Willingly. But you can't go around doing shit like this. It's not like you, Amy. And I get it. You're pissed over seeing Flynn with someone else. Man, do I get that. But you can't let yourself get dragged into a spiral of self-destruction.' He ran both hands through his mop of curls, frustrated. 'Great, now I sound like my fucking sister.'

Amy's gaze ran over him. His body was tense, his usually warm eyes guarded. 'What do you mean, you get that? Kenz is hardly seeing anyone else,' she mumbled.

'Kenzie? What does she have to do with this?'

'Is it Leona, then?'

'What are you talking about?'

'You like someone. Who is it?'

'What? No one. Just forget it, Ames.'

She stepped closer, her voice dropping. 'Come on. You can tell me, Luka.'

'No, I can't.'

'Why not? I thought we trusted each other.'

A gust of wind blew up the street, pushing Amy's hair into her face, but she stared through it, waiting. Neither of them moved. Then, slowly, Luka reached toward her and tenderly brushed the strands away. Torture filled his eyes.

'Because he's my best friend.'

Amy stared at him as the ground fell away beneath her. 'You're hot for Flynn?'

Luka's hand dropped. 'No, Ames. Not Flynn. Are you really that blind?'

⁕

Like the microfiche she'd used at the library, Amy's head spun back over the last few days, slowing down and zeroing in on moments she hadn't had cause to over-examine until now:

Luka saving her from the train ... rubbing her back while Flynn dressed her wound and cradling her while she threw up ... wanting to know if she'd hooked up with Flynn ... his look of surprise when she'd pulled him against the cafeteria wall ... and Luka this morning, coming to her house and holding her hand ... Luka ... Luka ... Luka.

Amy's heart beat in double time as she backed away. No, this was too much. It changed everything. *Everything.*

Why did he have to go and do that?

She needed space. The laneway with its Sunday morning coffee crowd was suddenly overwhelming. 'I have to go.'

'Ames, wait,' Luka called out, but she turned her back on him and ran.

She ran until her feet could run no more and slowed to a standstill on Queens Bridge. She turned around, unable to stop her eyes from seeking the large drain. She tried to imagine Valentina tipping bodies from that hideous wheelchair into the river.

Now that she'd met Marcel and his sister, she didn't want to believe the rumours. But what else could Valentina have been doing in that tunnel, other than dumping corpses? Luka had spoken of tunnels leading underground from the hospitals to the morgue, but Amy didn't believe Marcel had his own private death-dash to either of them. She wanted to find out the truth, but first, she needed to forget all about Luka and his theories.

Jogging over the bridge, she followed the path along Southbank and up onto Princes Bridge. There were markets in Federation Square, and she headed straight for them, needing to lose herself in the horde of tourists and families with children dripping gelato everywhere. Anything to take her mind off the tunnels until she could see Marcel again.

A band was on the stage playing covers of all the great British rock songs, and she stayed to listen for a while. It took her mind away from the onslaught of messages and missed calls from Luka. Eventually, her phone stopped buzzing, and she sent him a brief message, letting him know she was okay and that she'd see him at school tomorrow. Then, switching it off, she made her way back to Flinders Lane.

The street wasn't busy, but it wasn't clear enough for her to scale the fence in broad daylight, either. Thanks to the beautiful weather, the city was full of people. A homeless man had set up camp in the laneway next to Marcel's, and most pedestrians had crossed the street to avoid him. Amy wandered past him slowly, noting his possessions. A wicked idea formed in her mind.

Slipping him five dollars, she asked if he could hang his sleeping bag over the wrought-iron fence above Marcel's courtyard. It would look like he was airing it out, and it would give her some cover to slip over the fence beneath it. Although the stench from the stained fabric almost had her heaving on the tile inside, her plan worked. Not wanting him to follow, she locked the glass door behind her and raced up the stairs.

The door to the third-floor room was still ajar, and Amy pushed it open. Sagging onto the floorboards, she pulled the lancet from her pocket and sat, flicking the blade open and closed while her heart continued to hammer in her chest. What the hell was she doing? Crap, what had she just done? That homeless man could've been an undercover cop, a murderer, anyone. Many things could've gone wrong. *And yet they didn't,* answered the voice inside her head. *And here you are.*

'Here I am,' she said out loud, opening the lancet and running the blade down the back of her leg, right against the side of her scar. It actually didn't hurt that much, but it bled. And that was all that mattered.

⸺⊷✦⊶⸺

'Yes, here you are,' said a male voice from the doorway. Startled, Amy dropped the lancet. A tall, lean figure strode toward her, dark and brooding. Marcel.

Dropping to a crouch beside her, his fingers darted for the tiny knife and closed around it. The curtains of his hair swung open to reveal eyes like flint. He held up the lancet.

'Where did you get this?' A hint of menace laced his tone.

Amy braced her hands on her knees. 'Valentina gave it to me.'

'Did she?' He sounded amused. 'Clever girl.'

His eyes ran down the length of Amy's bare legs, following the trail of blood. Giving her the folded lancet, he stretched out a finger and touched it to her skin. Amy held her breath as he drew it away, his manicured fingertip glistening with her blood.

'I wonder what you taste like, Amy.'

She had no words as he brought the tip of his finger to his mouth and ran it along his plump lower lip.

'Rage? No. Perhaps lust?' He rubbed his lips together, smearing them with her blood like some kind of macabre lip gloss. 'Mmm, perhaps. But I'll wager my money on melancholy.' At that point, he opened his mouth and swiped his tongue around his lips, tasting her. It was both the sexiest and grossest thing she'd ever witnessed all at once. Her pulse thrummed throughout her entire body.

He stood and held out his hand to her, pulling her gently to her feet. Holding her at arm's length, he inspected her from head to toe. 'You know, I thought you were a street urchin, at first.'

Amy looked down at her shorts and top. A street urchin? Surely she didn't look that bad. The smell, however...

'What was the verdict?' she asked.

'I beg pardon?'

She jutted her chin forward. 'What did I taste like?'

His lips twitched, almost apologetically. 'Disappointment, Amy. You tasted like disappointment.'

He pulled her over to the chaise longue behind him, and Amy was too shocked to protest. Abruptly, the surrounding room became all too vivid.

'Never mind,' he said, easing her down. 'About three ounces should do it.'

Amy blinked faster. 'What?'

'Three ounces. Unlike melancholy, disappointment is only a mild affliction. If it continues, I can always let some more blood.' He opened a cabinet and took out a brass bowl.

'You're going to bleed me?'

'Is that not why you came?'

'No!' She sat bolt upright on the chaise, not caring that she was bleeding all over it. How much blood had stained this very fabric? She wanted to get up, but Marcel seated himself beside her, closing her in. So close that she could feel the heat from his body, the press of his knee against hers as he unbuttoned the cuffs of his long dark sleeves and rolled them to his elbow. 'I, I came to talk to you.'

'Talk?' He pivoted slightly in his seat to face her, eyes glinting like polished silver. 'I am not an alienist, nor someone who specialises in pillow conversation. However, I am certain we could come to an agreement.' His eyes flashed, and Amy was very much aware that his knee still pressed against hers. The man's mere presence was intimidating and thrilling as hell.

'Where's Valentina?' she asked, buying some time to look around the room. She had noticed little the last time she was here, surprised to find one wall contained several shelves of books, among other medical oddities. She got up and walked over to it, fingering the cloth spines. The books were mostly French and probably worth an absolute mint. She wondered idly what had happened to them. Fishing her phone out of her pocket and keeping her back to Marcel, she snapped a quick photo, the flash illuminating the wall behind the bookcase.

'She is out purchasing provisions. Do you wish to speak with her?'

'I like your sister,' she replied, ignoring his question. 'I don't have any siblings, although sometimes I wish I did. It must be comforting knowing that someone is always there for you.'

He sat in silence, watching her every move with shining eyes.

'But no, I want to know more about you,' she said, returning to the chaise.

'Very well,' he conceded. 'What do you wish to know?'

Amy's head was so full of questions, and it was spinning like a centrifuge. Momentarily dumbfounded, she blurted the first thing to filter through. 'How do you speak such fluent English?'

God, she could've face-palmed herself for wasting time with such a ridiculous question. But Marcel's luscious mouth turned up at the corners, and he seemed to relax back into the plush, tapestried cushions.

'When I first made the decision to leave France, I sought a teacher. An Englishman, in Versailles.' Ah. That explained the slight pompous lilt to his accent. 'He sought to silence his demons, and I sought to voice a new language. It was a mutual arrangement.'

'So why did you choose to come here, to Australia? Were there not enough people to bleed in France?' She smiled.

His mouth twitched again. She thought that behind Marcel's impeccable facade lay a wicked sense of humour, and she was eager to bring it to the surface.

'There are demons aplenty in Paris, Amy. No, Valentina and I were in need of a fresh start, and what better place to start afresh than halfway around the globe?' He smiled, but it didn't reach his eyes. Amy nodded, aware that he had artfully dodged her question and that she would need to tread carefully if she wanted to find out his truths. His *demons*.

She risked a glance at his scarred forearms. Marcel had demons, all right. But so did Flynn, she realised. And maybe, just maybe, she did too. We all have things that haunt us. It was an analogy she hadn't thought of before.

As her head whirled, Amy realised that the room was getting dimmer - more transparent, like a filter over a picture. Except it was happening right in front of her. The bookshelves dissolved, revealing a dull wallpapered wall, torn in places near the skirting board.

NO!

Her hand instinctively went to the cut on the back of her leg and came away clean. No, no, no.

The blood had dried.

Chapter Twenty-Three

W HEN AMY FOUND HERSELF sprawled on the dusty floor of Marcel's empty apartment, she could have screamed. She pushed on the wound, willing it to bleed again, but it had already congealed. Prodding it hurt like a bitch, and her phone was digging into her butt. Quickly opening the last photograph, she slammed her hand down on the floorboards as an image of the same blank wallpapered wall mocked her. There were no medical books or bookcases, nothing to prove what she'd seen. This couldn't be happening again. She'd been so close.

Consequences be damned. She ripped the lancet from her pocket and ran it down the other side of her scar. This time, she dug the tip in a little deeper and waited anxiously as the blood rose and chased gravity.

—❧—

This time, when Amy appeared in Marcel's parlour, it was during one of his appointments. Perplexed, she quickly crawled to hide behind the chaise and observe.

A woman dressed in a utilitarian dress and pinafore sat in a nearby wing-backed chair, her left sleeve unbuttoned and exposed to just above the elbow. Marcel tied a length of rubber tubing around her upper arm. A tourniquet, Amy realised.

Beneath the woman's arm rested the brass bowl that Marcel had fetched earlier. Blood from a minor cut in her inner forearm dripped into it steadily.

Marcel was speaking to the woman about her place of employment—a nearby garment factory, where she was a seamstress, and apparently quite convinced that her Singer sewing machine was going to stitch her mouth closed in her sleep. The poor woman was delusional. However, her rantings became less certain as the bowl filled until she was quite calm and strangely lucid.

Marcel released the tourniquet and bound her wound with a gauze bandage before redressing the buttons on her sleeve with tender care. The woman seemed placated and watched him with a slow languor that suggested she was drunk or completely under Marcel's charm. Valentina gave the woman a tiny glass of chartreuse coloured liquid to drink before leaving the room with the bowl of blood. Amy wanted to follow her and see what she did with it. Did she dispose of it? Fill a bath for Marcel to bathe in? Drink it? *Jesus. Don't be stupid.* Even though he'd tasted her blood, she knew the vampire rumour wasn't true.

The woman finished her liqueur and rose to her feet. Valentina emerged from the doorway and escorted her towards the elevator. Marcel began collecting his equipment and poured himself a large measure of what Amy now recognised as cognac from a wicker-covered bottle stashed in his bookcase. Pierre had many of them decorating the patisserie shelves.

'You may come out now,' he said matter-of-factly. Amy peered around the edge of the chaise to find those grey eyes trained on her. He sank down into the chair vacated by his client and crossed his long legs. Unable to stop shaking, she rose and skirted the edge of the lounge before he suggested she sit near him. 'Enjoy the show, did you?' He smirked as he lit another of those slim brown cigarettes.

'Is that what it was?' She frowned, batting away the plume of pungent smoke he blew in her direction.

'Cloves,' he said airily, showing her the cigarette before tapping it on a small dish. 'It helps to calm my nerves.' He then pointed it at her, his voice forceful. 'And you have no place interrupting my treatments.'

His sudden change of tone took her aback. 'I didn't mean to.'

'No?' He snarled, rising from the chair. 'Then tell me why you are here, Amy. Do you wish me to bleed you this time, or are you merely here for polite conversation?'

Amy shrank back against the cushions. This wasn't the version of Marcel she'd encountered before. She watched as he strode over to the bookcase and retrieved the bottle of cognac. Returning to the small table by his chair, he picked up the glass, knocked back the whole thing, and then poured another measure. Even though his demeanour was brusque, his body language was saying something else. His posture was proud, but his face was troubled. His hands shook slightly. To Amy, he looked tormented—a man haunted by his own demons. She felt sorry for him and a lot less threatened.

'Why do you help women like that, Marcel?' she asked softly, patting the lounge and gesturing for him to join her.

He huffed dramatically and sank into the cushions. 'Because they need me.'

'What's wrong with them?'

He turned to look her in the eye. 'They are damaged.' Her face must have belied her shock, for he hastened to add, 'The women I treat do not require specialist medical attention for any physical affliction. Unlike my contemporaries, I do not believe that the body produces excess blood that needs to be removed in order to maintain *balance*.' He practically spat the word. 'No. It is my understanding that letting blood relieves the mind and indeed, the heart of pain.'

That was an interesting notion. 'How so?'

'The darkness inside a woman must be allowed to escape. We must run our fingers through it. Feel its viscosity. Taste her pain.' His gaze fixed on something far away as his fingers were absently trailing across the scars on his forearm.

Amy swallowed. 'Why can you see me?'

He turned his silvery eyes to hers. 'Why indeed? I have pondered the same question.' Then he stood abruptly and went back to the table by the wing chair. The clove cigarette was still burning, and he took a long drag, the tip glowing furiously and sending a thin stream of smoke skyward. Turning his back on her, he removed his shirt and picked up the glass of cognac.

'Come. I shall give you a demonstration.'

In the candlelight, Amy admired the lines of his bare shoulders and arms as he tipped his head back and drained the liquor. He was much leaner than Flynn, but he had a wiry intensity that suggested strength and agility. Sitting down in the chair, he gave her a smirk as if to say, *like what you see?* Then, taking her hand, he placed it over his left pectoral. His heartbeat under her palm was strong. Even. Vital.

Tying a rubber strap around his bicep, he tightened the tourniquet with his teeth before opening a box on the table she hadn't noticed before. Concealing something in his palm, he positioned it at his inner elbow. Amy's eyes widened at the glimpse of brass before the tiny click of the ratchet blade broke out like a gunshot in the silent room.

Amy startled as Marcel's head fell back against the chair. The spring lancet fell to the floor as he moaned in release. A crimson ribbon unfurled down the inside of his arm, and he visibly relaxed, his long legs stretching out across the floor. His eyelids fluttered as his heartbeat softened and quickened, feeling to Amy as though he had a hummingbird caged behind his ribs.

Marcel lifted Amy's hand from his chest. 'I know not why I see you, but it is time for you to leave. Au revoir, petit démon.'

⁕

Putting a hand to her throbbing temple, Amy tried to sit up. She was lying on Valentina's bed with a merry-go-round of Marcel's words giving her a headache.

It is time for you to leave. Up.

Goodbye, little demon. Down.

Round and round we go.

Why had he called her a demon?

For the first time since she'd begun visiting Marcel, she wanted to go home. Wincing, she slid across the narrow mattress and lowered her legs to the floor. Her cut was no longer bleeding, so why was she still here?

Wobbling to her feet, she caught her reflection in Valentina's mirror. Something was wound around her head like a bandage. Had she fainted? Pulling it off, she realised it was the scarf she'd worn around her ponytail. Feeling thirsty, she ventured out into the hall. Marcel's bedroom door was closed. Was he in there? She'd check in on him later. First, she needed water. Still not trusting the elevator, she headed for the stairs and made her way cautiously up to the next floor. Her backpack was still behind the chaise, where she'd dropped it earlier. Pulling out a half-empty bottle of water, she sculled it in one go before noticing Valentina standing in the doorway.

She spluttered. Her head gave an almighty throb, making her stomach lurch. Wishing she'd packed some painkillers, Amy searched through her bag, finding nothing but an old chocolate bar. It'd have to do. She broke off half, holding it out to Valentina. The girl approached and gave the chocolate a cautious look before shaking her head politely. Amy shrugged (she wasn't asking twice) and shoved it in her mouth.

Tilting her head toward the wing-backed chair, she asked, 'Why do you always fix him up?'

Valentina looked confused, so Amy swirled her tongue around her mouth, getting rid of the last remnants of caramel before trying again. 'Why does Marcel bleed himself?'

Valentina looked sad. 'Les diables.' *Devils.*

Yes, Marcel had his demons. But what were they, and why did he think she was one?

She thought about the woman she'd seen today—the seamstress, who appeared to be hysterical, but who was most likely just overworked and exhausted. A common occurrence, she remembered, from her Industrial Revolution studies in history class. Cramped conditions, long hours, inadequate diet. No wonder these women were hallucinating.

The darkness inside a woman. Marcel's words haunted her, those fingers running along his scars. What woman could've hurt him so badly that he'd believe all women harboured darkness?

She risked a glance at Valentina. The girl was quiet and went about her duties with a cold efficiency at odds with her young age. But underneath, Amy sensed a warmth, a desire to help and nurture. And she clearly worshipped her brother. It wasn't the first time Amy had wondered about their parents. She had assumed them orphans and had been too polite to ask. But now, something was banging on the back door of her brain. And it wasn't her headache.

'Valentina? You will make an excellent nurse one day.'

'I am a nurse.'

'I know. I mean, you could work in a hospital or something. One day. If you wanted to.'

'Marcel needs me here.' It wasn't the first time she'd said that.

'But you need to have your own life, too. What if Marcel marries? What will you do then?'

'Marcel will never marry.' She seemed quite resolute.

'Why do you say that? He's still young. One day he might.'

Valentina shook her head firmly. 'He does not need for a wife.'

No, just hookers, then? *Oh.* She dropped her voice. 'Does he prefer the company of men?'

'On the contrary.' Marcel's deep, honeyed tone floated from the shadowy doorway. 'He most definitely prefers the fairer sex.' He stepped into the warm candlelit glow of the room. 'Still here, I see?' Amusement tipped the edges of his lips.

Her eyes narrowed. 'Is that why you only treat women?'

A flash of something crossed his face, then he smiled. 'I am completely professional with my treatments, mon petit démon. What I do in my private time, however, is my business.'

Amy thought back to the day she'd met him—lounging on the chaise with a couple of half-naked women, drunk, or high on God-knew-what, bleeding himself and lost to oblivion. He looked like a junkie. Only she'd been too surprised to see it at the time.

'What are you addicted to, Marcel?' she asked, thinking out loud.

'I beg pardon?' The pink flush on his cheeks gave her the courage to push further.

'It can't only be blood. Is it power? Do you feel powerful when you release the darkness, Doctor Boucher?'

A mask of indifference dropped over his face like a shadow. However, his eyes still glittered with a certain menace. Amy had hit a nerve. A woman had definitely wronged him at some time in his life. She pushed a little further.

'Tell me, Doctor. What darkness do I bleed?'

'I have already informed you. Disappointment.'

'No. I don't think so. There's more, Marcel, isn't there? You called me a demon earlier. Why was that?'

He inhaled sharply, his gaze flicking to her leg. 'I had consumed too much liquor. It was nothing but a mere fantasy.'

'*Au contraire.* I think you meant it. Now, if you won't offer me an explanation, then perhaps you can tell me why you refuse.'

He leaned in closer to her, and Amy lifted a brow. She didn't know why she felt so bold. This was madness. He could slice her open and leave her to bleed out all over the floor if he wanted to. And yet, she didn't seem to care. Deep down, she knew he wouldn't hurt her.

His lips parted, vanilla breath warming her face. Amy inclined her head even closer, staring at his mouth as if trying to read the words on his tongue. Everything else around them disappeared. Her attention hung on Marcel's lower lip and the slight glisten of his saliva as she waited with bated breath for him to form the words.

'Leave me, little demon.'

Marcel's eyes were the blackest she'd ever seen, full of malice. She blinked, and he was at the door. Head turned over his shoulder, he spoke again. His voice cracked, low and gritty. 'Leave me and never return.'

Amy gaped as he slammed the door behind him with such force it made her jump.

⸻ ❖ ⸻

It took Amy a few moments to realise she was standing in the empty room on the third floor of Marcel's house, staring at the door. It was closed. *Holy crap.* She touched her throbbing temple. The scarf she'd worn in her hair was tied around her head. Had she done that to herself, or had someone else?

Her eyes went back to the door. No way had she done that.

That door had definitely been open when she came in.

Chapter Twenty-Four

FLYNN THOUGHT ABOUT CALLING Amy all morning. He didn't like the way he'd left her last night. She seemed upset after he got called into work, but he couldn't figure out why and spent all night tossing and turning in his bed, thinking about it.

She was the one who said she couldn't do this. And then she went and invited him around for movies and popcorn? Okay, it probably wouldn't have been a big deal if she hadn't started the night off by flirting with him (the whole *licked-it-so-it's-mine* shit —did she have no clue what those kinds of words did to him?) only to go cold when he had to leave for work. Like he had a choice! He'd only worked two shifts so far. He couldn't turn anything down. God, women frustrated him.

When his phone began buzzing on the nightstand, he expected it to be Amy. But one glance at the screen had him groaning. Stacy. She'd wanted him to go with her to the markets in Fed Square today. He sat up and scrubbed his face. It was almost ten o'clock, and she was probably wondering where the fuck he was. Great, another woman he'd pissed off in less than twenty-four hours.

Yawning loudly, he hit accept on the video call and ran a hand through his dishevelled hair.

'Where are you?' She yelled through the noise.

Behind her on the stage, a band was playing a cover of Arctic Monkeys' *Do I Wanna Know*, and it sounded pretty good, making him wish he was there. He loved listening to live music. But that song. It always made him think of Amy.

Fuuuuuuuuuuuuuuuck... Now he truly couldn't get her out of his head.

'Still in bed.' He shrugged.

'You better not be. How quickly can you get here?'

'Probably half an hour. You still want me to come?'

'Yeah. Get your arse over here. I'll be waiting by the bridge, probably having eaten my bodyweight in curly fries and gelato by then.'

He grinned. 'Better leave some of that gelato for me, or there'll be trouble.'

'I'm not making any promises. Hustle.' She hung up.

He quickly showered, grabbed his skateboard, and headed for the train. While he waited for it to arrive, he pulled up Amy's number on his phone. Her smiling face and denim eyes watched him from the screen as her phone rang and went straight to voicemail.

'Hey,' he said to the recording. 'It's me. I hope you're okay. Call me if you want to.' Pause. 'Bye, Ames.'

It was a beautiful Spring day, not a cloud in sight. Heading down the steps at Flinders Station, Flynn crossed the road and headed straight for Princes Bridge. It was a popular meeting spot, but it didn't take him long to find Stacy with a bunch of organic re-usable shopping bags already at her feet.

'Where's my gelato?' He grinned, hugging her warmly.

'I ate it already. Do you want to get one? They're just over there.' She pointed randomly to the market stalls. Great directions, but fuck yeah, he wanted one.

He took a few steps, grinning. 'Do I need to drop breadcrumbs?'

'Hah! Seriously, though. Hurry, I want you to meet someone.'

Flynn laughed and dropped his board to the ground, slinging through the crowds until he found the gelato stand. He ordered a double scoop of salted caramel in a waffle cone and licked it all the way back to Stacy, who was chatting happily on her phone.

'You better pick up your board. There's security over there.'

'Sure.' He tucked it under his arm and tipped his chin at the guard, who was eyeing him from the perimeter of the square. 'Where're we off to?'

She gripped his elbow and picked up her bags. 'Just you wait and see.'

Pulling him back into the crowded markets again, Stacy weaved her way to a stall displaying some impressive street photography.

'Whoa,' Flynn breathed. The pictures were amazing. 'Dude, these are sick.'

'Thanks, man. You must be Flynn. My girl, Stace here, told me all about you.' Flynn raised his eyes from the photo to see a muscled guy with tattooed sleeves standing next to him, holding out his hand. 'I'm Jason.'

'Nice to meet you. Is this all your work?'

Jason scrubbed a hand over his shaved head and grinned. 'Yep. Every single one.'

'What do you think?' Stacy asked as she joined them, sliding her hand into Jason's back pocket.

Flynn gestured to a ground-level shot of a skater flipping an ollie mid-air. 'That's tight.'

'It sure is,' Stacy grinned as Flynn glimpsed her squeeze Jason's butt. 'But I was talking about you, not to you.'

'Huh?' Flynn turned to see Jason sizing him up.

'He's got potential.'

'Told you,' Stacy said, sending Flynn a cheeky wink. 'Jason needs a model for an upcoming portfolio, and I immediately thought of you.'

Flynn's gaze flicked uncertainly between Jason and Stacy. 'Um, thanks, I guess?'

Jason laughed. 'Relax, mate. It's all very chill. Stace tells me you do some manual work at the pub, shifting the kegs. Yeah?'

Flynn nodded. 'Yeah.'

'Perfect.' He stroked his sculpted beard and turned to Stacy. 'I'll clear it with Pat first, but I'd really love to get some shots of that. Black and white in high def would be so dope.'

'*So* dope.' She rolled her eyes, and they all laughed.

'Cheers, babe. I owe you.' Jason kissed Stacy on the lips while Flynn looked at his phone, giving them some privacy.

She grinned at them both. 'Exchange numbers, you two. I have stuff to do.'

They did, and Flynn left with Stacy, helping to carry her bags. 'Jason's cool,' he said as they reached her car. 'You look happy, Stace.'

She sent him that wide, dazzling smile. 'I am. He makes me so happy.'

'I'm glad. You deserve it, dog-breath.'

'But what about you? I know you're trying hard to look happy, but I don't think you are.'

'I'm doing okay,' he said, sliding into her passenger seat.

'*Okay* isn't exactly happy, though, is it?'

'It's not unhappy, either,' he retorted as she began driving to his place.

'Maybe you need to let loose a little. Have you got some mates you can hang with? Maybe invite them to the pub one night.'

He grunted. 'They're too busy with their girlfriends or studying for exams.'

'Just a thought. Think about it.' She turned up the radio, and they sang along for a bit until they reached his place.

'Thanks for the lift,' he said, reaching behind her seat for his board. As he did, she caught his face between her hands and stared at him with those piercing golden-green eyes. She reminded him of a snake, ready to strike.

'Flynn Powell, I'm going to tell you something. I won't seal this with a kiss because I have a hella-hot boyfriend, and I know you have a girl you're not telling me about, but always remember this. I care for you. Never doubt that even though I know you're strong. You've always been strong. You just need to find what makes you stronger.'

He swallowed, already knowing what that was, just not sure it was something he could have.

⋯⟡⋯

Flynn spent the next day at home studying. His mum came and went. They barely exchanged words, but she looked at him with more interest. Like she realised she actually had a son, not just a lodger. It was too late for any maternal feelings, and even though she said she'd given Mick the flick for good, he didn't believe her. He'd be back, just with another guy's face. There'd always be a Mick. His mum didn't know how to be alone.

That afternoon, he went to The Mission and helped Roger clean out the kitchen, ready for the rest of the week ahead. Amy would probably go to gym class tonight, but she still hadn't returned his call, so he was undecided about turning up. He still cared for her. Shit, he more than cared for her, but he didn't want to look like a lovesick puppy following her around.

He dipped the mop into the bucket of soapy water and sloshed around the storage room at the back of the kitchen. As he moved around the benches, thoughts of Amy imprinted the memory of that rainy afternoon on his brain. Fixing up her scraped hands, he'd almost kissed her.

But then she went and outright lied to him about having gone ghost-hunting. Even though she'd explained why she'd done it, it still hurt. And he was still letting it happen.

Even if she wasn't aware of it, Amy was still cutting him deeply by not trusting him to help her get through whatever she was struggling with. To be completely honest, he wouldn't have a clue where to start with improving her mental health. He'd hardly made the right choices himself, but the pain was something he understood only too well. And she had to be hurting. If only he knew what she was looking for, he'd try like hell to give it to her. Whatever the fuck it was, he'd do it. He just needed to get inside her head.

'Hey Flynn,' Roger popped his head through the door, 'could you run this plate up to Sonja, please? She's in her office on the second floor.'

'Yeah, sure. I'll just wash my hands first.'

Flynn took the food and stepped into the elevator. Sonja was one of the senior counsellors and the one who'd managed his program after the break and enter. He didn't see her much anymore, but he'd always enjoyed her company. She was easy-going but tough, and his favourite thing about her was that she dressed like a hipster, even though she was probably fifty.

She was on the phone when he knocked on her door, but her eyes lit up, and she eagerly gestured for him to sit. Putting the food down on her desk, he walked over to her therapy area and sat down on the cream fabric couch. He'd spent many hours in this corner of her office, and it still felt as relaxing as it did then. Sonja ended her call and rushed over to him, giving him a warm hug.

'Flynn! Look at you. Getting more handsome every time I see you.'

He rolled his eyes, gesturing to the split still visible on his cheek. 'I wouldn't say that.'

She frowned. 'Everything okay at home?' He nodded. 'How's school?'

He laughed. 'School's great. It's nearly over.'

'How are your grades going? I'm told you're still on track to graduate.'

Flynn had to grin at that. 'Good old Mr Jeffries keeping you updated, is he?'

Sonja turned crimson as she took a seat opposite. 'Well, he has a duty of care.'

Damn, it's like that, is it?

'Are you two...? Actually, don't answer that. I don't want that in my head. You look good, by the way.'

It wasn't a lie. With her denim vest, floral dress and Doc Martens, she looked exactly how he imagined Amy would in her older years. Except Amy didn't wear dresses.

Sonja threw a cushion at him. 'You always were a cheeky bugger.'

'Just trying my best.'

'Speaking of your best, have you given much thought to what you'll do after school?'

He ran a hand over his jaw. 'Not really. I've just landed a casual job working at a pub, so maybe I'll keep at that for a while.'

She eyed him thoughtfully for a few moments. 'You know, I think you'd make a pretty good social worker, Flynn. I've always thought that. You never acted like you were doing a public service from the day you first walked in here. It was as if you—'

'Felt right at home,' he interrupted. 'Yeah, I know.'

Frowning, he realised she was right. He enjoyed helping others, but was he a guy who had any right to give advice?

'I'm going to send some paperwork over to Matt. Have a chat with him, will you?'

He cocked a brow. 'Who's this Matt you speak of? He sounds almost normal, so it can't be Mr Jeffries.'

'Funny guy.' She grinned. 'Thanks for dinner, by the way. You staying to help Roger tonight?'

He usually did on a Monday night so that he could walk Amy home after her gym class. But now, he wasn't so sure. 'Maybe.'

Thinking hard about what she'd suggested, he asked for some advice. 'Hey Sonja, can you help me with something? I have a friend who I think might be... Fuck.'

He blew out a breath and scrubbed at his head. He didn't know how to describe Amy. 'She's totally obsessed with someone who's dead, but she's convinced they're not. It's like she's living in her head all the time. And I can't seem to reach her anymore.'

Sonja smiled tenderly. 'Is this friend grieving over a recent loss?'

'No, that's the point. That, I'd understand. But this? It's almost crazy. I'm not sure the dead guy even existed, but she's hell-bent on trying to prove that he did. To where she's no longer interested in anything else.'

'Would you say she has a pretty addictive personality? Like, does she normally get fixated on certain things she's passionate about?'

He gave her a half-smile. 'Oh yeah. She's passionate, all right. But I've always seen that as a good thing.'

'It is.' Sonja nodded. 'Her focus is likely a little misdirected right now, that's all, but it's definitely not a weakness. That sort of passion can be pretty powerful to observe. And if you're lucky enough to find yourself on the other side of it, you'll have a loyal partner for life.'

There was nothing he wanted more than to have Amy for the rest of his life, but right now, she was killing him. He looked at the floor, anguish twisting his insides.

'What if this friend is at risk of harming herself?'

'Do you think she'd be open to therapy?'

'Nope. She doesn't even think she has a problem.' He sighed. 'And to make things worse, she wants to deal with it all on her own because she thinks I don't believe her.'

'Do you?'

He chewed his lip and looked out the window. 'I don't believe in ghosts, no.'

'But do you believe she does?'

He turned back to her, confused. 'Are you saying I should encourage her?'

'Hell, no.' Sonja leaned forward and put her hand on his knee. 'You care for this girl, I can tell. What she needs more than anything right now is to know that you're there for her, Flynn. It doesn't matter if she believes in ghosts or unicorns that shit glitter. Whether you agree with her won't help, it's not the subject that's important here. It's that whatever she believes is important to you as well. That you validate her *feelings*.'

'How can I do that?'

She sat back and smiled. 'You be there for her. You don't belittle her beliefs, even when she's being fanciful. And if she's at risk of self-harm, you take away whatever she can use against herself.'

He nodded thoughtfully. That he could do. Hell, he'd done it already when she first spoke to him about seeing the ghost-girl. He'd told her he believed in her, and she'd been comfortable enough to confide in him. But then after that...

Flynn's body went rigid.

Because after that, he'd been so caught up in his own self-loathing that he'd left her with the lancet.

CHAPTER TWENTY-FIVE

F LYNN POUNDED ON AMY'S door.

Valerie Shipley met him dressed in a terry bathrobe in the vilest shade of pink and a towel wrapped around her head. Water trickled down the side of her face. He stepped back, embarrassed.

'Sorry to interrupt your shower, Val. Is Amy here?'

'No, love. She's studying with Leona.'

Bullshit. But he made a mental note to call Leona after he'd left and check.

'Oh, okay. Um, I think she might have something of mine. A little silver pocket knife. Have you seen it around, by any chance?'

'A pocket knife? Really, Flynn?'

He winced at her disappointment.

'No, I haven't. But you're welcome to look in her room. Just lock the door on your way out, hey?' She disappeared back into the bathroom.

Flynn raced to Amy's bedroom and had a quick look around. Her room was always neat, so it wasn't like he had to sift through piles of clothes and makeup on every surface. He felt like an absolute tool, but he even had a peek in all her drawers to see if she'd stashed the lancet in with her underwear or something.

Leaving empty-handed and frustrated, he called Leona. She confirmed Amy was at her place and wasn't going to the gym tonight because they had to wrap up their science project. He asked her to look out for Amy and make sure she got home. But Leona was super curt to the point of being downright rude. Obviously, she still hadn't gotten over him confronting her outside school the other day. The girl sure knew how to hold a grudge and was more than likely to put a curse on him if he enraged her any further.

But Flynn couldn't sit still after going back to The Mission and helping with the dinner queue. Thinking about Stacy's suggestion of a boys-night-out, he called Jimmy and Luka to see if they wanted to come out to the pub tomorrow night. They were graduating in a week, exams were in full swing, and it would be a good way to finish the study block. Luka wasn't legal drinking age yet, but he was close enough, and Flynn hoped Patrick wouldn't mind so long as none of them got shit-faced.

⚬✦⚬

The following afternoon, Flynn met Jason and Stacy in the car park behind the Terrace Hotel. Jason wanted to use the golden hour to take some outdoor shots of Flynn hefting some kegs with the sun lowering at his back. Stacy stayed to watch for a bit until her shift in the bottle shop started, and even Patrick stepped out too, joking about Flynn being his new calendar boy.

After a few takes wearing an open shirt and then a singlet, Jason had Flynn do a few shirtless ones. Even though the kegs weren't heavy when empty, it was enough to show the muscle Jason was keen on highlighting. Luka and Jim turned up, and even though they teased him mercilessly, Flynn was enjoying himself. It helped that Jason was super chill and had a dry sense of humour they all appreciated.

'That's it mate. Just prop it on your shoulder, like you're going all caveman,' Jason instructed.

'Shit, if Amy was built like that, I'd be letting her do the heavy lifting,' Luka quipped.

Flynn laughed out loud as he hefted the keg, hearing the shutter of Jason's camera firing on his every move.

'Yeah, little Flynny-boy always was a bit of a lightweight. Bet your mum misses me carrying her to bed like that.' A gruff laugh accompanied the crude statement, and all four of them turned to the source of the voice. Flynn gripped the edges of the keg till his knuckles turned white. *You've got to be fucking kidding me.*

Mick was standing at the edge of the car park, an ugly sneer across his sweaty face. 'Isn't that right, pretty boy? But not so pretty now, are you? Yeah, I split that cheek.'

'Can't believe you still want to go me.' Flynn put the keg down and flexed his fists. 'How are you breathing through that broken nose, old man? Careful, or I'll land a hit in your windpipe next.'

'Guess I'll have to use my ears to breathe then. Had plenty of practice between your mum's legs.'

Motherfucker. Flynn launched at Mick. He got a good swing in before Mick punched him in the ribs, and then two sets of powerful arms wrapped around him and pulled him back. Jason was standing in front of Mick, warning him to leave. But the prick was still mouthing off, so as soon as he shook Jim and Luka off, Flynn charged forward and aimed a kick under Mick's chin, cracking his head back and making him fall to his knees on the bitumen. 'That's from Mum.'

Jason ushered them inside and fetched Stacy, who cleaned up Flynn's scraped knuckles, and gave him a bag of ice for his ribs.

'Dude, you have some serious fighting skills,' Jim said, handing him a beer.

'Flynn always was up for a dogfight as a kid,' Stacy grinned.

Luka sidled up to her as she stood next to Jason, who was flicking through his camera roll. 'Tell us more. No one ever has dirt on this guy.'

'Not my stories to tell, I'm afraid.' She held up her hands, and Flynn sent her a look of silent thanks.

'You're no fun.' Luka got up just as Leona walked in. 'Oh look, my Uber's here,' he taunted. In true Leona-style, she walked right up to him and shoved her middle finger in his face before turning to glare at Stacy, her mouth hanging wide.

'You're her.' She pointed.

Stacy gave a mischievous grin. 'That depends. What've I done, first?'

Leona then told them all about the photo that Amy had seen, and Flynn sucked in an excruciating breath.

'So you two only work together, right?' she asked.

Stacy laughed. 'Afraid so. I mean, we are old friends who haven't seen each other for six years. But this fine hunk of male specimen right here is my partner.'

Leona looked at Jason, who was regarding Stacy with an amused grin. 'Yeah, I can see now why there's no competition.'

'Oh, nice!' Flynn hurled his bag of ice at her.

'How are the ribs?' Jason asked, getting up and coming over.

Flynn winked. 'I'll live.'

'Do you think you could sink a few balls at the pool table? I'd really like to finish with a couple of close-ups of those fingers.'

Stacy went back to work, and the rest of them shifted into the billiard-room. Jason ended up taking more than just a few photos of the boys playing. When he showed them to Flynn afterwards, his favourite was a front-on shot of his busted hand lining up the shot, while his still-blackened eye held focus near the felt.

Jason was explaining to him all about depth of field as Leona came around to listen in.

'You're pretty good,' she enthused.

'Thanks.'

'So, everyone—' Leona raised her voice, 'Here's the thing. I've decided we're all going to go into the CBD and get some pre-grad photos done in the graffiti laneways. You know, the six of us, all dressed up. I reckon it'd look swag against the grungy backdrop.'

'Swag? What are you, twelve?' Luka chuckled.

Leona tossed her hair. 'On a scale of one to ten, yes.'

Jason nodded. 'Actually, that's a really cool idea. Would you like me to be your official photographer?'

'He's quick, this one.' Leona jerked her thumb at Jason before turning her focus to the rest of them. 'As for you three, you better scrub up. Your girls have some amazing dresses. And you—' She pointed straight at Flynn, '—need to get off your arse and ask Amy properly.'

He frowned. 'Ask her what?'

'To be your date, you dick.'

He turned to Jim and Luka. 'I thought we were all going together. Why do I need to ask her?'

Jason chuckled. 'Oh man, you have a lot to learn.'

⁕

After Leona's constant digs about the grad dance, Flynn called Pierre. He realised he needed to get some dress pants and a nice shirt and damn if that Frenchman didn't have great style. They made a plan to meet up on Thursday when Flynn had a free study day to go shopping.

Frenchie ended up taking him to his personal tailor, which had Flynn freaking out as the guy measured him all over. Pierre laughed and told him to stop scowling, or he'd scare all the customers away.

'What style are you thinking of?' The tailor pointed to various posters around the store.

Flynn had absolutely no idea. He shrugged, turning to Pierre. 'What do you think Amy would like?'

'Forget about what she wants, mate. This is about you. What do you like?'

'The fuck does it matter? Like I'll ever wear this again.' He rolled his eyes. 'Help a dude out, Frenchie, come on.'

'What sort of shoes do you plan on wearing?' the tailor asked.

Flynn stared at the man like he was a complete moron and pointed to his scruffy black Vans. 'These.'

Frenchie tried to cover a grin. 'Fine, but let's get you some brand new ones.'

'Sure, so long as you're buying.' Flynn grinned back.

He ended up choosing a pair of slim-legged pants in a dark petrol-blue that (according to Frenchie) brought out the colour in his eyes, and a slim-fit white shirt with a full placket, which was just a fancy way of saying the buttons were covered by a panel of fabric. He didn't care either way, but Frenchie told him it was more versatile. Whatever. There was no way he was going to button it all the way to the collar, anyway.

Leaving the shirt partly undone, he put on his best puppy-dog face and snapped a selfie in the dressing room before adding the words "Be the Elle to my Noah?" hoping Amy would get the movie reference and fired it off to her.

⸎

Later that afternoon, Flynn called into the patisserie to take the leftover bread to The Mission. After sending her the proposal, he still hadn't heard from Amy, but he knew that she was in exams all day, but hoped to still catch her before gym class.

Frenchie caught him as he came through the door, ushering him through to the back. He held up a bag and handed it to Flynn. Inside was a new pair of light grey Vans.

'Really?' Flynn couldn't hide his astonishment. 'You know I was only kidding, right?'

Pierre grinned and slapped a hand on his shoulder. 'My treat.'

'But you already paid for the rest of the clothes. I can't let you do that.'

'Of course you can, son. And before you tell me I can't call you that, just let me say that I'm not trying to replace your father. Only that I care for you, and if I were blessed with the ability to be a dad, I'd be proud to have a son like you.'

'Fuck, Frenchie. That was deep.' Flynn stepped forward and enveloped Pierre in a man-hug. 'It's okay. You can call me *mon fils*, anytime.'

He slapped the Frenchman's back affectionately just as his phone pinged in his back pocket. Pulling it out, his heart sped up at the notification from Amy. *Please say yes. Please say yes.*

Inside the message was a photo of the front of the patisserie. He stared at it, confused until his phone pinged again with a message.

TURN AROUND!

Grinning like an idiot, he spun and looked through the front windows to see Amy leaning against the wall across the laneway.

Jogging outside, he slowed to weave around a few pedestrians. When he reached her, she was holding up his message on her phone.

'Noah Flynn, from *The Kissing Booth*. Could you get any more cliché?'

He didn't care if it was cliché, cheesy or contrite, because she was smiling, and that's all that mattered. 'So?' He risked tucking a stray curl behind her ear.

She let him, but her smile became less certain. 'You're not about to move halfway across the country for college, are you?'

He laughed. 'Definitely not.'

'Are you sure it's me you want to take?'

He looked down into those denim eyes, so unsure, and shifted his hand to hold her cheek. 'I'm sorry you had to see that photo without knowing the history behind it.'

'Leona told me you're old friends and that she's absolutely fucking gorgeous. Her words.'

Fucking Leona. 'I've wanted to tell you about Stacy for a while. We grew up in the same neighbourhood, and she works at the pub too, because Patrick has a thing for giving street kids second chances. I reckon that's the only reason he gave me the job, and I don't want to blow it, Ames. But I can tell you with absolute certainty that nothing is going on between her and me. Besides, she's like, nearly twenty-one. That's so old. Practically an adult, and fuck knows I don't want to grow up anytime soon.'

He offered her the grin that never failed to make her pupils dilate. 'I'm sure.' He watched her eyes widen as they traced his mouth.

'Well, in that case,' she rolled her eyes, suppressing a grin, and leaned into his palm as he cupped her other cheek, 'I never could resist a bad boy.'

'That's great to hear, because—' He leaned down to press his lips to hers '—there's no one in this world I want to be bad with more than you, Amy Rose Shipley.'

She pulled back, creating a space between them he wanted to be closed just as quickly. 'Walk me home tonight?'

'Always.'

They parted ways then, as Amy wanted to see her coach about something, and Flynn really needed to get to The Mission before the soup kitchen opened.

⟡

He met Amy after her gym class, as promised, with a cardboard tray of Pierre's rolled sweet crepes. Amy's eyes were on him from the moment he walked in, and it was tough not to sneak one when she turned her back. They smelled so good.

He watched her talk to her coach for a bit before she finally came through the gate towards him.

'How was class?'

'Tough. My leg has been stiff.'

'Still?' He frowned. It'd been almost a fortnight since she'd cut it on that damn rooftop sign at the Butcher's House. It should have healed well and truly by now. He hoped it wasn't infected. 'Want me to take a look?'

She shook her head. 'It's fine. I think I've just been favouring it a bit, you know?'

'As long as you're sure. You know I'll never knock back the chance to examine you.' He waggled his brows suggestively, and she punched him in the arm. 'Fine, no crepes for you.'

'What, there're crepes? Give me. Now!'

She made little grabby hands that almost had him tossing the tray to the ground and pinning her against the nearest wall. Crepes be damned. *He* wanted to be her food.

Instead, they shared Frenchie's delectably good dessert all the way to the train station while he told her about shopping for graduation clothes and trying to get her to tell him what her dress looked like, but she wouldn't spill. Not a single word. But she wrapped her hand in his as they walked through the park towards her apartment.

The closer they got to the swings, the slower their steps became. This time, Flynn sat on the swing beside Amy's, anchoring his feet to the ground and rocking back and forth lazily. He felt good again. More than good. He felt strong.

'I'd like to have a re-do,' Amy said suddenly.

He turned to her, confused.

'The last time we were here, like this? Everything went to shit.' She dropped her head and gazed at her lap. 'And the time before that, I should have told you something. Only I didn't get the chance to because it just didn't feel right and then I told you in a roundabout way but not how I really wanted to and I'm seriously rambling now so I should just shut up and say it.'

Flynn's mouth twitched. She was so adorable when she was flustered.

She took a deep breath.

Flynn was already holding his.

Chapter Twenty-Six

'I LOVE YOU.'

People always spoke about the gravity of those three little words, about how much weight they held. But now that Amy had spoken them out loud, she felt lighter than ever. As if helium filled her body, she grasped onto the chains of the swing to keep herself grounded.

Flynn's chest collapsed as he exhaled, relief writ large across his whole body. Silently, he reached and pulled her from the swing to sit on his lap. His arms came around her. Warm. Tight. She stared into those ocean eyes that made her want to drown willingly, and if she didn't hold on, they'd pull her under. She put a finger to his lips.

'Don't.' Her eyelids fluttered closed. 'Please don't say anything. You need to hear me out, first.'

She watched him nod slowly, pressing his lips against her finger in a gesture so intimate it made her want to cry.

'I don't want there to be any secrets between us. I'm sick of hiding. Of the lies I've told. Of the hurt I've caused.' She opened her eyes but kept them on her lap, where her fingers twisted together. Flynn pulled her closer to his chest, his heart thudding against her shoulder. 'I've been back to the Butcher's House. To see Marcel.' Flynn's body stiffened against her. 'Flynn—' She risked a glance at those eyes. In the light from the park lamps, all she saw was her own reflection. 'I'm going to give you a choice to walk away if you want to.'

He shook his head. 'Not happening.'

She took a breath and continued. 'I don't have all the answers to what I'm searching for yet. And until I do, I need to keep going back there. I know this sounds insane, but I don't believe he butchered those women. History has it wrong, or at the very least, the rumours are false. I've seen things, Flynn.' Her fingers found him and held on tight like he was the safety bar on a Ferris wheel, and she was at the very top in a stiff wind. She knew he would never let her fall, but it didn't make it any less scary. 'I've not only seen things. But I've heard them. Felt others. Things that I know seem unbelievable. Crazy, even.

'When I first went ghost-hunting with the others, I was sceptical. But when we failed to raise Elodie's spirit, I didn't feel relieved. I felt really sad, because that poor girl died alone, on the train tracks, and no one cares why. They don't care about the reasons that led her there. Whether she jumped or was pushed, they only care about her death. Elodie was a ghost before she even became one. Nobody sees her as an actual person, Flynn.

'So after I cut my leg in Marcel's house and saw that girl, and realised that somehow she could see me too, I knew I owed it to her to find out her truth. I know what it's like to be unseen. To be the new kid who arrives in the middle of the term, only to leave again before the year is out. To have your past made up before you even show up. Everyone thinks they've figured you out, but they don't know you for shit. And the worse thing is, they don't even care.' Flynn squeezed her tighter.

'Call me mad. But I can't let it go. Elodie's a lost cause, but Marcel and his sister Valentina—the girl I saw—need to have their story told. They deserve to be more than another urban myth told in locker rooms or at slumber parties. They were actual people with genuine histories, and I'm really close to finding out what those were.

'As for the cutting, I don't understand the logic behind it, but my blood is the key. It connects me to them. We can't see each other unless I'm bleeding. And I know I'm not explaining this very well, but I guess what I'm trying to tell you is that even though you think this might be all in my head, I will not let it go until I have all the answers. And I'm not expecting you to be okay with that. I just needed to tell you right now, in case I don't get the chance again. I love you, Flynn Powell. I love you so much.'

She held her breath. *Come on, Flynn. Say something.*

Keeping his dark gaze on hers, he unwrapped his arms from her waist, and, despite the balmy night air, Amy's body went cold. Whatever he was feeling, she'd have to accept it. She couldn't expect him to tag along while she rode the crazy train. Resigned, she turned away.

Suddenly, an arm slid around her back, another underneath her knees as Flynn stood up, cradling Amy honeymoon-style as he began walking towards her apartment.

'What are you doing?' she asked breathlessly when they reached her front door.

His face remained impassive. 'Key.'

'What?'

'Key.' He stared straight at the door. 'You'll have to unlock it. I have my hands full.'

She huffed out a short laugh and felt around in her backpack pocket for her house key. Once they were inside, Flynn carried her all the way through to her bedroom, where he kicked the door closed and shucked off his shoes. Then, sitting on her bed, he removed her sneakers and tugged the covers aside before sliding into her bed, still holding her spooned against his chest.

'Ask me again what I'm doing,' he whispered in her ear, sending both goosebumps and a flush of heat across the back of her neck.

'Just what the hell *are* you doing, Flynn? My mother will kill us both if she finds you in my bed.'

'I'm staying the whole night to prove to you I'm never going to let you go, no matter what. I promise you, I'm here for the long haul.' His lips pressed against her skin.

'But what if Mum finds out?'

'I'll take full responsibility. Besides, you're a risk worth taking.' He nibbled at her earlobe. 'That, and she's staying over at Frenchie's tonight.' She felt him smile into her nape.

The lightness in her chest returned. 'Never going to let me go, huh?'

His arms tightened around her. 'Nope.'

'What if I have to use the bathroom?'

'Then I'll have to come with you. Please tell me you have to take a shower.' He kissed her bare shoulder, and even though everything about him was lighting her on fire, the night's conversation had taken its toll, her body now weak, exhausted. She stifled a yawn.

Flynn snuggled into her back. 'Let's leave the shower till morning because I've always wanted to fall asleep with you in my arms.'

⸻❖⸻

Friday morning dawned clear and warm. It was the last official day of school, and graduation was just a weekend away. Amy had woken exactly how she'd fallen asleep—with Flynn's arms wrapped around her and him snoring softly.

Now he sat across the kitchen table from her, eating cereal and watching her from under dark hair, still wet from the shower they'd just shared. They had done nothing more than admire and explore each other's bodies, but the memory still brought a flush to her skin.

'Whatcha thinking?' Flynn grinned like he knew exactly what was going through her head.

Amy couldn't believe that this guy, who was not only awesome but had a scorching hot body (as she'd just found out), was really hers. 'That I am one very lucky girl.'

He threw a spoonful of cereal in his mouth. 'I wouldn't say that yet, but you will be soon. Trust me.' He followed that with a wink that had her biting her lip in anticipation.

'What a glorious morning!' A shadow fell across the front entrance as Amy's mum breezed through the open door. 'Honestly, could it get any better?'

Amy threw Flynn a quick smirk. 'You're home earlier than expected. Everything okay?' She busied herself putting the kettle on for coffee, so her mum wouldn't see the heat in her cheeks.

'More than okay, love. Pierre gave me the morning off.' Her mum hugged her, then turned to Flynn with a smile. 'What a pleasant surprise, Flynn. I wasn't expecting to see you here so early. It looks like both the Shipley women scored this morning.'

Flynn made a small choking sound and coughed into his bowl. 'I wanted to walk Amy to school for the last time,' he said, still clearing this throat. 'Since you don't live next door anymore, I thought it'd be kind of nice.'

'Aw, you're sweeter than my Nutella profiteroles.' She stepped over to him and ruffled his hair while mouthing at Amy to *marry this boy.*

Flynn held Amy's hand all the way to school and most of the day as well. They didn't have any regular classes, just lots of presentations on moving into the workforce and university life. They both had last-minute appointments with Mr Jeffries, and the guidance counsellor graciously allowed them to sit in on each other's session.

Amy had found that in the last two-and-a-half weeks, her interests had shifted considerably. Although her love of research had her previously applying for the History programs at all the major universities, she'd now discovered a new passion for mental illness and anthropology. So with Mr Jeffries' help, she put in a late application for Health Science as well. If she was successful, she'd be able to join the mid-year intake the following year. And he gave Flynn the approval on his request to be sponsored by The Mission to complete an online Counselling Diploma.

Amy squeezed his hand in excitement, but Flynn didn't hesitate to pull her in for a breath-taking kiss right in front of Mr Jeffries. Amy was sure her face had turned bright red, but Flynn only winked and said, 'Thanks, Matt. By the way, Sonja says hi.'

It wasn't until they'd walked out of the office that Amy confessed to Flynn that she was going to stop her regular gym class at the end of the term to take on a coaching role with the tiny tots over the summer break.

'So that's what you were talking to your coach about last night?'

'Yep. I've been thinking about it for a while now. The little kids seem to like me.' She shrugged.

'Of course they do. What's not to like?' He grinned. 'So will that mean I'll have to bring extra treats when I pick you up?'

She swatted his shoulder. 'Don't you dare! They'll end up liking you more than me.'

'So what do you want to do for the rest of the day? I have to work tonight, but I think the entire year level is heading to the arcade for pizza and ice cream. You know, living out the last hours of their youth like it's going to evaporate by Monday or something. They're mad.'

'Sounds like fun. But you have to promise me one thing,' she said.

Flynn rolled his eyes. 'Here we go. Don't start abusing your position already.'

'And what position would that be?'

'The one that says I'll do anything you want.'

'Well, in that case, you're playing Dance Rush with me.'

'What, you mean that motion game like the one in The Kissing Booth? Who's being clichéd now, huh?' She caught the grin he tried to suppress before agreeing. 'Fine.'

When Amy and Flynn walked into the arcade with their hands still interlaced, Leona jumped up and grabbed Amy around the waist, trying to spin her around.

'Oh, finally! We've been waiting all year for you two to get together, and you wait till the last fucking day. Unbelievable. But I'm still so excited for you both,' she squealed.

Amy laughed and squeezed into the booth beside Kenzie. She watched Flynn with open appreciation as he high-fived and fist-pumped the boys, who were still standing around the edge of the booth.

'You know that we've kissed before today, right?' she said, low enough for just the girls to hear, their mouths dropping open in a collective gasp.

'When? We need details. On the table, now.' Kenzie tapped a manicured fingernail on the laminate surface.

'The night we broke into the Butcher's House. When I cut my leg.' Amy could feel her cheeks heating under their combined gazes.

Leona's gaze sharpened. 'Let me guess, when he took you home?'

Amy nodded, biting her lip.

'Was it good?' Kenzie's eyes were shining, but they kept flicking to Luka.

'Have you seen that boy's lips? Of course it was good,' Leona gushed before whispering to Amy. 'It was good, right? Please tell me it was good.'

Amy giggled again, giddy with all the attention. 'Amazingly good.'

The three of them sat back against the booth and sighed.

'So what happened between then and now, Ames?' Kenzie asked.

Leona smacked her bare arm. 'Shut up, bitch. It's not your business.'

'It's okay,' Amy said, sighing. 'It's been complicated, that's all.'

'That fucking photo.' Leona leaned in and put her arm around Amy.

She laughed. 'I'm fine. We're fine. More than fine,' she added with a glance at Flynn. He sent her that lopsided grin, and she flushed all over.

When he took her hand and led her to the Dance Rush platform later on, she almost combusted on the spot. She already knew he was an excellent dancer, but he also had great coordination and some seriously impressive footwork. He shrugged when she complimented him, citing that 'Skateboarders are totally underestimated.'

They played another couple of rounds, and then he needed to leave for work. Walking him outside, Flynn pressed her against the wall by the door and kissed her so deep she felt it all the way to her toes.

'I don't want to go,' he breathed, resting his chin on her head. 'I feel like I'm breaking my promise to you already.'

'You might not have your arms around me, but you still have me wrapped up tight. Right here.' Amy pointed to her heart.

'That's for sure.' He kissed her again. 'I'll call you later. Have fun.'

'Oh, she will,' Leona taunted from the open doorway. 'Come on, girlfriend. We're going up against Kenz and Luka in laser tag.' Leona linked her arm through Amy's and pulled her back inside.

'What colour team are we on?'

'Red, of course. We're gonna give those fuckers a bloodbath.'

Chapter Twenty-Seven

FLYNN SPENT ALMOST THE entire weekend at Amy's place, except for the eighties prom-com movie marathon held at Luka's on the day before graduation. There was only so much pink and douchebag heroes that a guy could handle before he slipped out to use the bathroom, joining Jimmy and Luka at the pool table.

'So, who's looking forward to tomorrow?' Jimmy asked as he set up the triangle and shook a bottle of numbers for their game of Kelly pool.

Flynn pushed the little ball etched with his secret number (10) into his pocket and grinned. For ten months, he'd been secretly in love with Amy. 'I'm just so fucking glad it's over.' There was double irony in that statement.

'You're shitting me, right?' Luka struck the white to start the game. 'You haven't even put in the minimum attendance all year.'

Flynn watched the balls roll around the table, not needing to look for the numbers to know which ball was his. He knew the colour off by heart. Denim blue, just like Amy's eyes. 'You seem to forget that I repeated Year Ten, so technically, I've put in more than my fair share already, thanks.'

'Oh shit, dude. I forgot about that.' Jimmy laughed, slapping him on the back as he passed. 'No wonder you can't wait for tomorrow.'

'Nah, he's just hanging out to see Amy in a dress, aren't you, mate?' Luka pocketed Jim's ball, making him curse out loud. Flynn bit down on a smile. He was looking forward to this stupid dance more than he wanted to admit. And it didn't matter to him what Amy's dress looked like—the girl could make a hospital gown look beautiful.

'You're so full of shit, Luka. You're the one who's been stressing all week about matching Kenzie.'

'Dude, you *know* Leona will rip us a new set of balls if we ruin her precious photo shoot.'

'True.' Flynn winked at Jim and laughed. He knew the big guy was totally shit-scared of Leona. He'd seen feral cats with less fight in them than her, but Flynn knew she wouldn't dare boss them around tomorrow. Besides, with Jason's skill as a black and white photographer, it wouldn't matter what colours they wore.

⋯⟡⋯

Before the group session, Flynn met Amy in the park near her apartment for their own private photoshoot. Jason was keen to do some outdoor portraits, and Flynn wanted Amy to meet Stacy away from the prying attention of the other girls.

He sat on the swings, chatting with her for a bit while Jason fiddled with his camera settings. Even though his new clothes were comfortable, he felt strangely stiff, and it took a moment to realise he was actually nervous. The grad dance wasn't a big deal, and neither he nor Amy put much weight on the actual occasion. It was more that this marked the beginning of fresh territory for him. With his life, his future career, and with Amy. He was desperate to protect it with everything he had.

Stacy's head lifted, and she tilted it toward Amy's estate as two figures began walking toward them. Valerie and Frenchie. But where was Amy? Panicked, Flynn stood. She was trailing behind them, shielded from view. He glimpsed golden curls piled high on her head and white lace, but that was all. His heart began thudding, and he smoothed his hands down the front of his pants.

Calm the fuck down. This isn't your wedding day.

Valerie and Frenchie parted, and his heart literally slowed down. Everything did. The birdsong disappeared, the wind in the trees died, and time seemed to hold still as the girl of his dreams walked towards him. *Holy shit.* Beautiful wasn't a strong enough word.

She lifted her eyes to meet his, her cheeks lightly flushing the same shade as the skirt of her dress. His gaze ran the length of it, making him long to bury his head in all those soft folds and forget about the damn graduation.

'Amazing Ames.' He pulled her to him and leant down to kiss her glossed lips.

'Don't you dare!' Stacy yelled. 'You'll ruin her makeup.'

He growled at her to get fucked, and bent his head to Amy's, sinking into the sweetest kiss he'd ever tasted. 'What is that?' He licked his lips and went back for more.

Amy giggled. 'Salted caramel.'

'You realise I'm going to be eating that off you all night.'

She bit her luscious lower lip. 'That's okay. I have plenty more.' Her hand disappeared within the layers of her dress before it reappeared, clutching a little silver tube.

He cocked a brow. 'Where did you pull that from?'

Jason guffawed loudly, and Stacy slapped his arm. 'Her pocket, dipshit. I'm Stacy, by the way. It's so good to meet you finally,' she said, hugging Amy, before throwing Flynn a mocking glare. 'Why didn't you tell us she was so gorgeous?'

'A guy's gotta keep some things just for himself.' He smiled, his heart warming as Amy and Stacy giggled together.

Jason, who had been candidly snapping shots the entire time, piped up. 'Well, you're a good-looking couple, that's for sure. So, how about we get these photos done so that you can relax for a bit.'

Wanting to keep the child-like memories alive, he had them pose on the swings, with Amy sitting on Flynn's lap. It was while he held her close that Flynn realised she wasn't actually wearing a dress as he'd initially thought, but a top and skirt. He groaned as his hands brushed against her warm, bare skin.

'How am I supposed to keep my hands off you now?'

She giggled and whispered close to his ear. 'What if I don't want you to take them off me?'

'Then I'm taking you inside right now, and everyone else can go to hell,' he replied in kind.

'Okay,' Jason interrupted. 'Just one more guys, with Amy sitting on the swing and you standing behind her.'

Amy shifted off Flynn's lap, but he pulled her back down, addressing Jason. 'I can't right now, dude. I'm going to need a minute. Know what I'm saying?'

Jason smirked. 'Look over there. It might help.'

Flynn swung his head around to catch Frenchie and Valerie smooching near the trees. *Jesus.* 'Yep, that's better than a cold shower. I'm good.'

Jason and Stacy drove them into the city, where they met up with the rest of the gang. The plan was to do the photoshoot and then train it into school to meet their parents, ready for graduation.

They had loads of fun in the graffitied laneways, and the girls adored Jason. Flynn could see why Stacy was so enamoured with him. Clutching Amy's hand a little tighter, he pressed a tender kiss to her forehead and murmured, 'There's something I want to tell you before the night's over.'

She looked up at him, those denim blue eyes sparkling with happiness. 'What's that?'

'You'll have to wait. The time's not right yet.'

She pouted, and he swooped onto those lips, unable to resist.

'Hey Jase, what about that little lane off Collins with the Italian joint in it? You know the one with the fairy lights overhead?' Stacy suggested, with a quick raise of her brows to Flynn. Jason nodded and led them through the city streets, attracting much attention with their formal wear and loud antics.

After heading up from the Flinders Lane end, they congregated near the top of Collins, where the taller buildings gave the appearance of dusk, even though the sun was still setting. Jason was practically lying on the ground, taking photos of each couple hugging with the lights and twilight sky overhead.

'This is so magical.' Amy wrapped her arms around Flynn's neck and looked skyward. 'I am so happy right now.'

'Oh, Ames, I know something else that will make you happy.' Jimmy grinned at them. 'I almost forgot to tell you. They've started work on the Butcher's House. Lee and I saw it on our way here.'

Flynn felt Amy tense in his arms. 'What, already?'

'Yeah. Scaffolding's up and everything. I hear they're going to turn it into a hotel. You guys should spend the night there, sometime.' Jim winked. He actually fucking winked.

Flynn's arms tightened around Amy's waist as he felt her flight response kick in. She tilted her face up to his, pleading. No way. This wasn't happening on his watch. He shook his head.

'Please, Flynn,' she whispered. 'I have to.'

'Not right now, you don't. It's graduation.'

'Don't you see? If I can't get in there before they rip walls out or whatever, I'll never know! And I have to know, Flynn. I have to. I'm sorry.' Her voice broke on a sob.

Not tonight. He had this all planned. 'Amy, this is utter—'

'What, madness? Is that what you were going to say?' She put her hands on his chest and pushed herself from him, taking a step back. 'Do you really think I'm mad?'

'No, baby. You know I don't think that. I'm just worried about you.'

'What's that supposed to mean?'

'Flynn.' Luka's voice was cautionary, but Flynn ignored him.

'You're deliberately hurting yourself. I've seen the cuts on your hand, Amy. Do you think I don't recognise self-harm when I see it? You think I don't know what to look for?'

Luka grabbed his arm. 'Flynn.'

He shoved his mate back, pulling his arm free. 'Stay the fuck out of this, Luka.' He was almost yelling now, and Amy put a hand to her mouth, shocked. 'This isn't how I wanted to say this tonight... but I love you. So fucking much, Ames. I don't think you realise just how much.' He took a step toward her, his voice scraping inside his throat. 'Do you hear me? I fucking love you, and I will not sit back and watch you destroy yourself.' He stepped closer again, ready to get down on his knees and beg her to stay if he had to.

Amy looked from him to everyone else. He knew they were all congregated behind him in uncomfortable silence. Fucking hell, this night had gone to shit. He'd planned to confess to Amy under the fairy lights. He and Stacy had coordinated the whole thing. It was going to be perfect. If only Jimmy hadn't opened his fucking mouth. *Fucking Jimmy.*

'You!' In under a second, he was up in his friend's face. 'This is all your fucking fault.'

'C'mon, man.' Jimmy stepped back, putting his hands up.

Flynn shoved his sleeves roughly to the elbow. 'You still can't learn to keep your mouth shut, can you, Jim?' He rounded on him, throwing his fist inches from Jimmy's face, and holding. His whole body shook. Fuck. He was turning into everything he hated.

'Fellas,' Jason warned, launching forward and grabbing Flynn's forearm just as Stacy called out.

Flynn turned in time to see Amy disappearing down the laneway towards Flinders Lane.

'Fuck!' He wrenched out of Jason's grip and propelled himself after her.

Dodging and weaving through pedestrians, he gave up and began tearing down the road instead. The cars were easier to miss. And who the fuck knew girls could run so fast in heels? Amy was already a full block ahead of him, running against the traffic, and despite everything, he felt a twinge of pride knowing she'd also had the same thought to abandon the footpath.

Another block and a half, and he was there—the Butcher's House.

Jimmy wasn't wrong. Scaffolding covered the entire building, masking that cream façade, so he'd almost sprinted past it. And crawling up the steel fretwork like a bloody spider, was Amy.

Fuck me. His visceral need to go after her was like a living thing, clawing its way through his limbs, but Flynn's feet remained rooted to the ground in fear.

'Amy!'

She paused and looked down at him, her skirt bunched up around her waist like a ballerina's tutu. He watched helplessly as she hauled herself up another rung and shuffled sideways to the boarded-up window on the third floor. Adrenaline made him antsy, and he jumped from foot to foot like a boxer, weighing up his options.

Luka had told him that Amy once got in over the iron fence. Peering through the safety netting, he could see the glass courtyard door beyond, just like he had that night they broke in. That had only been a fortnight ago. Jesus, it felt like a lifetime.

A splintering crack sounded overhead as Amy kicked at the board covering the open window. Another crack rang out, and Amy disappeared through the hole in a tangle of legs and blush fabric. Flynn braced his arms on the scaffold and pulled himself up the nine feet to reach the top of the iron fence. Then, standing on top of the spikes in his new Vans, he launched off, landing on the tiles below.

He braced his knees like he'd done from the half-pipe so many times before and pushed to his feet to propel himself at the door.

But the handle remained steadfast, his shoulder slamming into the glass. 'Fuck!'

He rattled the handle. Locked. There was no time to think about picking it open or anything else, except getting to Amy. With no regard for what he was about to do, Flynn swung his elbow back and smashed it hard against the glass, shattering a hole large enough to slip his arm through and unlock the door. From somewhere inside, an alarm sounded, but he didn't give two fucks.

'Amy! Amy!' His voice was desperate. A stranger to his own ears. Searching through each room, he found her on the third floor, in a large room near the stairs that led to the roof. He remembered hardly anything from the last time he was there, but he'd thought the door to that room was locked.

'Flynn.'

She stood near the window that faced the alley. Her skirt was still puffed out around her thighs, and a few curls of hair had come down around her face. Despite the manic gleam in her eye, she looked beautiful. And eerily calm.

He knew he wouldn't win this fight. Defeated, he asked, 'What do you want me to do, Ames?'

'Believe me.'

His breath was loud and erratic. 'I believe you.'

She smiled sadly. 'No, you don't.'

'Yes, I do.' He took a few steps determinedly towards her. 'I love you. So, I'm going to ask you again. What do you want me to do?'

Her head bent to the floor, and she winced. 'Will you hold me while I bleed?'

'I won't watch you cut yourself. Ames, I can't do that. Fuck, anything but that.' Tears pricked his eyes.

'Even though you've seen it all before? Twenty-seven times. You know, I never could quite understand the compulsion. But I think I do now.' She tilted her head to the side.

He followed her gaze as it slid to the pocket that concealed her right hand. A red stain was already spreading through her skirt as he crossed the space between them. She withdrew her hand to reveal the lancet clutched in her palm. The blade had pierced the inside of her wrist.

No!

'I'm sorry, Flynn. It's too late.'

She fell into his arms as he sank to his knees on the floor, his anguished roar loud enough to wake the dead.

Chapter Twenty-Eight

AMY BLINKED SLOWLY. HER vision blurred, then pulsed. The wooden floor was hard beneath her, and someone wailed nearby. Loudly.

Instinctively, she put her hands to her mouth in case it was her.

It wasn't.

Then she smelled the blood. Cold and metallic, it invaded every inhalation until it was all she could think about. Fear gripped her. Was she hurt?

Crap, how badly had she cut herself? Could she actually be dead?

No, her head throbbed too much, and she was pretty sure that death wasn't supposed to be painful.

Movement from the corner of her eye made her twist around. Through her hazy vision, she made out three figures. One of which was firing a rapid volley of French and pacing in front of the arched window. *Valentina.* The other two were on the floor, like her.

Taking deep breaths through her mouth, Amy pushed herself up and crawled shakily towards them. Marcel was on his knees, hands clutched to his head. The horrible sounds were coming from him.

Reluctantly, her eyes shifted to the other figure lying prone on the floor. A young woman. In a pool of blood. Amy tasted bile as her vision snapped into vivid focus.

Holy fucking hell.

She tore her eyes away and took a long, proper look at Marcel. He was rocking back and forth, eyes closed, shirtless—his lily-white skin covered in blood. Whether it was the woman's or his own, she couldn't tell.

'What have you done?' she whispered.

The only sound came from the dead woman. Wet, sucking sounds crawled around Amy's head and down her spine. But she had to be dead. There was no way this woman could still be alive. There was far too much blood. Valentina was hauling her up and into the crude wheelchair. *Oh, God.*

This was real. And it was happening right in front of her. This was what she'd wanted all along—to find out the truth. But now that she was face to face with it, Amy wasn't so sure she wanted to.

Valentina pushed the slumped woman towards the elevator shaft with an ease that suggested she'd done this more than once. Her movements were precise, ordered, *practiced.*

Amy wanted to help her, to find out exactly what happened to the women who bled out, but the chance to be alone with Marcel was too important to lose. There were too many unanswered questions. Plus, she was so lightheaded, she couldn't move. When Valentina and her pitiful cargo were out of sight, Amy returned her attention to Marcel.

He lay face-down in the pool of blood as if emerging from it. Her stomach lurched. Each time he tried to push himself up, he slipped back down into it.

'Help me.' He stretched a red dripping hand towards her. She looked away, not knowing whether to scream or be sick. 'Devil, please!'

Amy dragged her gaze back to him. Jesus, what if some of that blood is his? He was visibly shaking. Whether from shock or anger, she couldn't tell, but did it really matter? She couldn't leave him there like that, wallowing in his own despair. And she needed answers.

Dragging herself slowly to her feet, she shuffled around the entire level, looking for the bathroom. When she couldn't find one, logic drove her down to the floor below. Nestled behind the bedrooms was a narrow door. Pushing it open with great trepidation, Amy nearly wept to find a small claw-footed iron tub. She immediately wrenched on the taps. The dull clanging of pipes in the wall told her at least there was water flowing, and not knowing how long it would take to come through, she went back to fetch Marcel.

She found him halfway to the door, having pulled himself along the floor, leaving a large streak of congealing blood in his wake. The smell was overpowering, and Amy held her breath as she planted her feet on either side of him and cupped her hands under his armpits, trying desperately to get him to stand. He was heavier than he looked.

'Ma petit démon, what are you doing?' he smirked as she moved to the front of him and pushed at his chest to roll him over. Then, cross-bracing one arm over the other, she grasped both his hands and pulled him up to a sitting position.

'Get up!' she yelled in a mix of frustration and fear.

He grinned at her, his mouth wet and bloodied. 'Have you come for me, Devil?'

'I'm not the Devil, Marcel.' She kicked at his boot. 'Move.'

He laughed as if drunk. 'Only the Devil can help me now.' A sneer replaced the smile, and then, nothing. His face became completely blank and grey as stone. He was going into shock.

Fine. If he believed only the Devil could move him, then the Devil she would become. Kicking his boot as hard as she could, she put her face inches from his, narrowed her eyes and told him to get the fuck up.

If he could go even paler, he did. His pupils constricted, his eyes becoming dull, like silver coins. It was unsettling to watch, and Amy trained her focus on his scarred forearms instead as she helped him to stand.

What darkness do you conceal, Marcel?

No matter how desperately she wanted to know, her questions would need to wait until she could thaw him out a bit. Wrapping one of his arms around her shoulders, they shuffled toward the stairwell. Even though she'd seen Valentina use the elevator, Amy didn't trust it. Shoving open the door with her shoulder, she and Marcel stumbled down the stairs to the floor below.

The bathwater was running hot when they reached the tub, so she dropped in the plug and adjusted the temperature until tepid. As much as Marcel needed warming up, she didn't want to scald him or have him pass out on her and drown. While they waited for the bath to fill, she pulled off his boots, trying to chafe warmth into his cold and bloodless feet. Her eyes took in the whiteness of his skin, accentuated by the fine black hairs dusting the tops of his toes. It all seemed suddenly too intimate.

Jumping to her feet, she directed him to sit in the water, pants and all. The water immediately turned pink, and by the time the bath was full, it was distinctly red. The entire room was thick with the coppery scent of blood; Amy could feel it flowing down her throat, choking her.

Marcel sat with his head bent forward, resting on his knees. He was clearly too big for the tub and appeared childlike inside it. Amy dipped her hand under the water and lifted each of his arms, inspecting them for any bleeding cuts. She found none, meaning all the blood had belonged to that poor woman.

Marcel looked at her with something like fear in his eyes. 'Why have you come for me, Devil?'

'Marcel, I told you I'm not the Devil. *Je suis ton ami.* I am your friend.'

'*Non, vous êtes un diable,*' he whispered. 'You must be a demon, dressed as an angel. How else could you appear and disappear? Clearly, you are here to torment me. Did Maman send you? I always knew the Devil would bleed me in the next world.'

Maman? He wanted to know if his mother had sent her? Amy's head reeled. Had his mother been the one to hurt him? And if so, what the hell had she done?

'I'm not here to bleed you, Marcel.' She showed him her wrist, still pulsing blood from the lancet's puncture wound. 'See? I only do it to myself.'

He visibly flinched. 'You're just like her.'

'Your mother?' She took his hand, running her fingers up his forearm. Tracing his scars, as she did with Flynn, she hoped it would get him to talk. 'What did she do to you?' Her eyes softened as they bored into his. 'Maman. Did she do this? Did she cut you?'

He shook his head. 'Non. That was my doing. She... cut herself.' He hung his head, running his free hand through his hair in a way that reminded her of Flynn. Tears pricked her eyes. Both of them were so damaged. So broken. It was beyond unfair. At least she and Flynn had each other, but who did Marcel have? A fourteen-year-old sister who was already so desensitized to pain that she could clean up a homicide without blinking an eye.

She clutched his hand tighter. Brought it to her lips and pressed them to the blue veins that so prominently ran across the inside of his wrist. He watched every move she made. 'So she was like us?'

'I don't understand.'

'She bled herself to achieve a higher purpose. Like I bleed to come to you and Valentina.' She pulled his forearm closer, scrutinising those crisscrossed white raised lines. Just like with Flynn, she realised they were tallies. 'And I think you bleed to make amends. To make yourself suffer for having wronged your own expectations.'

He wrenched his arm away. 'She did no such thing!'

'Then what did she do, Marcel? Tell me what she did to you. You'll never be free of her demons if you keep them locked up inside your head.'

He glared at her, the colour finally returning to his face. 'She did nothing to me. It was Valentina who she wronged. Valentina, who was just a child, and blamed for Maman's weak disposition. Valentina, who witnessed Maman bleed herself.'

This time, Marcel grabbed Amy. His fingers dug into the skin around the wound on her wrist, making the blood spill faster down her arm. 'Can you believe it? She intentionally expired in front of her child!'

Oh hell. Marcel's mother had slit her wrists in front of her daughter.

No wonder Valentina was so detached.

And Marcel? He was carrying the weight of his mother's mental illness, seeking redemption by bleeding out the madness in a bevy of misinformed and unsuspecting women. As if by saving them, he was saving his Maman, time and time again. Absolving himself of some self-imposed guilt. He wasn't just a quack or a charlatan. He was a broken young man parading as a doctor. And that made him very dangerous.

'Oh, Marcel.'

Amy's head spun to the doorway, where Valentina stood just inside the bathroom, her gaze running over her brother. He hung his head again as if ashamed. Amy looked between them. Just who was looking after who, here? Valentina was definitely the stronger of the two siblings. Given what had happened to her, Amy was understanding why. And why Marcel was so lost. He was just as wounded by his mother's death, and yet they were both trying to make amends in their own distorted ways.

'What happened here today?' She asked Valentina.

The girl lifted her shoulders sadly. She looked impossibly small. 'An accident.'

This was no accident. This was insane. All so bloody insane. 'How can you call a woman bleeding to death in front of you an accident?'

She hadn't realised she'd said it out loud until Marcel turned in the bath to face her. 'Sometimes, the patients bleed more than they should. It was quick.'

'Define quick.'

'Less than five minutes.' This came from Valentina. 'Marcel is not to blame.'

'Why are you protecting him?' Amy turned back to Marcel as the full extent of what happened hit her. 'How is this not your fault? You pretended to be a doctor. She trusted you to help her. But you couldn't fix her.' Her vision swam. 'You didn't help her. *You murdered her.*'

'She may be dead, but she escaped the voices, the visions. The pain. The torment. The—'

'Madness.' The word spilled from Amy's lips and hung in the air between them.

⸺◈◈⸺

Amy sank slowly onto the tile, resting her head on the edge of the bath. Marcel genuinely cared about the women he bled. They, too, were damaged and trying to escape their own horrors. She looked at her wrist. What had she done to herself? Blood drenched her graduation outfit. She wasn't any better than those women. Than Marcel. Or Flynn. And Valentina? She was only protecting her brother. Amy knew she'd do the same for Flynn. Were they really all that different underneath?

Marcel laid a tender hand on her cheek. It was cold. No, she was the cold one. Freezing. He pulled her into the bath with him. Pushed her down. Water filled her ears and stung her nose. Bubbles streamed from her mouth.

Under the surface, the bloodied water didn't cloud her vision. She could see Marcel clearly, tears on his cheeks, as he held her down. Amy was crying too, but lost her tears in the water that surrounded her.

God, she was tired. So, so tired. Relaxing into his embrace, she closed her eyes.

Until Marcel pulled her up and grasped her to his bare chest, his mouth on hers—

—and her lungs opened.

CHAPTER TWENTY-NINE

AMY WOKE WITH A gasp.

Flynn sat by her side, dark blue eyes shining with relief. He cupped her left hand in both of his and squeezed gently. 'Hey.' His voice shook.

She gripped his fingers, pulling him towards her, only to realise she had something stuck in the back of her hand: an IV cannula. Deliberately, her eyes followed the length of tubing to a half-deflated bag of yellowish liquid hanging on a metal stand next to her bed. She was in a hospital. Panic flared in her chest.

Flynn pulled her chin towards him and brought his lips to hers.

'You're okay, Ames.' He sat back down and pointed to the IV bag. 'It's only plasma.'

He smiled weakly as a nurse in dark blue scrubs materialised over his shoulder.

'Sleeping Beauty awakes at last! That must have been some kiss.' She winked at Flynn, who reddened.

Amy tried to speak but had trouble forming the words. Her mouth was so dry. Flynn poured her a cup of water from a plastic jug and held it to her lips. She could only manage a few sips, but it helped to ease the aching in her throat.

'How are you feeling?' the nurse asked with a warm smile.

Amy tried to swallow down the sob and apology that threatened to choke her. 'Tired,' her voice croaked. Single words were her limit.

'That's not surprising. You've lost a lot of blood, young lady.'

Amy's eyes flicked from the nurse back to Flynn. He was watching her carefully.

'Now that you're awake, can you tell me your full name and date of birth?' As Amy answered, the nurse reached under the blankets and carefully pulled her right hand out. It was bandaged at the wrist. The nurse checked her patient ID bracelet, then tucked it away from view again, patting her forearm. 'I'll be back again in fifteen.' As she reached the end of the bed, she turned around to address Flynn. 'Now, no more raising her heart rate, Prince Charming.'

Amy blinked away tears. The boy sitting by her side really was her Prince Charming. Not only had he woken her with a kiss, but he'd also saved her life. She closed her eyes at the irony of the fairy tale. *A sleeping spell induced by the pricking of her finger.* How blind she'd been. She'd also been living in a dream for far too long. It was time to wake up and start living. A kingdom with her prince awaited.

With clarity she hadn't possessed in weeks, Amy realised it no longer mattered if Marcel's legend was real or not. As awful as his truth was, there was nothing she could've done to prevent it. And in doing so, she'd almost lost Flynn. Had almost lost *herself.*

She squeezed Flynn's hand and looked at him properly for the first time since she'd woken up. His shirt was blood-streaked and completely ripped open down the front. Her cheeks warmed at the sight of his bare chest.

'You checking me out?' He smirked, making her cheeks flame harder.

'What happened to your shirt?'

'You don't remember?' His voice was gentle but hurt burned in his eyes.

She smiled. 'I remember you saying that you loved me.'

He smiled back. Not his usual lopsided grin, but one that was a little wobbly around the edges.

'I remember everything up until this.' She held up her bandaged wrist. 'I'm sorry that I ran from you.' More tears welled, and she tried to blink them back. 'That I ran to him.'

Flynn's smile disappeared. He swallowed and moved his chair closer. Leaning his elbows on the bed, he brought her fingers to his lips. 'I thought I was going to lose you.'

She ran her other hand through his hair while he spoke.

'There was so much blood, Ames. This is nothing.' He gestured to his ruined shirtfront. 'Guess these shirts really are more versatile because I had to cut a strip off with that *fucking blade* to bind your wrist. Luka called Frenchie, and I did nothing but hold you till he came. It was like you'd fallen asleep.' He let go of her hand. Wrapping his arms around her, he rested his head on her chest. 'But you were so cold. And I was so scared you wouldn't wake up.'

Her hospital gown grew damp and she realised he was crying, too.

They stayed like that, wrapped up in each other until the nurse returned. Two other sets of footsteps followed her into the room.

'Is she still asleep?'

Amy turned her face toward the familiar sound of her mother's voice.

'Oh, my baby girl!' Her mum immediately enveloped her in a massive hug. 'We just ducked home to pick you up some clothes.'

Pierre stood back, hands in his pockets, and Amy smiled at him over her mum's shoulder. 'Merci,' she whispered.

'It's not me you should be thanking, cherie.' He strode over to Flynn and placed a hand on his shoulder.

The nurse grinned. 'That boy hasn't left your side all night, you know.' She checked the flow rate on the IV and typed something into the tablet she was carrying. 'Now, someone from mental health will come around to talk to you shortly. They'll assess your risk, and if you're cleared for release and all the paperwork is complete, you can get dressed and go home.'

Amy watched her mum thank the nurse and ask about when to have the stitches removed. But she was only half-listening because the crazy train had stopped and was backing up fast.

Mental health? Assessed for risk? Cleared for release?

Amy squeezed her eyes shut. 'I'm on suicide watch?'

'It's just a precaution,' Pierre assured her.

This couldn't be happening. 'But can't they see I wasn't trying to take my own life?' It was obvious, surely. Did they think she was that unstable?

Her mind went into reverse hyper-speed, spinning through memories from the last two weeks.

The first time Valentina made contact with her, Amy had collapsed against Luka as Flynn bound the wound in her leg.

Mate, I think she's going into shock.

Every other time when she'd cut herself, she was alone and had woken dizzy and disoriented. Except for tonight. Tonight, Flynn had been with her the entire time.

It was like you'd fallen asleep.

The nurse left to speak to someone just outside the room and Amy overheard her explaining that she'd been falling in and out of consciousness ever since presenting at the emergency department a few hours ago. Could she really have been passing out from shock or blood loss each time? Amy swallowed. She hadn't imagined Marcel, surely.

No. It wasn't all in her head. *He wasn't.*

'Hello, Amy.' A young woman's voice stirred her back to the present, the sounds of the busy ER suddenly loud in her ears. 'We're from the Mental Health department. The clinician will need to give you an assessment so that we can get you out of here and on the path to recovery. Are you happy for your friend and family to step out for a bit while we have a chat?'

Amy's mum nodded, giving her a kiss on the forehead. She joined Pierre at the foot of the bed, clutching him as they left the room.

'I suspect Pierre's already filled her in,' Flynn said in a soft voice.

The clinician looked him over, clearly taking in Flynn's ripped and bloodstained clothing, and lifted his brows. 'Sorry young man. We need to speak with Amy for a moment.'

These people might seem friendly enough, but Amy didn't care. Flynn wasn't going anywhere. She latched onto his arm protectively. 'He stays.'

'Okay then. If you're completely sure, we can proceed. Amy, can you tell me *in your own words* what happened tonight?'

Flynn slipped his warm palm in hers and laced their fingers tight. Amy took a deep breath, garnering strength from him, and talked about her recent cutting. She stressed that this wasn't about getting attention. That it wasn't about trying to harm herself, or about managing her emotions. It was simply a means to an end. A way to connect with someone who'd passed, and now that need was over. She would not become a repeat offender.

While his assistant took lots of notes, the clinician asked her lots of questions, finally determining that she was low risk and not a threat to herself. They also spoke to her about getting some support from an external psychologist, as the urge could likely surface again.

Flynn spoke up. 'We have someone in mind.' He glanced at Amy with a smirk. 'Sonja Walker. She's Mr Jeffries' ... lady friend.'

'Oh.' Amy snorted.

Once they were alone again, Amy changed into the sweats her mum brought, and Flynn bundled her bloodied clothes into a paper bag. 'Here's your phone,' he said, pulling it from the other pocket of her skirt. She didn't ask what happened to the lancet. She'd be happy never to see it again.

Her graduation outfit was a mess, but according to Pierre, his tailor knew of someone who specialised in removing difficult stains. Including blood, apparently, which had Amy raising her brows. Pierre really did have the dodgiest acquaintances.

'I'm sorry I ruined graduation,' she said, as they waited for Pierre to bring the car around. Her phone was full of messages and photos of Leona and Kenzie.

'Ames, don't.' Flynn took the phone from her grasp and replaced it with his hand.

Pierre pulled up, and they all piled in. As they drove towards Amy's apartment, Luka called Flynn. They spoke for a few minutes in hushed tones.

'He wanted to know you were okay. He was pretty upset when we ran off.'

Luka called Frenchie. Amy frowned. 'How did he find us?'

'He followed me. And thank Christ he did.' Flynn tipped her head to rest on his shoulder.

'He's a good friend.'

'The best.' Beneath her cheek, she felt him take a deep breath. 'He told me, you know.'

Amy lifted her head. 'Told you what?'

'About crushing on you. It really upset him, thinking he'd fucked us both over.' Flynn threw his head back and exhaled loudly. 'Luka wears his heart on his sleeve. He deserves to find someone as amazing as you.'

Amy smiled and snuggled into his side. 'I might just be able to help with that.'

CHAPTER THIRTY

F OUR NIGHTS LATER, FLYNN led Amy up onto the roof of their old unit complex. It wasn't easy to climb the last of the stairwell with one of his hands covering her eyes, and she stumbled in her heels. At least she had the foresight to tuck the hem of her long graduation skirt (that looked brand new thanks to Pierre's tailor) into the legs of her knickers, or she'd have face-planted into the concrete.

'Nearly there,' he said, an obvious smile in his voice. 'One more step to go. Okay now, no peeking.'

She felt him move around behind her, his warm chest pressing against the thin lace of her top. She stuck her tongue out, giggling when it contacted with the salty skin of his palm.

'Hey! No licking either.'

'But I licked it, so it's mine.'

His breath tickled her ear as he chuckled, sending goosebumps across every inch of her bare shoulders and neck. 'You got that right, Amazing Ames. Are you ready?'

She nodded and bit her lip. He lifted his hand away.

'Surprise!'

Leona, Jimmy, Kenzie, and Luka stood in the centre of the rooftop, dressed in their graduation outfits. The twilight sky behind them shimmered in deep purples and pinks, and they had laced the edges of the concrete surround with fairy lights. It was nothing short of magical.

Flynn slipped a warm, steadying hand under the lace covering her lower back. 'I figured we both missed out on the grad dance, and these guys were keen for a second one.'

Amy spun and flung her arms around his neck, jumping up and locking her legs around his waist. Burying her face in his neck, she whispered, 'Thank you.'

'Hey, I'm all for this, but just remember we have an audience,' he whispered back, making her laugh. 'Let's save it for later.' His mouth was on her neck, and her whole body melted.

'How much later?'

'Give me the word, and they're gone. I'll tell them to fuck off now if you want.'

She laughed. 'Not yet.' Hugging him tight, she unwound her legs and slipped her feet to the ground. 'We have to party first.'

She ran over to the girls, squealing. They squealed back, hugging her tight, mindful of her bandaged wrist. None of them spoke about it, and Amy was glad for the chance to forget, if only for one night. She'd already decided not to let one mistake define her, but it was still early days.

The night was balmy and clear, stars popping out one by one. Jimmy had brought his kick-ass speakers, and they played all their favourite songs, dancing together and singing loudly. They ordered pizza, and when they were done, Flynn produced a fancy bottle of champagne, 'courtesy of Frenchie' and six plastic flutes.

They all cheered when Flynn sent the cork flying over the neighbouring block of flats and excitedly raised their cup of bubbles.

'To us,' Luka said. 'May we all stay the best of friends, even though we'll no longer see each other every day.'

'To us,' they toasted, drinking deeply.

'Oh God, that's bad.' Jimmy's face screwed up.

Flynn spat his on the ground. 'Tastes like cat piss.'

'I like it,' Kenzie protested, but they all agreed it had to go. Flynn collected their glasses and tossed everything off the roof, flutes and all.

It didn't escape Amy's notice that Luka scowled at Flynn behind his back, but Kenzie pulled him away, laughing. Amy smiled, watching them dance together. Luka's hands were on Kenzie's waist, and he had a massive grin on his face. Maybe tonight would be a new beginning for them, too.

Flynn spun Amy around and put his forehead to hers. 'Having a good time?'

She melted into him. 'The best. Thank you, but you didn't need to do this.'

'Yes, I did. And there's more.' He hesitated. 'I've done some digging around these past few days. Well, Frenchie has. I've only advised him.' She pulled back a bit, looking directly into those night ocean eyes. Trepidation swam in their depths. 'I've found out some things you might want to know.'

'What sort of things?'

'We found them.' He gave her a nervous smile. 'Marcel and Valentina.'

What? Amy's mouth dropped open, and she took an involuntary step back. 'Are you sure?' Her heart pounded double-time.

He nodded. 'Want to sit for this? Yeah. I think you'll need to.' He led her gently over to the wall, where they sank to the ground and rested their backs against the concrete, just like they'd done so many times before.

He gripped her hand tightly in his. 'Frenchie researched some Euro ancestry sites and found a passenger list from a ship's voyage from Melbourne to England in late 1896.'

'England?'

'Yeah. There was definitely a record of both Marcel Boucher and Valentina Boucher departing Melbourne. Valentina disembarked in Marseille, but Marcel...' She gripped his hand harder when his voice took on a sombre tone. 'Marcel didn't make it. He perished en route to England of septicaemia. That's—'

'Blood poisoning.' Amy felt herself deflate. 'The irony, huh?'

She thought of the Marcel she'd seen. The man she'd spent time with had been full of confidence, charm... and blood. A young man who, despite everything, deserved to know that life could be so much more. She felt incredibly saddened, but she refused to shed any tears tonight.

Flynn touched her cheek. 'Are you okay?'

'Yeah. I think I am.'

'I'm glad because we found out something else.' He stretched out with a mischievous grin, clearly enjoying himself. 'Did you know Boucher is the French word for *butcher*? Coincidence, I think not. How about this—Frenchie's surname, Fournier, means *baker*. I mean, what are the odds, right? Now, I know you won't believe this, but guess who Valentina married?'

'You really found her?'

'Uh-huh.' He was full-on grinning now.

'Let's see. A butcher. A baker. Don't tell me a candlestick maker?'

He laughed out loud. 'No, Ames. She married a doctor. And it gets better. She became a midwife, so she brought new life into the world instead of disposing of it.' He gave her a little nudge. 'Thought that would make you happy.'

She smiled. 'It does. But—'

'But Marcel didn't make it, I know. I'm really sorry, but we thought it best that you knew.' His voice dropped, kissing the spot beneath her ear.

'You're right. It is for the best. It's finally time to close that chapter of my life.'

'Are you sure you're ready?'

'Completely. Because I have a brand new one, to begin with you.' She turned to face him and looked deep into his eyes. 'Right now.'

'Right now?' His lips quirked up at the same time as his brow.

'Uh-huh.'

Flynn stood and clapped his hands to get everyone's attention. 'Guys and gals, it's been grand, but don't overstay your welcome. Ubers are on me.'

Amy giggled as her friends came over to kiss and hug her goodbye. It would be hard to accept that this chapter of her life had ended. But, they were all on the cusp of the rest of their lives, and Amy couldn't wait to begin hers, with Flynn by her side.

Waving from the roof, she waited until all the cars had left before making her way back to Flynn. He was dragging something from the shadows out into the middle of the rooftop. As she drew closer, she realised it was an inflatable mattress, and he was busy tucking in sheets, arranging pillows and blankets. Her mouth dropped open.

'Are we—?'

'Spending the night under the stars? In the exact spot where we first met?' He sent her one of those lopsided grins. 'You bet.'

'Oh my God, could this night get any more perfect?'

'You're about to find out.' He took her in his arms, and she ran her fingers down the front of his new white dress shirt. 'You know, I don't think Frenchie will buy me a third shirt if you end up ripping this one.'

'Well, I'd better take it slow, then.'

'We've got all night,' he breathed into her neck as she reached up to his collar.

Carefully undoing his shirt, button by button, Amy revelled in each heave of Flynn's abdominals as his breathing quickened.

'I've been waiting to do this since that first day, you know.'

She looked up into his darkened eyes. 'Me too,' she said.

Once they'd removed everything that kept them apart, they lay together under the blankets, skin to skin, looking up at the twinkling stars above. Flynn rolled over her and braced himself on his forearms, his chest against hers, feeling the beat of each other's hearts. Ocean eyes burning deeply into hers, he declared, 'Amy Rose Shipley, I'm here for the good times. The bad times. The in-between times. I'll always be here for you.'

True to his word, he had been; from that very first day when he helped carry her suitcase up the stairs. She reached up with her lips and dragged his mouth down. After several minutes of breathless kissing, she broke away.

'Are you sure you want on this ride? It could get pretty insane.'

He blinked dreamily. 'Are you kidding? I've been holding onto this ticket for ten whole months.'

'Ten months? You must be crazy.'

'You have no fucking idea.'

He smiled down at her. Another one of those lopsided grins that she loved so much, with those lips she longed to kiss every night. She'd been a fool not to choose him—this amazing boy who wanted her so badly but didn't believe himself worthy of her love. He had it completely wrong, though. She belonged to him, and tonight she was ready to make that pact. Not with her blood, but with her body and her heart.

The hours drifted by in a haze of bliss. A gentle and skilled lover, Flynn took her to places she'd never been. Over and over and over again.

When dawn broke over the horizon, she snuggled into his bare chest; his arms wrapped around her, their legs and hearts entwined. In a few hours, they would be attending her first therapy appointment together, but Amy was too happy to sleep. Beneath her, Flynn's chest rose and lowered slowly as he drifted off.

As the sky turned blush above, Amy let her eyelids close and whispered goodbye to Marcel's ghost. Whether she'd imagined him or not, without those moments of darkness, she'd never have learned her truth.

This was where she was always meant to be. With the only man who mattered.

Safe. Seen. Loved.

It's Okay Not to be Okay

If you or someone you know is at risk of harming themselves, help is always available. Please reach out. You are not invisible.

In Australia, the following organisations can offer support and assistance:

LIFELINE: 13 11 14
www.lifeline.org.au

SUICIDE CALL BACK SERVICE: 1300 659 467

KIDS HELPLINE: 1800 55 1800
www.kidshelpline.com.au

BEYOND BLUE: 1300 22 4636
www.beyondblue.org.au

HEADSPACE: 1800 650 890
www.headspace.org.au

ACKNOWLEDGMENTS

To David, whose belief in me from the very beginning has meant *everything*—thank you. Your constant support and unwavering faith in my ability to write (and finish) a book worthy of publication means more to me than I show. For your selfless dedication to working every day just so I can follow my dream—I will forever be indebted. I hope to be able to return the favour one day soon. You are the Flynn to my Amy.

To Hannah and Ben—never give up on your dreams. Be passionate about something, and then pursue it relentlessly. Thank you for being self-sufficient and taking my stress-induced bad moods with good humour. (Your "shut the fuck up—I'm working" sign for my office door was particularly appreciated.) It may look like I always have my head stuck in a book, but *I see you*. Never forget that.

To my best girls—the *Romantics with Attitude*—Jenny Westgarth, Heather Epstein, and especially Jacqui Greig for convincing me to "STOP EVERYTHING YOU'RE DOING AND FINISH THIS BOOK IMMEDIATELY"—I will forever be grateful.

Your constant comments, critiques, suggestions and support have made Amy and Flynn's story what it is today. I could not have done it without the laughter, the banter and the long-running gif trains. Our daily messaging keeps me going. I couldn't ask for a better tribe.

To my early readers—Elouise Tynan, Kristy Fairlamb and Kylie Templeton—thank you for your belief in this story and your early suggestions on how to make it even better. And to Christina Darwin—for your intuitiveness and for completely understanding the reasons behind this book.

To Aaron Delaney, for answering all my late-night questions regarding emergency mental health procedures. I'm thankful to have a nephew who's worked in both hospital psychology and emergency departments. Any misinformation is total poetic license on my behalf.

To my parents, friends and family—thank you for supporting my love of reading and not rolling your eyes too hard whenever I request bookstore vouchers as gifts. Huge thanks to Antonietta Neighbour, Helen Caswell, Mary-Anne Ashton and Robyn Heath, for your constant enthusiasm, support and promotion.

And finally, to you—the readers, bookstagrammers, fellow authors and #yalit championeers—thank you for everything you're doing. Every rating, review, email, photo, post and word of mouth recommendation is deeply heartfelt and appreciated beyond measure. *Thank you for helping me to be seen.*

About the Author

Melanie Pickering is an Australian author of genre-blending young adult novels full of the twisted, the morally-grey and the lovesick.

Her urban fantasy romances often blur the lines between reality and fiction, and contain lots of kissing, swearing and real issues.

She lives in a sunny sub-tropical city on the east coast of Australia with her family and a couple of rescue pets in a ninety-year-old former workers cottage that is possibly haunted. When not writing, she enjoys reading, photography and spending time with her family. While writing, she enjoys eating copious amounts of dark chocolate and daydreaming about swoony heroes.

Sign up for her newsletter at: www.melaniepickering.com

www.ingramcontent.com/pod-product-compliance
Lightning Source LLC
Chambersburg PA
CBHW050147120726
47903CB00002B/529